SWITCH PLAY

MASTERS OF MARQUIS

GOLDEN ANGEL

Cover Model: Nick Fitzgerald

Cover Photographer: Golden Czermack

Cover Designer: Eris Adderly

Edited by Personal Touch Editing

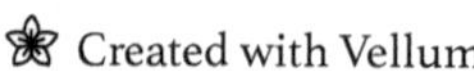 Created with Vellum

PROLOGUE – 6 MONTHS AGO

Samantha

"You! What are you doing here?"

Samantha froze at the hostile tone, all the feelings of being an imposter, of being in the wrong place, of trying to pretend she was something that she wasn't, reared up and made her want to turn and run right back out the door.

I'm not really a Dominant. I don't belong here.

No one else gets to decide that but me.

The voice in her head was immediately countered by another voice, a voice she respected, and a voice she'd been hearing a lot more often in her head when her own internal voice got out of control. Mistress Olivia was a force to be reckoned with, and Sam heard her sardonic tones every time her own uncertainties got too loud.

She blinked and her eyes narrowed on the incredibly attractive black man who had spoken, the one who was staring at her in shock. There was something incredibly familiar about him...

Sam's stomach turned over.

Now she really did feel like running out of the room. She just wanted to learn how to be a Dominatrix—at least get a feel for the

Dom side of things because she hadn't quite felt like she fit in as a submissive—not be confronted by a ghost of high school past.

Either way, she had never let Quinton Bright boss her around in high school, and she wasn't about to start now. He might be the last person she'd expected to find in Marquis' How-to-Dom class, but she wasn't going to let his presence stop her from getting what she wanted. Just as she hadn't in high school.

"Excuse me, Quinton?" She hid her satisfaction at his flinch. Still didn't like his name, huh? "I'm a *member*. What are *you* doing here?"

As soon as the question was out of her mouth she wanted to wince because duh... what else would he be doing at a kink club's Introduction to Dominance class other than learning how to be a Dom? Could she have asked a more inane question?

Not that she let it show on her face.

Channeling her inner Olivia, she drew herself up, keeping her expression coldly impassive and doing her best to slow her pounding heart rate. Brushing her hands over the blue skirt of her dress, at least she knew she looked damn good.

"Quinton?" The dark-haired girl behind Q looked both interested and amused at the confrontation going down in front of her. Samantha had seen her around Stronghold, Marquis' sister club, though she hadn't seen Q. What was her name? Iris. That was it.

"Don't call me that, Samwise," Q snapped.

Oh, he did not. Sam glared at him, her hands automatically going to her hips. Olivia wouldn't run screaming just because someone brought up a crappy high school nickname that had been used to taunt her. So, what if she was a bigger girl? She still loved potatoes, nearly as much as she'd hated that stupid nickname, and she was well past the age where she was going to let anyone make her feel bad about it.

"Then don't call me that stupid nickname. We're not in high school anymore. Grow up." There, that had told him. She couldn't help muttering, "Ass" under her breath. Yeah, she might have started it, but there was a difference between calling someone by their actual legal name, no matter how much they didn't like it, and using a taunting nickname.

Especially since she knew he'd hated being called "Quinton" in high school was he'd hated being teased about being a nerd. "Quinton" sounded like a nerd name, he'd said. Even though he'd been a nerd, he hadn't embraced it the way she had.

He looked even better than he had back then. His close-cropped black hair was similar to the cut he'd had in high school, but the scrawny limbs had been filled out with what looked like pure muscle bulging under his t-shirt. The shirt said, "One Lab Accident Away from Being a Supervillain," so he seemed to be more comfortable with his nerd side.

Which wasn't too surprising. Being a nerd had somehow become cool since they were in high school. Sam was still trying to reconcile that with her memories of being teased for knowing anything about superheroes and Game of Thrones.

It would have been nice if he hadn't grown up to be quite so hot, but at least she knew she looked good, too. She'd dressed the part today, going for the pin-up look, which made the most of her curves, with a blue dress and a wide red belt that cinched in her waist an extra inch or so. While she might not be exactly an hourglass without a corset, she could make herself look more like one.

"I take it you two know each other?" That question came from Chef Nick, whom Sam immediately recognized. He was the head chef at the restaurant downstairs.

Marquis operated as a regular restaurant on its first floor and a kinky hotel on its second. Sam loved coming here. Not that she didn't love Stronghold, which had been the first club before Marquis was built, but she'd spent more time here. Marquis made her feel classy, elegant, and... hot. She liked that she could hang out at the bar downstairs without feeling self-conscious about who was checking her out and who wasn't.

Stronghold's bar was full of Dominants who decided whether to ask one of the submissives hanging out in the Lounge area to play. Sure, there was some crossover, especially among couples, but for the most part, they stayed well apart. Sam never felt as though she fit in with either side, so Marquis—with its mix of kinksters and totally vanilla people who had no idea about Marquis' naughty side—suited her better.

Not answering, Q turned around and sat down, as though she wasn't even there. Samantha had to blink back the tears that threatened to surge upward. Yeah, that was a little too reminiscent of their past.

High school had been a decade ago, though. Shouldn't they be able to put their past behind them?

"Hi, I'm Nick," the chef said, waving when Samantha didn't move closer. "This is my girlfriend, Avery, and that's Iris."

"I'm single and ready to mingle," Iris said with a friendly grin. Samantha made herself smile, but her stomach turned over again when she realized there was a good chance, she was going to have to watch Q play—scene—with another submissive during training.

Not over a high school crush, huh? Pathetic.

Yeah, it really was since she hadn't seen him since graduation. It wasn't that she wasn't over a silly little crush, she just had some what-if thoughts. Not regrets exactly, just curiosity over the path not taken.

Not that it was worth dwelling on.

I'm not that girl anymore.

"I'm Samantha, but I go by Sam," she said, giving herself a mental shake, trying to make her wayward emotions straighten out.

"Welcome to the party." Iris seemed completely unperturbed by the interaction between Q and Sam, which was good, though Nick and Avery appeared to be a little uncomfortable. Hopefully, the introductions would get them all past that, though by sitting so far away from Q, she'd also put a bunch of space between her and them.

Ugh.

At least they knew what she liked to be called, so hopefully, things would get less awkward. Samantha had always felt too formal. She'd liked the more casual Sam, even when kids had teased her about it being boyish.

Friendlier.

Hopefully.

She'd hated Samwise. Just because she'd loved Lord of the Rings didn't mean she'd wanted to be known as the fat hobbit. She'd been too tall to be a hobbit, anyway.

Thank you, Q, for sticking me with that name.

It grated that it still had the ability to get under her skin a decade later.

The room had been set up with a small semi-circle of chairs around the circular stage in the center of the room. The booths that were used for dinner, eating, and watching the stage shows were along the edges of the room, their heavy curtains currently drawn. Samantha recognized the setup from when she'd taken the subbie class.

The stage was where demonstrations were done and on weekend nights, actual kinky sex shows happened for the titillation of the watching diners. Sam had come once with one of the girls from the submissives class. She and Morgan weren't besties or anything, but they'd formed a friendship, despite their differences.

It hadn't been the same as seeing a show with someone she was actually interested in, which was still on her list of 'things I want to do sometime soon.'

Finding someone she was interested in romantically would be step number one. Maybe she'd have better luck finding a submissive than a Dominant. That's why she was here. Olivia thought Sam might be a 'switch,' someone who could do either or both.

Sam was willing to explore. She loved being a submissive a lot of the times, but sometimes, it just didn't suit how she felt. She wasn't a brat, which someone had suggested. It had taken Morgan pointing out Sam sometimes acted like a Dominant when a Dom was trying to scene with her. Sam had decided to talk things out with Olivia.

"Okay, everybody's here!" Freddy's cheerful voice filled the room as the entrance door opened again. Sam twisted around in her seat to see the flamboyant submissive, who also ran the host station at Marquis, and was apparently a shark of a divorce lawyer by day.

Freddy had volunteered to be her submissive for the class.

Samantha liked him a lot, but there wasn't a spark between them. Still, she had someone to practice on. She occasionally found women attractive, but not enough to consider herself bisexual, and she really preferred men.

Freddy was also smart as hell. Sam saw his eyes flit around them, taking in where everyone was seated, and he frowned for a fraction of a second before his smile returned. She knew that meant he would be questioning her about it later. She would have to think of something to tell him other than "I had a crush on a boy in high school, and ten years later I didn't want to sit too close to him."

Behind Freddy was Morgan and a huge man well over six feet, considering Morgan came up to his chin in heels. Morgan and Sam were both taller than average, so Sam was sure she would feel petite standing next to him. Morgan was a stunning redhead with a model's body, while Sam was blonde and 'pleasantly plump,' as her mom liked to say.

They went through another quick round of introductions while Freddy went to get Master Law and Mistress Julie, who would be teaching the class. Sam wished Mistress Olivia was instructing since she didn't know Mistress Julie. She'd hoped for some mentorship, but she knew Olivia was busy running Marquis. Plus, Olivia's boyfriend and submissive was Nick's older brother, so she didn't think Olivia would jump to teach this particular class, even if she didn't have a huge workload.

Morgan sat next to Samantha, giving her a bright smile, while Connor sat down next to Morgan. It wasn't as if people were choosing sides, but Samantha felt a little better having people next to her.

If Morgan and Connor had left the seat beside her for Freddy, it would have been understandable, yet also made her feel like even more of an outsider. Not that it was anyone's fault. She'd chosen her own seat.

Just once, she wished she could feel like she was making the right decisions instead of floundering like a fish out of water.

It was going to be an interesting class.

1

---

6 MONTHS LATER – AN
INTRODUCTION TO SUBMISSION

Q

It was going to be an interesting class. He'd thought that when he'd first signed up for it, after completing the Dominance class, but he hadn't known at the time exactly how interesting it would be.

Q was doing his best to listen to Master Law and Mistress Julie as they welcomed everyone to the Introduction to Submission class, but his eyes were on Samantha Dupre, who preferred to be called Sam. She'd also been in the Dominance class, both of them learning that side of kink, but now he was going to learn how to be a submissive, and she was practicing being a Domme.

Mistress Sam.

Samwise.

He squashed the voice in his head. She really hated to be called that, and he hated feeling like the kid on the playground, tugging on a girl's pigtails to get her attention. That wasn't the kind of attention he wanted from her, and he should really be more mature by now.

I should also be over her by now.

Who knew a high school crush could have such longevity? They were completely different people now, yet he was still attracted to her. Maybe even more so than he'd been in high school.

To be fair, she didn't dress like that in high school.

Tonight was the first class, and Sam had signed up to be one of the Dominants. Law had checked with Q beforehand to make sure he was okay with having Sam hands-on with him in the class, since he preferred a woman Dominant. Pretty much everyone in the club had become aware of the friction between him and Sam. Friction he'd helped along by doing stupid things like changing her phone's ring tone to Lord of the Rings theme. In retaliation, she'd covered his car in Post-it notes... like, completely covered bumper to bumper and even the tires.

Looking at her now, one would never guess she had a mischievous streak. She was wearing a corset that lifted her substantial breasts up like a shelf. Q was pretty sure he could rest a drink on it. Though what he really wanted to do was burrow in and hibernate for the winter. He'd noticed her boobs in high school, of course, but they were even more incredible now. The long skirt she was wearing had slits up the sides, flashing her legs every time she moved.

With her long blonde hair pulled up into a no-nonsense French twist, she looked like a hot librarian Dominatrix.

"Tonight, you'll practice negotiations with all of our Dom volunteers," Mistress Julie said, sweeping her hand out to gesture at Sam and the others. Almost a foot shorter than Sam, Mistress Julie still had no problem appearing threatening. She was a petite Asian woman and a force of nature, from her spiked boots to the tip of the chopsticks in her hair. Q was pretty sure she'd gotten her corset, with its mandarin inspired neckline, from his friend Angel.

Angel was the reason he knew what a mandarin inspired neckline was. She was also the reason he'd gotten into kink in the first place, after he'd found out what she and her now-husband were up to. Q hadn't thought places like Stronghold and Marquis really existed.

Now, here he was attending his *second* kink class, since he already knew how to be a Dom. At least, he'd completed the course and Mistress Olivia had signed off on him being able to play in the club. But there had been something missing. Eventually, he'd realized that he'd really enjoyed doing the submissive part of the Dom class and wanted to explore it more.

"Are we being paired with one of them?" Noelle, one of his new classmates, asked. Q looked back and forth between her and Master Law with interest. He was ninety percent sure Noelle was Master Law's girlfriend's ex-roommate and best friend, and he was dying to know what she was doing here, of all places. If he was right about who Noelle was, Q couldn't tell from Law's expression. Law looked as stoic as he normally did as he met Noelle's eager gaze.

"Not tonight," Law said impassively. "Tonight, you'll be practicing with everyone. That way, you can get a good feel for how negotiations might go differently with different people. Next time, we'll pair you off." His eyes flicked to Q for just a moment.

He doubted anyone else was going to have difficulty with whoever they were paired with for the class. He'd chosen to have Sam as his partner. Unlike everyone else in the room, he'd been consulted beforehand.

There was no way his answer would have been anything but 'yes' for a myriad of complicated reasons, but the top two were that he had never backed down from a challenge from Samantha Dupre in his life, and he was so damn attracted to her, he couldn't think straight. He was happy to take an opportunity to get her hands all over him. Whether there would be any sex involved would depend on their negotiations, but he could always hope.

"Okay, everyone, split up. You'll have fifteen minutes to talk through your limits and work on negotiations before you'll move on to the next partner." Mistress Julie's dark gaze moved over all of them, then she motioned to the other Dominants.

Standing, Q moved his chair to the side. He'd expected his first negotiation would be with Sam, so he was a little surprised when Connor stepped up to sit down with him. Over the past few months, he and the big Dom had become friends—they'd gone through the Dom class together—but he hadn't expected the other man to choose him first. He could tell Connor was nervous. Maybe he just wanted someone familiar before he had to tackle the unknown.

"Hey, man," Q said, sitting down. Connor sat across from him. A big burly guy, he was close to six and a half feet tall and built like the Hulk. When they'd gone to the Maryland Renaissance Fair in the fall, Connor had dressed up like a Viking and looked every bit the part.

"Hey." Connor had a clipboard, which looked toy-sized in his giant hands. He glanced nervously to where Mistress Julie was talking to Law about something. "So, uh, I guess we're supposed to pretend we don't know each other. Hi, I'm Master Connor."

"Hi Master Connor, I'm Q." Q grinned, hoping to ease his friend's anxiety.

He glanced over to where Sam was sitting with Steve and chuckled. Steve was gay and would have as little sexual interest in Sam as Q did in Connor. That was going to be pretty common this evening, though. Their little group was more sexually diverse than the Dominance class had been.

Q was the only straight guy. Noelle and Cassidy hadn't said whether they were straight, but if Noelle was Iris' ex-friend, Q knew she'd had a boyfriend. Cassidy had also had a boyfriend before he'd gotten kicked out of the club for ignoring Cassidy's safeword. He wasn't sure why Cassidy was here. He'd thought she was an experienced submissive, albeit with a shithead for a Dom.

The other submissives were Steve and Emery. Steve was a friend of a friend's brother, who Q met in passing at group gatherings, which was how he knew Steve was gay. He hadn't met Emery, and they were the only non-binary person in the class. They hadn't said what their sexual preferences were, but since Sam was the only woman Dominant, Emery would be paired with a man for the class. Q knew the other Doms by sight and name—in addition to Sam and Connor were Leo, Trey, and Eric.

"Q? Did you need a minute? Oh crap, were you hoping to talk to Sam first?" Connor's face fell, his expression turning apologetic as he realized where Q had been looking.

"No, this is good. I can practice going through everything from this side before I have to talk to the person I'll be scening with." He turned his attention back to Connor. Sam would be by eventually, and until then... well, it really didn't hurt to practice.

"Okay, cool. So, um.... let's talk about limits." Connor's smile widened, his eyes crinkling with amusement. "I see that you've put cock and ball torture as a soft limit."

Q pointed a warning finger at his friend.

"For you, that's a hard limit."

Connor's chuckle made him smile as the big man finally relaxed.

---

*S*AM

"It was nice to meet you," Sam said, giving Steve a wave as she got up from her seat. This was kind of like speed dating except with hard limits and a lot more talk about sex than she would normally put up with from a stranger. Steve had been a total sweetheart, though, and going first with him had shaken loose a lot of her nerves.

The Dominants all moved, as if by unspoken agreement, in a clockwise circle, heading to the next submissive. Q would be her last stop, and she didn't know how she felt about that.

"Hi, I'm Sa... Mistress Sam," she said, quickly correctly herself when she almost left off the honorific. She sat across from a pretty blonde sub. With their similar coloring, at first glance, she bet a lot of people would say they looked like sisters, though the sub was shorter and much skinnier than Sam.

All the Dominants had a list of each sub's limit list for the evening so they could be prepared. She'd spent three times as long looking over Q's as she had anyone else's.

"I'm Noelle." The blonde smiled back at her, leaning forward slightly. "I love that you're a female Dominant. I am all about female empowerment." She held up her hand for a fist bump, which Sam returned somewhat bemusedly. It didn't feel very respectful, but at the same time, Noelle was being super friendly, and she didn't want to discourage that.

Making friends had never been one of her strengths, and it had gotten even harder over the years. She couldn't remember having a best friend, even though she'd always wanted one. And it wasn't like she was actually going to be dominating Noelle, since they weren't attracted to each other.

She decided not to take offense at the lack of formality.

"Thanks," she said, trying to smile as naturally as she could. "Actually, I'm a Switch. I kinda go both ways, Dom and sub."

"Oh, cool!" Noelle appeared surprised but interested. "I wonder if I'm a Switch. I bet I could be. I'm not sure about this whole sub thing, but I wanted to get into it." Waving her hand to indicate the room around them, she definitely didn't seem very submissive. Maybe she was a Switch, too.

"Well, the class will definitely help you figure it out." Samantha's smile felt more genuine now. "I know it helped me. I've done both classes, but I wanted to get more practice being a Dominant." She'd had plenty of practice being a submissive before she'd realized she might be interested in both.

"That would be great. I lost my best friend because I didn't understand this whole lifestyle thing, so I wanted to try to understand it. I just wish she'd been more willing to explain things to me, but I know stuff like this can be a sensitive subject."

Noelle looked so sad, Sam wanted to reach out and hug her. That probably wasn't appropriate though, right?

Ugh. This was why she was so bad at the friend thing.

"It can be," she agreed sympathetically. "I'm happy to answer any questions you have, everyone will. I don't know all the Dominants in here, but Stronghold and Marquis are really careful about their membership."

Though, even as she said the words, her eyes shifted over to where Cassidy was tucked in on herself, barely looking at the Dom who was trying to engage her. Unfortunately, assholes snuck in unexpectedly, but she trusted Master Patrick and the other owners to take out the trash.

"Thank you so much," Noelle replied effusively, reaching out to put her hand on Sam's knee. Sam blinked in surprise, but she didn't really know what to do. "You're so nice. I'm sure we're going to be friends."

"Um, right." She smiled, relaxing again as Noelle sat back. So, she was a little more touchy-feely than Sam was. That happened. She was nice, and she wanted to be Sam's friend. Sam held up her clipboard with the limits on it. "I think so, too. Um, would you mind if I practiced some of this stuff? I need it."

Not just because she was going to be facing Q in a few minutes. Part of the reason she'd volunteered to be a Dominant for the subbie class was because she needed more practical practice with it. Striking up a conversation with someone she didn't know, for the purposes of negotiating a scene, was absolutely something she needed more experience with.

It was also one of the reasons she'd started to worry maybe she wasn't really a Dominant after the previous class she'd taken—if she was a Dominant, shouldn't that mean this should all be easier?

Part of what had appealed to her about being a submissive was not having to make any of the decisions, but eventually, she realized that wasn't always what she wanted. Sometimes, she wanted to be in charge. She wanted to have a man on his knees and play with him the way she wanted instead of the other way around.

Or a woman, she supposed. Kink wasn't always about sex, which was why she needed to regain control of this conversation with Noelle.

"Absolutely. I'd love to help you practice." Noelle sat up straight, her hands in her lap, eyes sparkling at Sam. She looked like an eager submissive, and Sam inwardly breathed a sigh of relief.

"Great. So, it's nice to meet you, Noelle. I was looking over your limits list and saw you have a lot of 'would like to try' items marked off, especially with impact play, but that you say you're experienced with spanking. I'm assuming bare handed?" Sam tilted her head, giving Noelle the professional smile she would give a new patient at her job.

"Yes, and between you and me, it was more like a swat or two here and there, not like a 'putting me over his knee' situation." Noelle giggled, then winked. She'd leaned forward a little again, as if letting Sam in on a secret.

"Well, we can definitely do more than that." Sam smiled. "Are there any implements you had at the top of your list to try?"

Settling into the questions, she stayed focused on the woman, despite being able to practically feel Q's presence from all the way across the room.

2

———————

MISTRESS SAMANTHA

Sam

In hindsight, saving Q for last might not have been the best tactic. By the time she got to him, her anxiety had wound tighter and tighter with each 'practice' session with a different sub. It might have been better to rip the Band-Aid off, so to speak, and get him over with first.

Too late now.

She kept her practiced smile on her face as she sat down across from him. Did her expression feel a little tighter than it had for anyone else? Yes. Not that she would admit to it.

He's just another sub. He's just another sub. He's just another sub.

Except he was looking at her with heat in his eyes that none of the other subs had. His eyes weren't on her face, they were on her breasts. Sam felt the heat rise in her cheeks as she blushed.

Dammit.

He wasn't supposed to be looking at her like that.

It was much easier to deal with him when they were operating on the hostility left over from high school. When he was looking at her like he actually wanted her...

Crap. It wasn't just her cheeks that were heating.

"Hello, I'm Mistress Samantha," she said, crossing one leg over the other. She realized, about halfway through the evening, being called Samantha made her feel a little more like an actual Domme, more formal. Speaking had the fortunate side effect of drawing his attention back up to her face, which she hoped he wouldn't realize was a little flushed. If he was disconcerted at being caught staring at her boobs, he didn't show it.

"I'm Q, Mistress Samantha." The charming smile that flashed across his lips was enough to make her blush a little more. "It's nice to *meet* you."

It had been that smile that had first attracted her in high school.

Clearing her throat, Sam adjusted the clipboard on her lap to give her something to do with her hands. This felt a bit like sexy stranger role play except she wasn't sure she wanted to find Q sexy. From his reaction to her appearance in the Dominance class a few months ago, she'd assumed he'd lost any interest in her. Actually, he'd been pretty hostile.

Then the prank war had started.

Mistress Julie had checked in to make sure she'd be okay being paired with Q for this class while he learned how to be a submissive.

'Okay' wasn't exactly the right word, but she hadn't wanted to back down, hadn't wanted him to feel as if he'd scared her off.

She probably owed him an apology from high school, which she hadn't cared about giving him when they'd first run into each other at Marquis because he'd been such a jerk. Or while they were messing with each other... but now that he was looking at her like this, she was uncomfortably aware of their past. He looked a bit too much like when he'd asked her to prom.

They had limited time right now, and it was more important to go over his sheet and limits than anyone else's since they already knew they'd be paired together. That's what she told herself.

Chicken.

Yup. Bwok, bwok, that was her. She had a first-place ribbon in avoidance.

"Is there anything on your 'want to try' list you're most interested in?" She got right down to business rather than trying to start an awkward conversation.

"Not really." Q leaned back in his chair, watching her closely. "I'll admit, I am more interested in the domination part than any particular toy or implement. Being spanked didn't do much for me when I had to try it during the Dom class. I liked being bossed around by a woman who knew exactly what she wanted."

His grin flashed again, and Sam did her best to ignore the impulse to squeeze her thighs together.

"Do you have any particular objection to being spanked? Or whipped?" She was curious since he hadn't put either under a soft limit.

"No objection, though I'm definitely not a masochist. I'm more of a hedonist."

Interesting. Personally, Sam liked a bit of pain with her pleasure, but she could work with that. During the class, they'd go over a lot of the things Q professed he didn't have much interest in. That could be good practice for her since he would probably have a pretty low limit on what was pleasurable or arousing for him.

She looked down at the clipboard again, even though she didn't really need to. She practically had his limits list memorized.

"Yet you indicated an interest in cock and ball torture?" That didn't sound like something a non-masochist would be interested in.

Q's grin widened.

"Curiosity killed the cat. I'm not sure I want to know, but since it's an option, I have to know."

Lifting her head to stare at him, Sam pressed her lips together in amusement, trying to hide her smile.

"You were one of those kids who burned their fingers on the stove after they were told not to touch, weren't you?"

"Twice." Q laughed at her expression. "I had to make sure it was the same the second time. I'm guessing by the way you phrased the question that you weren't?"

"No." Sam had always been cautious to a fault. She'd been a good girl, not wanting to cause her dad any trouble when they already had enough issues. "I didn't even touch it the first time."

"That was probably the smarter thing to do," Q admitted. "But then, I always knew you were smart."

Dammit. She shouldn't like being complimented by him so much. She was losing control of this little interview.

Q

Q knew he wasn't being a very good submissive, but he didn't seem to be able to help himself. Sam had always had a way of making him fumble over his words... and he wasn't feeling particularly submissive tonight. Which was a problem.

Despite her outfit, he had the strongest urge to peel her out of the Domme attire and find the sweet subbie underneath.

Bad Q. Wrong night. Try again some other time.

As if she heard his thoughts, she sat up a little straighter, her hazel eyes turning flinty. Damn. That was hot. She'd gone from uncertain and nervous to Mistress Samantha in a heartbeat.

Okay, now he was feeling a little more submissive. The change in her had triggered a change in him, and he found himself automatically sitting a little straighter, his eyes dropping, and his attention sharpening.

"What's the most painful thing you've experienced that you also enjoyed?"

"Nipple clamps." Those had hurt, but they'd also felt good. At least until they came off. He hadn't loved how sensitive his nipples were afterward rubbing against his shirt, but he could tolerate it.

Mistress Samantha nodded thoughtfully.

"Do you have a preference for what you'll be called during the class?" She hesitated, trying to figure out the right words to use, and Q realized what she was talking about.

"Q, when you're talking to me, but I like being called a 'good boy.'" While he understood the derogative connotations some black men would feel about the terminology, he'd felt nothing but envy when he overheard male submissives earning the accolade in the club.

He'd wanted to be told he was someone's good boy.

Sam nodded, relief sparking in her eyes, but only for a moment, then she looked away again, down at her notes.

"It's not marked on the sheet. Do you have any sexual limits for the class?"

It was a standard question and one Q had thought long and hard about once he knew he would be paired with Samantha. A lot of casual sex had gone on during the Dom class, but it wasn't really for him. By the end of the class, he'd kept any sensual play to toys and fingers. He'd planned to do the same for this class... until he found out who his Domme would be.

High school Q was all for fulfilling that old fantasy, the one where he'd take her to prom and lose his virginity to her on prom night. Not that he was still a virgin, but just knowing this was a second chance for the night he'd wanted... yeah. That wasn't something he could turn down.

"No limits." He met her gaze, smiling at her. "I'm here to pleasure you however you wish."

They stared at each other for a long moment, the magnetic attraction simmering between them growing exponentially as their gazes held and the front of Q's pants tightened.

Hands clapping made them jump. Mistress Julie was back on the Marquis' stage with Master Law beside her, and she was smiling at all of them.

"Great job today, everyone. I hope you enjoyed your practice negotiations. Next week, we'll be doing some hands-on practical work. If you have any questions about limits or your negotiations, Master Law and I will hang around for a little longer. Otherwise, thank you for being here, and we'll see you next week."

That was that then.

Damn. Q had been enjoying himself and wasn't quite ready for it to be over.

"Want to go down to the bar and get a drink?" The words were out of his mouth before he could think them through, but he didn't regret them.

Sam blinked, turning from Mistress Samantha back into Sam with that one movement.

"A drink? Like a date?"

She sounded more surprised than put off, so Q tried not to be insulted. Especially since, before tonight, they'd had a pretty volatile relationship. It was probably time to call a truce before the cock and ball torture started happening.

"Not a date..." Yeah, he didn't need a repeat of what had happened when he'd asked her to prom. The sting of rejection had faded, but that didn't mean he was going to set himself up to do it again. "Just... I thought maybe we could talk. Clear the air as it were."

He waved his hand, and Sam nodded slowly.

"You're probably right." She took a deep breath, appearing more uncertain of herself than she had all night. "Sure, let's do a drink."

Something in Q's chest squeezed. *She said yes!* And it wasn't as though she would change her mind tomorrow because they were doing this *right now.* Maybe he'd even finally find out what had happened all those years ago when she'd said yes at first, then changed her mind.

"Great." Q hopped up to his feet. He glanced over at Law, wanting to ask Law about Noelle, but Law was in the middle of a discussion with Emery and he didn't want to give Sam a chance to run. It was better to stick by her side to make sure the drink actually happened. He met her gaze again and offered her his arm.

"Let's go."

With her hand securely wrapped around his arm, he felt a lot better about his chances of keeping her around for the conversation.

"Let me just grab my jacket," she said, slowing when they stepped into the lobby. Q didn't argue. It was fucking cold out, so he'd worn a coat as well, but he was surprised when he realized she meant an actual jacket in addition to her coat. As she pulled it on over her corset, he realized why she'd wanted it.

It covered up the corset and most of the tops of her breasts. Even though her skirt was leather, it blended well enough to make it look like she was a regular person out on the town, wearing a sexy black top and dress, but not like she had just been at a kink club. He'd been so preoccupied at the idea of getting to talk to her, he hadn't considered that, but thankfully she'd come prepared.

Since it was a Monday night, the bar was pretty quiet, though the booths were filled up. Marquis was a popular restaurant, so the dining room still had a fair amount of people.

"Corner?" Q asked, nodding his head toward the corner of the bar where they'd be able to sit perpendicular to each other instead of side by side.

"Sounds good." Though she still appeared nervous, Sam quickly took a step in the direction indicated, tugging slightly on his arm as she got a little ahead of him, but Q quickly fixed that. In her heels, she was almost exactly his height, which he liked, so he lengthened his stride to stay at her side.

There was only one other person at the bar, a woman sitting on the other side, staring at her phone. Q didn't recognize her, so she probably wasn't a member of Stronghold or Marquis. She didn't glance up when he and Sam sat down, so he doubted he had to worry about her listening in.

"Hello, how are you two doing tonight?" Shane seemed to be a permanent fixture behind Marquis' bar. About Q's height, he was completely bald but had a well-trimmed salt and pepper goatee and sharp brown eyes that seemed to see more than most people.

"We're good. Just came from class. Do you ever take a night off?" Q helped Sam onto the bar stool before he took his own seat.

"No, Olivia owns my soul," Shane said, so matter-of-factly, Q wasn't entirely sure he was joking. Sam giggled, though.

"Slow night?" she asked, and Shane shrugged in answer.

"It's a Monday. What can I get you?"

They both ordered a beer from the tap, chatting with Shane while he poured. He headed back to the kitchen for something, and they were left alone in increasingly awkward silence. Q took a sip of his beer. He wanted to talk to Sam but had no idea what to say or how to get started.

"So, I guess you want to know why I changed my mind about going to prom with you?" Sam was staring down at the wooden bar top, not looking at him, tracing circles with her fingertip in the water from the condensation on her beer glass.

"I wasn't going to go straight for that, but I have to admit, I am curious." Q twisted on the seat, turning so he could give her his full attention.

One side of her lips lifted in a resigned smile.

"I was too poor," she said bluntly, making Q blink.

His mind immediately went back to high school. Though she'd always been withdrawn in school, he'd assumed she was introverted and focused on her studies. He hadn't noticed anything that would indicate that.

"I couldn't afford the dress, much less my part in any of the stuff that goes with prom."

"I would have paid for all the stuff, though it might have been a little weird if I'd offered to pay for the dress," Q said softly, reaching out to touch her hand. She stilled, no longer drawing on the bar top. She finally looked up to meet his eyes, her smile sad. He wanted to wipe the sadness away and bring back the spark he'd seen earlier.

"I didn't want you to. I was too proud. I never wanted anyone to know we were struggling. Plus..." She sighed, looking away again. "The day you asked me, we had that big test in AP English that afternoon, remember?"

"I do." When they'd gotten their tests back the next day, she'd stared at the piece of paper, then shoved it in her backpack. It was the first time they hadn't compared grades on something.

"I got a C minus." She stared down at the bar, her shoulders hunching in on themselves, then lifted her glass to take a long drink while Q blinked rapidly, trying to understand.

Sam *never* got Cs. They had both been straight-A students. She had been the only student to even rival him for grades. They'd both had a thirst for knowledge, a love of learning, and good test-taking skills—a combination hard to beat.

She took a deep breath.

"I got a C minus because the night before I was too busy trying to figure out how I was going to afford everything and researching prom dresses to study the way I needed to. Then my dad came home, and he was worried about being laid off, and I realized it would add another financial burden to him." Even now her voice was thick with emotion.

Q squeezed her hand tightly. He wanted to reach out and pull her into his arms, but he didn't know how she would react. Everything about her body language screamed that she didn't want to be touched.

"Sam, it's okay—"

"He wouldn't let me get a job," she cut him off, the words pouring out of her like she'd been holding them back for too long and now she couldn't stop them. "My job was to get good grades so I could get scholarships so I could go to college. Then I got a C minus on my test because I was too busy obsessing over one night with a boy I liked." She looked up at him again, and this time he could see the sheen of tears in her eyes. "So, I took back my yes, but I was too ashamed to explain why. I'm really, really sorry because I think I hurt you a lot more than I meant to, but I just couldn't explain."

That did it. Q hopped off his bar stool and wrapped his arms around her, pulling her against him so her head nuzzled into his shoulder.

There. Much better.

3

LET'S TALK ABOUT IT

Oh my God, could I be more pathetic, crying over something that happened a decade ago?

It was something that had stuck in her head all these years. Even after she'd gotten the scholarships she needed, gone through college, and started working as an occupational therapist, she'd never told anyone. She'd been too busy with schoolwork to have friends, and she'd never wanted to add to everything her single dad was going through to give her the life he thought she deserved. After her mom left them, they'd been a team, and she'd been determined to be a benefit, not a detriment.

But she'd felt bad and always wondered 'what if.' That 'what if' had hurt sometimes, especially after she'd taken back her yes, her and Q's mostly friendly rivalry had taken on a hostile edge. She'd been just as bad as him, partly because she'd been mad he'd stopped being friendly, even though she understood why, and partly because she'd resented him for that C minus. It had taken her a while to unpack that and realize her teenage brain had blamed him.

"Sam, it's over, it's in the past, and I get it. I wish you'd told me then, but I get why you didn't." Q's hand rubbed up and down on her back in soothing circles, and she sniffled but wasn't *crying* crying, and her tears were already drying up, but this felt... nice.

It was the most cuddling she'd gotten outside of after care in months. She wasn't sure she wanted him to let her go, even though this was probably a bad idea. Emotions could get complicated enough between kink and sex without their baggage.

Would it really be the worst thing?

No, no it would not.

God, he smells so good, I wish I could just lick him...

"You okay, Sam?" Shane's cautious tone made her sit up. His expression was neutral, but the look he was giving Q still managed to be repressive. He didn't want to step on any toes, but he was also willing to give Q a stern talking-to if necessary.

"I'm good, sorry." She gave Q a wan smile as she straightened. "Sorry."

"Hey, feel free to press your boobs against me any time, I am here at your disposal." Q grinned as he shifted back, regaining his seat and making Shane chuckle and relax. He turned to go take care of the other customer, and Q gave her a mock scared look, dropping his voice to a whisper. "For a second there, I thought I might be in trouble. I felt like I was facing someone's dad."

"Bartender Daddy," Sam whispered, giggling when Q cracked up. She could totally see Shane as reluctant Daddy. He'd probably protest the entire time.

"Seriously though, Sam, I was upset and felt rejected as a kid, but I was fine. You did nothing wrong."

"I did, though." She sighed and took another long drink of beer. The pleasant, cool bitterness slid down her throat, helping with the heat of embarrassment. "I could have told you."

"We were dumb teenagers." He shrugged. "Besides, if things hadn't gone down the way they had, I would have never known that someone could Post-it an entire car."

Sam snickered at his mention of the prank. She'd had help, but she and two of the submissives from Stronghold—one of whom was good friends with Q—had literally covered his car in Post-it notes while he was in the club. It had been hilarious watching the security feed when he went outside and just stood there, staring at his car, unmoving, for five long minutes.

"I only did that because you changed the ring tone on my phone."

"I know. It was pretty hilarious. Makes me a little scared to tempt fate and see what else you have up your sleeve."

Rather than answer him, Samantha smiled enigmatically. The truth was she had a few more ideas. Including some she wasn't sure how to implement since Master Patrick, the main owner for Stronghold and Marquis, had forbidden anything to do with glitter in the clubs.

It seemed like she and Q had called a truce, anyway.

They chatted about everything they'd been up to since graduating high school. She told him how she'd decided to go into occupational therapy because she didn't think she could afford the bills to become a surgeon like she wanted, then discovered that she loved being an OT. He told her about how he'd been a proposal writer until one of his friends had got him a job working with video games at Storm-Cloud in Bethesda.

Shane came by, and they ordered a second drink before Q got up to take a bathroom break. Sitting at the bar, smiling into the nothingness while she waited for him to return, Sam jumped a little when Noelle appeared at her elbow.

"Hi again! I was on my way out and saw you sitting here," Noelle said, glancing at Q's empty glass.

"Q and I decided to get a drink to keep talking things through," Sam said, answering the unasked question.

"Oh, I guess you two will be paired together? That makes sense. I wish I knew who I was going to be paired with." Noelle smiled, but the way she was staring at her made Sam feel a little uncomfortable, as though she was accusing Sam of having insider knowledge. Then again, she guessed she did, but only for herself.

"They asked us before the class if we'd be okay with being paired with each other since we, um, have a bit of past history. We knew each other in high school." The words kept coming as Noelle stared at her. Finally, the other woman nodded, her eyes brightening with understanding.

"Okay, got it." She sighed. "I guess I'll have to wait till next week to find out my partner. I can't wait though. I think this is going to be a lot of fun."

Noelle seemed a little awkward, but maybe Sam was projecting. Maybe this was why she had no friends other than Morgan, who was more of a very friendly acquaintance. Sam didn't know how to relate to people. Maybe Noelle came off as a little too friendly because Sam was too unfriendly.

Maybe she needed to try harder.

"I have a lot of fun with it," she offered. "I wasn't sure when I first started coming to Stronghold, but it's really satisfied something inside me."

She'd first signed up for classes because she'd been reading a lot of romances, which led to her looking for local clubs online. She'd done a ton of research and determined Stronghold was the one she wanted to go to, then found their introduction class, which happened to be at its sister club, Marquis. The idea of a classroom setting had made her feel more comfortable, though she'd quickly discovered it wasn't at all like being in a conventional classroom.

But she'd enjoyed it.

She enjoyed kink and liked having somewhere to go on the weekends where people were friendly, even if she wasn't really friends with any of them.

"I can't wait. I have to get going but maybe we could get together before class next week? Have a drink ahead of time?" Noelle smiled expectantly.

Samantha mentally pulled up her calendar. Mondays she only worked till five, so that should be fine.

"Sure, that'd be great."

Maybe she was getting better at this making-friends thing.

Q

Coming out of the bathroom, Q ran into Law, who had just exited the stairway at the back of the hall and was headed to the main dining room. The back stairs were right next to the back entrance of Marquis, which was for members only, and tucked around the corner from the hallway where Q was standing.

"Hey, how was your first night?" Law asked. "You and Sam seem to be getting along better."

"It was good," Q said, bemused. "Did you come all the way down to check on me?"

"Yeah. Shane texted that you were at the bar with Sam."

Q shot a dirty look toward the bar, not that Shane noticed. He frowned when he realized Sam wasn't alone, and who she was with.

"Hey, so... Noelle..." He let his voice trail off, turning his head slightly so he could see Law. The other man's jaw tightened with seeming annoyance.

"Noelle." The way he said her name, confirmed Q's question and told him she was exactly who he'd thought.

"You guys let her application go through after what she did to Iris?" He was more than a little surprised. His understanding of the situation was that Iris had moved in with Law because Noelle had ended their lease agreement with their apartment building without even notifying her until after it was done. Sure, it had worked out between Law and Iris in the long run, but it had been a shitty thing to do.

Iris didn't say much about her, but the overall impression Q had gotten from Iris' other friends was not a positive one.

"We have to keep the personal and professional stuff separate. If she's a submissive in need and she checks out in all the other ways, we have a responsibility to ensure she can explore in a safe environment. That means personal feelings have to be left at the door." Law said the words like he was reciting them.

"Trust me, if I could keep people I don't like off the membership list, everyone's lives would be easier." Olivia had followed Law downstairs and apparently, overheard what he'd said. The Dominatrix was a stately redhead who wore a lot of red, and tonight was no exception. She managed the whole of Marquis and was dressed for the part in a red pantsuit with some dangerously high stilettos. "Truckstop would be at the top of the list, but she's like a bad rash, she just keeps coming back."

Q choked back a cough. 'Truckstop' was Olivia's name for her friend Jared's ex. Jared's fiancé, Leigh, was one of Q's friends and he did remember there was a lot of drama around Jared and Leigh getting together since Marissa was also a member at Stronghold. She hung around with a small group of submissives, one of which was pretty nice and the other whom Q couldn't stand.

"I get it. Just seems weird." He shrugged.

"It's super weird and super frustrating, but trust me, the second one of them steps out of line." Olivia grinned and dragged her finger across her throat, her silvery eyes glowing with anticipation. "One day. Truckstop has already come close a few times, but the worst she got was probation."

"If she causes Iris any trouble in the club, she's gone," Law said, though his expression was pained. "And she won't have the opportunity to do so outside the club."

"Is Iris okay with it?"

Law and Olivia exchanged a glance.

"Iris insisted on it." Law sighed and rubbed his hand over his bald head with aggravation. "She doesn't want to give Noelle more of a reason to resent her, even though they aren't friends anymore, and insists that she should be given the same chance as everyone else who applies to the club."

"I'll help keep an eye on her." The offer wasn't entirely unselfish. He was a little concerned about the way Noelle was cozying up to Sam. All three of them watched as Noelle said goodbye, waving to Sam before walking away. Q quickly waved to Law and Olivia and headed over to regain his seat.

Sam smiled as he slid back onto the stool next to her, just as Shane appeared on the other side of the bar with Q's beer. She already had hers.

"What did Noelle want?" he asked bluntly, though he tried to keep any hint of his feelings about the other sub out of his voice. Sam's eyebrows rose, so he didn't think he'd been entirely successful, but she still answered him.

"Just to say hi. She's super friendly. We're going to get together for drinks next week before the class." There was a hint of challenge in her voice, though he wasn't sure why. Might just be the way they used to spark off each other. He'd hoped they would be sparking off each other in a different way by now.

Definitely time to end the Noelle talk.

"That's nice." He might not entirely mean it, but he would be keeping an eye on things with her. Maybe Noelle deserved a chance to meet everyone without her past hanging over her head, but from what she'd said about losing her best friend over kink... it seemed a little revisionist. He didn't want to piss Sam off, though. He'd learned a long time ago not to get between a girl and her friends.

"So, you were telling me your new office?"

With the change of subject, it didn't take long for Sam to relax and for them to find an easy rhythm to their banter again. It was almost as if no time had passed between them, except he couldn't quite say that because they had never been this congenial in high school. The night flew by and he walked her to her car because it was dark out and... well, because he didn't want the evening to end.

It was way too soon for shit like that, yet here he was.

"So, um, thanks," Sam said, fiddling with her keys. "I think it was good we talked this all out."

"Me, too." Q stared at her. The urge to lean forward and kiss her was growing stronger, but he didn't know if that was the right thing to do. Didn't know if she'd want him to. This was the first time since they'd re-met they hadn't spent the encounter sniping at each other. "Um, thanks for talking with me."

"You're welcome." Heat suddenly colored her cheeks. "I mean, you don't need to thank me. I'm glad we did. It should make the whole class thing easier."

"Yeah. Okay, well then, I guess I'll see you next week in class." He smiled, but deep down he knew he was trying to get her out of there because if he didn't, there was a good chance he would go in for the kiss.

Which was a really bad idea. What if he did and she wasn't into it? Or rejected him? Just because she was willing to top him in class didn't mean she'd be interested in anything more than friendship outside of it.

Better not push his luck before class had even started. If she wasn't into it, that would just make the entire course a shitshow of awkwardness.

"See you next week." She stared at him for a moment longer before turning to open her car door, and the opportunity passed.

Q closed the door behind her, feeling the oddest mix of relief and disappointment.

4

WHAT ARE FRIENDS FOR?

Q

He was in the middle of working through some of the code behind Glorg the Destroyer's dialogue when his phone buzzed. Glancing down at the screen, it was his friend, Angel. Crap. He'd meant to text her last night when he got out of the class to let her know how it went. She was the reason he'd ended up at Stronghold in the first place. They'd been friends for a long time and after she'd met her Dom and now husband, Adam, Q had finally gotten up the courage to ask her about the club.

She'd been thrilled to get him in touch with Patrick, the owner of Stronghold and one of the three owners of Marquis, and get him started on his membership. She was also a relentless busybody and likely brimming with impatience to hear about his first class as a sub.

Opening the message, he wished he could have placed a bet on that. He was one hundred percent right.

Angel: *I have been waiting patiently ALL NIGHT AND ALL MORNING and I get nothing from you! Nothing! Proof of life, NOW!*

Q chuckled, shaking his head.

Q: *Some of us have real jobs, Angel.*

His phone buzzed almost immediately.

Angel: *Which is why you should have texted me last night. Suck it up, buttercup. And don't blame me just because you weren't smart enough to get a job with a flexible schedule.*

Q: *I'll show you flexible.*

Angel: *And I'll show Adam my texts if you don't start spilling deets! I'm home alone with a toddler, Q. I need to live vicariously through someone. Take pity on me.*

Q: *Send the toll.*

He wasn't actually worried about her showing Adam their texts. It was an empty threat, and they both knew it. First of all, Adam wouldn't care. Adam was used to Angel's banter, especially with her close friends. He was completely secure in his relationship with Angel and knew there was nothing between her and Q—even though at one time, Q had wished there would be. Second of all, she was probably going to tell Adam about this entire exchange later, anyway. He wouldn't be surprised if she read the texts aloud to him, mocking Q the entire time.

This time when the text message sounded, Q grinned before he opened it, knowing what he would see.

Baby Melody, Angel and Adam's daughter, grinning at the camera. She was the cutest little thing, happy to be standing and climbing on things, though she didn't appear particularly interested in walking just yet. She was content being carried around—and no wonder when there was never any shortage of volunteers.

Q was usually at the head of the line.

Q: *Damn she gets cuter every day.*

Angel: *Toll paid, now spill!*

Laughing, Q glanced at the clock. It was close enough to lunch time and would be easier to talk on the phone than texting for this conversation. Saving his work, he pushed his chair away from his desk and got up to close his door. Not that many people walked in unannounced, but still. He wanted the warning knock that someone was there.

Picking his phone up, he dialed Angel's contact and wasn't the least bit surprised when she picked up before the first ring was barely over.

"Tell me everything!"

"Do you have a point where you wanted me to start at?" he asked dryly, laughing.

"Yes, skip over everyone else and tell me about Sam. Was it weird? Did you two talk at all? Did you find out what happened? Do you think it's going to be awkward?"

Shaking his head, Q sat and leaned back in his chair as he told Angel about the evening. He didn't bother going into all the others in the class. She would probably be interested later, but right now, she was focused on him and Sam. He'd learned telling Angel everything she wanted to know usually led to some pretty good insights.

It didn't take long for him to work his way through the entire evening, including talking with Sam at the bar.

"Oooh, poor thing. It sounds like she was embarrassed," Angel said sympathetically.

"Yeah, she seems okay now, though."

"Does she?" Angel sounded a little dubious. "She's pretty stand-offish. Not that it's always a bad thing. Some people just don't like others getting too close, but she struck me as someone who wants to make friends but doesn't really know how to."

"Is that why you helped her Post-it note my car?" Q asked dryly.

"If I was to do such a thing, and I'm not saying that I did, it would probably be because I was trying to make friends with someone."

As far as Q knew, Angel had never had any trouble making friends with anyone. When she wanted a new friend, she made one. She was like a friendship octopus, but it sounded like Sam had escaped her tentacles.

"I can't believe you didn't pull her into your group." Angel had a whole group of close friends at Stronghold who spent time together, both in and out of the club.

"I don't think she's much of a group person. Even with Lexie and I both trying to bring her into the fold, she was never comfortable. You can't make someone be your friend."

True enough. He could see it. Sam had been standoffish in high school as well. Now he knew why. She had been focused on her studies to the exclusion of all else. Something he could sympathize with, even if he hadn't experienced it himself. Angel's group of friends could be overwhelming. They were a big group and most of them were pretty loud.

Yeah, he could see where Sam would be hesitant to be pulled into all that. It would be a lot.

"I'm surprised you didn't try to drag her in, anyway." That would be far truer to Angel's M.O.

"I'm a little busier than I used to be." She sighed. Yeah, motherhood had changed her. Not a ton, but enough that she didn't have the time for everything she used to do, and her priorities had definitely shifted. She was a damn good mom, though, and Q had a feeling she and Adam would be adding to their family before long. Which would probably mean more changes and even less time for her to seek out new friends.

Well, that was okay. He was making friends with Sam and would bring her along to the things he went to.

Which reminded him of the other person who had been trying to make friends with Sam. He was about to ask Angel what she knew about Noelle when he heard the sound of a baby's wail.

"Hey, little fussy thing, did you fall down? I gotta go, Q, I'll talk to you later. Keep me updated!"

"Will do," was all he got out before the phone hung up.

Yeah, things had changed, but that was okay. He'd get her opinion later. Right now, he needed to get some lunch, then get back to work.

---

*S*AM

"You did great today, Ryan, high five," Sam said, showing the little boy out of her therapy room. He was grinning widely as he slapped his palm against hers. "Good progress."

Ryan was a good kid who'd been injured in a car accident last year, which had caused him some delays in motor development. It was something they'd been working on for a few months now, and he was getting much better at his fine motor skills.

"Thanks, Sam!"

"Thank you, Sam," his mother echoed as she walked past, a tired but warm smile on her lips.

"Of course," she said, giving them a wave. Out of the corner of her eye, she saw Rose, the office manager, watching from down the hall before disappearing. Sam sighed inwardly.

For some reason she and Rose had never hit it off. Maybe because while Rose was not an OT, she'd been working in the practice long enough, she thought she knew more than some of the people who actually were OTs. While Sam didn't want to put on airs or cause trouble, she wasn't going to do what Rose said just to keep the peace.

She also didn't want to rock the boat too much because she needed this job.

I need a raise is what I need.

A raise that wouldn't be coming this year. Sam pressed her lips together and turned to go back into her room. She'd already asked for an end-of-year raise and been told it wasn't practical for this year, but that she should be getting one next year. Unfortunately, the cost of living still went up every year, even if her income didn't.

She was coming to a point where she was either going to need to get a second job, ask her dad for help, or start cutting expenses. Unfortunately, the first thing that would get cut would be Stronghold and Marquis. Even though she had a discounted membership right now because she was helping out with the sub class—which had been part of her reason for signing up—that wouldn't last forever.

Sure, she could keep volunteering for things at the club, but that was like taking on a second job that only got her one thing. Still might be worth it.

Some people would find it laughable that she was so reluctant to cut a membership to a sex club out of her life, but it wasn't as though she spent money on anything else for fun. She'd already cut out pretty much all of her entertainment expenses, but she knew from her childhood that some people expected poor people to live without anything that fed their soul.

It was so easy to say, 'of course, just cut out television, a phone plan, a club membership' when you weren't the one having to do it. She'd heard all sorts of advice throughout her life.

The 'get a second job' was another one of those well-meaning tidbits. As if it was that easy to work another job into her day. Her current job was already physically and emotionally draining. Adding something else on top of it...

Dammit.

"Just move." That was another goodie. Just move to somewhere with a lower cost of living. Because of course, moving didn't cost money. Not to mention leaving everything she knew behind.

How had her dad done it? He'd worked two jobs, raised a daughter by himself, and he'd never lost the smile on his face.

Logically, she knew there must have been times he'd felt like this, but she'd never witnessed it. And she really didn't want to ask him for help now. After everything he'd done, he deserved to spend his money on *him*. If he was rolling in it, it might be different, but he had enough to keep him comfortable and go on a few vacations—which was all she really wanted.

It shouldn't be this damn hard.

What I wouldn't do to win the lottery...

Of course, she had to play to win. More money.

Her phone buzzing with a text message was a welcome distraction. Sam's eyebrows rose at the message, which was from Noelle.

Noelle: *Hey, girl! Want to go to Stronghold with me this Saturday?*

Sam smiled, some of the tension in her chest relaxing. She'd never gone to Stronghold with anyone other than Morgan.

Sam: *Sure, sounds good! What time did you want to get there?*

After a moment she sent a second text, because now Morgan was on her mind.

Sam: *Do you mind if I invite my friend Morgan, too? Or we can keep it just us.* She didn't want to step on Noelle's toes, but the idea having a little group to hang out with really appealed. Other people went and hung out at Stronghold in groups.

Man, she really did not want to give up her membership. Maybe when she was there, she could talk to Patrick or someone about getting a paid job that would also cover membership fees. Whether that was something they did, she had no idea, but she could at least ask.

Her phone buzzed again.

Noelle: *Please do. I'd love to meet Morgan!*

A few minutes later, Sam had confirmation from Morgan that she would be there. And there it was. Sam was getting together with friends on the weekend. She couldn't remember the last time she could say that.

No, leaving Stronghold wasn't an option. She would just have to find some way to make it work.

Glancing at the clock, she saw that she had about ten more minutes before her next appointment. If she was really quick, she could type up her notes and maybe start looking at some job sites.

5

LADIES' NIGHT

<u>Sam</u>

Stronghold ended up being more than just Noelle and Morgan. Sam found herself sitting in the Lounge area with a bunch of Morgan's friends as well. She'd met them but never actually hung out with them. Noelle seemed thrilled to have found herself smack dab in the middle of a group of ready-made friends, which was about all that kept Sam from running.

If Noelle, who was completely new to all of this, could hang out with them, Sam could find the courage to as well.

She'd never been comfortable in groups of people, but with Noelle on one side of her and Morgan on the other, it was definitely easier. At least she was already friends with Morgan, and Noelle and she were in the same situation of not knowing anyone else, so that helped.

Caroline, Marissa, and Amy had been coming to Stronghold for a long time, so Sam had seen them around. They hadn't been particularly friendly to her, but they hadn't been unfriendly, either... though they'd snapped Morgan right up into their little group. Caroline and Marissa were both slim and stunning and gave off a kind of mean-girl vibe, which had intimidated Sam. Amy had always been super nice when Sam had run into her, but they just hadn't hung out or anything since Amy already had her friends.

Tonight, Amy and Morgan were kind of acting as a bridge between everyone, with Caroline and Marissa sitting on one side and Noelle and Sam on the other.

"What's the Dominance class like?" Amy wanted to know, leaning forward with her eyes alight.

"Pretty much the same as the submissive class," Sam told her, smiling wryly. "Just from the other side of things. Master Patrick is a big believer in making sure all the Doms have experienced what they want to put a sub through."

"Master Patrick is a control freak," Marissa said, rolling her eyes. It wasn't the first time Sam had heard such a thing, his own sub said it all the time, but there was something different about Marissa's tone when she said it. It lacked any fondness or patience for his quirk.

"I think most Doms are," Noelle said, laughing. She didn't seem to see anything wrong, so Sam smiled. Maybe she was overreacting again. Or maybe that was just how Marissa always talked.

"That's true," Caroline smirked, tossing her dark hair back over her shoulder.

Sam was trying so hard not to be judgmental, but she wasn't sure how she felt about Caroline. More than once, Caroline had mentioned her husband waiting at home, but Sam *knew* she'd seen Caroline scening with and having sex with people at Stronghold. *Not my business.* They might have an open relationship. She wouldn't make assumptions.

"It's always fun seeing if you can make them lose it. I don't think I've ever seen Patrick really lose it except the time that Lexie scened with Michael. That was hilarious."

"Lexie scened with Master Michael?" Sam asked, surprised. She couldn't imagine that.

"Yeah, forever ago, right before she and Patrick got together," Caroline said, leaning forward with the juicy gossip. "That's what pushed Patrick to finally make his move."

Marissa snorted and leaned back in her chair. She had a sharp angled face, but she was very pretty, with long light brown hair that flowed down her back. The blue corset she was wearing made the most of her small breasts, though she was so skinny, she didn't really need it to make her waist any smaller. She could actually lounge in her corset, unlike Sam, who looking forward to when she could get home and take the damn thing off. It wasn't the lack of air, the way the movies made it seem, it was just that sitting up this straight for so long wasn't comfortable. She wanted to slouch and twist.

"Patrick will do anything to stay in control," Marissa said.

The familiar way she spoke about him and Lexie made it seem like she knew them, but there was a definite edge to her voice. Well, Sam thought there was. Should she ask? She wasn't sure, so she took a sip of her drink.

"Amy, what are you doing?" Caroline asked exasperatedly, thankfully changing the subject. Everyone looked at Amy, who blushed hotly as she tugged on the tight top she was wearing.

"I... my top doesn't fit me right anymore," Amy mumbled. She hunched her shoulders forward a little, but her blonde hair was pulled back from her face, so she couldn't hide behind it the way it seemed she was trying to do. "I've been putting on weight, and I don't know what to do."

"Stop eating cheese fries?" Caroline snickered. No one else laughed, so Sam didn't feel bad about not doing so.

"I have," Amy replied miserably. "I've been trying to get in shape for the wedding, you know that. I've been dieting and exercising, and I wasn't losing, but now I think I'm actually *gaining*."

Marissa frowned.

"You should probably go see a doctor about that."

"Yeah, maybe." Amy looked forlorn, which Sam hated to see. She'd had her own struggles with her weight over the years until she'd finally realized she was happy in her body and fuck whoever didn't like it.

Amy had seemed that way, too, but weddings definitely did do that to people. If Sam ever got married, would she want to lose weight? She wasn't sure. She didn't think so, but who knew? Not that she was anywhere near getting married. Sam's eyes drifted across the main room of Stronghold, taking in all the people packing into the space.

Would she find someone she could have a kink and romantic relationship with? Some people didn't. Caroline kept hers completely separate. Sam had seen plenty of people who scened together without letting emotion get involved, and she'd seen plenty of people who became partners in every way.

If she was being honest with herself, that was what she wanted… but she wasn't sure she'd be able to find it.

Awareness tickled the back of her neck, and she turned her head, feeling like someone was staring at her.

Dark brown eyes bore into her from across the room. Q was there, standing with Angel and Master Adam, and he was watching her. She could hear the others beside her talking, giving Amy suggestions, but none of it really registered as Q held her gaze.

<u>Q</u>

"Go ask her to scene."

"What?" Q jerked his gaze away from Sam's, wincing as Angel's elbow jabbed into his side.

"Go ask her to scene. You're not going to get anywhere just trying to eye fuck her from across the room." Angel grinned up at him as Q pinched the bridge of his nose. Sometimes Angel gave him a headache.

"I am not eye fucking her."

He kind of was.

For some reason, he didn't want to admit it. He also wasn't sure if he should go over. Sure, they were paired together during class, but that didn't mean she would want to do anything outside of it.

It wasn't as if they'd talked or anything since Monday after he'd walked her to her car. Not that she'd ever given him her number, but he had it. He'd needed it to change her ringtones, which didn't make him sound like a creeper at all.

Ugh.

"You were definitely eye fucking her. Wasn't he?" Angel turned to Adam for support, widening her eyes as she looked up at him. Her dark curls bounced slightly from the movement, and she leaned toward him to give him the best view of her cleavage. In her heels, she was nearly as tall as her blond Viking of a Dom, so it was quite a view.

Not that it had the effect she wanted.

Adam shook his head at her, and she pouted.

"You're incorrigible." He looked at Q, expression apologetic, then reached up to smooth his fingers over his goatee. "As much as it pains me to agree with her…"

"YES!" Angel pumped her fist.

"I would say you and Sam were definitely eye fucking each other." Adam grinned at Q's chagrin.

Sometimes, he wished for friends who weren't quite so blunt.

"You should go over there and ask her to scene," Angel insisted.

"I'm supposed to be meeting Asad and Connor."

Angel rolled her eyes at him. "Like they won't understand. You know, at some point, Asad will ditch you to scene with a sub, anyway."

"Just like we're about to ditch you." Adam grinned as he stepped away from the table, tugging on Angel's arm. Unsurprisingly, she dug in her heels, clearly not wanting to retreat until she had what she wanted. Very Angel.

"Go over there, then you won't have to stand here alone. You could at least see if she's— AH! Adam!" Tired of waiting for his wife, Adam had spun her around and flipped her up over his shoulder.

"She's not wrong, you know," he said to Q before turning to stride away.

"Hey, it's just like old times!" Angel slapped Adam's ass as he walked, then started giggling and using both hands to play his cheeks like a drum. Encased in his leather pants, the sound was not terrible. "Butt bongos!"

The laughter that followed them didn't quite cover up Angel's squeal when Adam took his revenge by administering his own hard slap to her upturned butt. Q watched with envy as they headed up the stairs. That kind of relationship was what he wanted.

So, listen to Angel and go get it, dumbass.

Right. That would make sense. His gaze cut back across to where Sam was sitting.

Did he really want to try with *her*?

On the other hand, it wasn't like he'd met any other sub here he felt a connection with. He also didn't know if he and Sam would keep that chemistry in the bedroom. What if it fizzled the moment they actually touched each other? What if what they were feeling was left over from high school?

Only one way to find out.

He could wait for Monday, but that was a classroom situation. There would be a lot going on in terms of new experiences for him. Not really the best scenario for trying to test out an attraction.

Shaking his head, Q went over to the bar and lifted a hand to catch Andrew's attention. Another of Angel's friends, he didn't work the bar as much as he used to but stepped in on nights when they needed help.

"Hey, if you see Asad and Connor, can you tell them I went to scene?"

Andrew's grin lit up his face, his teeth flashing white against tanned skin.

"With Sam? Good luck."

Q almost asked how Andrew knew, then shut his mouth and shook his head. Angel's group of friends made gossip an Olympic sport. Heck, the whole club did. If Angel was pushing him to make a move on Sam, he wasn't at all surprised the rest of their friends knew about it.

Headed to where Sam was sitting, he saw her shooting him a few small glances, then her eyes widened when she realized he was making his way to her group. He knew all of them. She was sitting with some of the people Angel and her friends didn't get along with.

Angel's best friend Leigh was now engaged to Jared, Marissa's ex. Q's understanding was Marissa hadn't been thrilled about letting Jared go, even though they'd been broken up when he met Leigh. They'd had an on-again off-again relationship similar to what Leigh had been going through. Leigh and Jared had leaned on each other while getting over their exes—a rebound story that had actually worked, much to everyone's surprise and relief.

Well... not everyone. Marissa and her bestie, Caroline, who was also sitting with Sam, didn't stir up drama but they weren't pleasant. Caroline was a real piece of work on her own. She had no problem coming to the club to cheat on her husband and bragged about how he had no idea.

They'd latched onto Morgan for some reason, who had been so excited to have real friends, no one had the heart to tell her that her friends could be pretty awful people. They had been good friends to Morgan since meeting her, so there wasn't a real reason to try to pull her away from them. They were trying to let her make her own decisions, and no one wanted to undermine her confidence in being able to do so.

The person that didn't make sense in their little group was Amy, who was one of the sweetest people Q had ever met. On the other hand, that sweetness allowed Marissa and Caroline to push her around. Amy was always trying to smooth over the messes they left behind. She was also the one Morgan hung out with the most, which might be another reason no one intervened. Amy was a good friend for her to have.

Sam would be, too.

Q was a lot less sure about Noelle, but he would try not to judge without reason. He still didn't know the full story about what went down between her and Iris. He did notice that both Caroline and Noelle sat up a little straighter as he approached, Caroline smiling with interest while Noelle eyed him curiously. Like he'd ever scene with Caroline. That hadn't stopped her from trying.

He gave everyone else a noncommittal nod, focusing his attention on Sam. The confusion on her face was adorable.

"Hey, Sam, I was wondering if you'd be interested in scening tonight?"

She blinked as if she wasn't sure she'd heard what she thought she'd heard. Morgan elbowed her in the side when she didn't answer.

"Oh, um... now? Who's in charge?"

He grinned wider.

"I am."

6

AN UNEXPECTED INVITATION

Sam

Holy crap, holy crap, holy crap.

It wasn't like no one had ever asked her to scene before, but she'd never had someone she was actually *interested* in ask her to scene. All her other scenes had been platonic, or they'd agreed to use toys or whatever. From the heat in Q's eyes as he looked down at her, she didn't doubt for one moment that he was asking her *because* he wanted her. Not just someone to scene with, but her specifically.

As if coming up to ask her when she was surrounded by a bunch of willing, attractive, single subs hadn't indicated that already. He'd chosen *her*. It was a little like being singled out from the herd by a predator, except she actually wanted it.

Especially with the authoritative way he said he would be in charge tonight.

Being honest, as much as she was looking forward to having Q on his knees for her in class, she'd also fantasized about having him take control ever since she'd walked into Marquis and seen him for the first time.

"Say yes," Morgan hissed in her ear, nudging her with her elbow.

Sam glanced at Noelle. She didn't want to just ditch the other woman, but Noelle grinned and nodded.

Well, okay then.

"If you'll excuse me," she said, glancing around at the others. Caroline had a pinched expression as she nodded back, but Marissa gave her a thumbs up, and Amy made a little shooing motion, her eyes alight with encouragement. No one but Caroline seemed to mind, and, well... Caroline wasn't Sam's problem.

Taking Q's hand, she let him help her up from her chair. To her surprise, he didn't let go once she was standing, holding onto it as he led them toward the stairs.

"Upstairs or downstairs?" he asked, glancing at her.

"Can we even get a room upstairs?" she asked, bemused. It was a Saturday night after all. If you wanted a room, you had to plan ahead. Wait... had he planned ahead for this?

"No. Downstairs it is." Q grimaced, but Sam didn't mind.

If he'd planned ahead, she might not have felt as special since he could have just been looking to use the room and not necessarily with her. The spontaneity of his invitation made her feel on top of the world. He wasn't just looking for a sub to fill a slot.

He wanted *her*.

Even after everything they'd talked about on Monday, even hearing the reason she'd changed her mind about prom. Even after he hadn't kissed her goodbye when she'd thought he was going to. Maybe he'd just needed a little more time to think about everything.

Regardless, tonight, he was asking her to scene with him.

Yes, that made her feel giddy.

"Any hard limits I should know about?" he asked, giving her fingers a small squeeze as they went down the steps, drawing her attention back to the present.

"I've seen your list, and all of mine are covered by it," she replied, giving him a sideways smile. "When it comes to humiliation, I don't mind being called a naughty, bad girl, or a toy, but I've got way more of a praise kink."

"Me, too." Q winked at her, making her laugh. Yeah, she could see that about both of them. With the way they worked to excel in high school, both of them liked getting rewards more than punishments.

Although Sam didn't mind a little role play now and then.

The staircase emptied out into the dungeon, which was full of people, though not everyone was doing something. Some people were just walking around and watching the scenes rather than participating.

Stronghold's dungeon was full of possible places to scene. Spanking benches were arranged throughout the center of the main floor. Along the walls were various nooks with chains hanging or occupied by St. Andrews' crosses. A quiet nook was filled with couches, a mini fridge, and a basket of blankets for aftercare. And, of course, there were the private rooms, which were all occupied.

Interrogation, the Doctor's Office, and the Jail were located on this floor. The second floor had more options, like a Locker Room, a movie room, a school room, an office, and things like that. One day, Sam would love to use a private room, here or at Marquis, with someone who had reserved the room with her in mind. Not when it was part of the class, because that didn't count.

"How do you feel about a little spanking?" Q asked, his steps slowing as he took in the benches. They were spaced far enough apart to avoid feeling crowded, and there were a few that were currently open. A club submissive was wiping down the closest one to them.

"Have I been naughty?" she asked flirtatiously.

They came to a halt, Q turning to face her, but never relinquishing her hand.

"Well, you were never properly punished for leaving me without a prom date." His voice had turned to a low, husky growl, but his eyes simmered with heat and promise. Guilt threatened, but when he was looking at her like that, she knew he didn't really mean it.

This was going to be a funishment. Role play. Though she probably did deserve a spanking.

Widening her eyes, she tilted her head. With the heels she was wearing, they were basically the same height, so it was no trouble to meet his gaze.

"Oh, you're right... I'm so sorry, Master Q." She made her voice syrupy sweet, which had the added effect of making her sound entirely insincere.

His lips quirked.

"You're certainly going to be Ms. Dupre."

* * *

Q

Talk about fantasies coming true. Not that he'd fantasized about spanking Sam after she'd changed her mind about prom. He hadn't known enough then to even fathom such a thing. But if he'd known about kink back then, this was exactly what he would have fantasized about. Her wide eyes and pouty, half-parted lips made his cock throb. He was already rock hard, his body eager for... well, everything.

"I suppose you want me to make it up to you?" Her mischievous smile demonstrated as little regret as her tone had.

"Yes. Yes, I do."

He was being completely sincere. While he might not have known about kink, he'd had plans for that night. Pretty innocent plans since they hadn't been dating or anything, but still. A dance. A kiss. Maybe the chance to tell her how much he liked her, if he'd been able to make himself that vulnerable.

They had been going off to separate colleges after graduation. He hadn't been about to suggest anything like being boyfriend and girlfriend and trying to do long distance, but he'd wanted some memories to take with him. Maybe a little hope that they'd meet again in the future, after college, older, wiser, and with the attraction still firmly in place.

That last wish had actually come true, and he sure as hell wasn't going to squander it.

Which was why he let go of her hand to cup her face in his palms.

They'd gone over his limits at the last class—sex was on the table, and kissing was as well.

He'd waited years for his first kiss with Samantha Dupre.

Her eyes widened right before their lips connected, and he felt her tense, but only for a moment. Then she relaxed, hands pressing against his chest, and she leaned into the kiss.

Fuck.

The simmering attraction between them exploded. Q's right hand slid from her chin to the back of her neck while the other dropped to wrap around her waist and haul her against him. She gasped, her lips parting, and he took full advantage, delving between them with his tongue and getting his first proper taste of her.

She tasted like lemons, which brought to mind the water with lemon she'd been drinking upstairs. Or maybe this was how she always tasted. Sweet and tart at the same time, which summed her up perfectly. She kissed him back, just as needy, just as hot for him as he was for her.

A small cough beside them made both of them jump, Q staring at her for a moment before tearing his gaze away to look at the club sub who had been cleaning the spanking bench near them. She was grinning widely.

"Sorry to interrupt, but if you wanted a bench, I'd grab this one now," she said, giving them a wink before skipping away.

Good thing she'd cut in because Q saw several people eyeing the bench as he shifted Sam closer to it. He didn't have to get her on it immediately, of course, but just by standing next to it, they were staking their claim. In the past minute or so, while they'd been flirting and kissing, all the other benches had been taken.

"I'm not sure if I should thank her or curse her," Sam joked, looking down at the bench before cocking her head at him. A lock of blonde hair fell across her eyes, and Q reached up to brush it away before she could, letting the tips of his fingers stroke over her face.

The hot blush that followed in its wake made him feel like a king.

It was also making him feel a little out of his element. He'd never scened with anyone that he was this into. He'd been attracted to the other submissives he'd scened with, but not like this. Not this white-hot attraction that made him forget where they were when they kissed.

I am so fucked.

"Well, I want to thank her for ensuring I get to bend you over this bench." He grinned even wider when she snorted and shook her head. "Okay pretty girl, on your knees with your hands up behind your head. I want to get this corset off you."

She blushed even harder when he called her pretty girl, but she didn't get on her knees right away. For a moment, he thought she was going to fight him on it, but a considering expression fell over her features, and she slowly got down on her knees. Interesting.

Q decided to take a moment to walk around her. He wanted to look at her and wanted to drive home who was in charge. He wasn't sure if her hesitation was because it was him or because she struggled to submit because she was a Switch—he felt like that was how it would be for him—but he figured taking his time couldn't hurt either way.

It also meant he got to enjoy the view.

With her on her knees, her breasts pushed up by the corset, he wanted to dive in between her pillowy breasts and snuggle in for the winter. If only. The skirt she was wearing got in the way of being able to see her lower half, but he still liked seeing her on her knees, with them spread wide apart. It was a hell of a tease to know he would be able to see everything soon.

Thanks to Angel and her penchant for corset making, Q knew how to lace and unlace a corset properly, so he decided to ignore the quick release front. Coming around behind Sam, he tugged at the knot.

Sam turned her head to look over her shoulder.

"You know you can just undo the front, right?" she asked, hands already moving to show him.

"Hands up," he snapped, taking hold of her hair and using it to pull her head back. Sam's eyes went wide, her lips parting in surprise as her pupils dilated. "I'll take care of the corset, pretty girl, you just sit still and let me."

With her head tipped back like this, her lips were impossible to resist. Bending, he claimed another kiss. Damn, he liked kissing her, especially when he felt her lips soften beneath his.

But bending over wasn't completely comfortable and as much as he liked kissing her, he was way more excited about finally getting his hands on that sweet ass of hers.

Straightening, he smiled when she put her hands back behind her head, twining her fingers behind her neck.

"Good girl."

With those words, he got to watch her melt a little. Running his hand down her upper back, he let go of her hair so her head could drop forward again. This time, she kept her hands firmly in place as he expertly unlaced the back of her corset, loosening it from the center outward, and she sighed with relief as the tight constraint around her body relaxed.

"Hands up."

Sure, he could undo the quick release in the front, but there was something satisfying about pulling the whole corset up and off. Her hands dropped to the back of her neck, thrusting her breasts forward with the movement, and Q's cock throbbed. He was actually going to get to second base with Samantha Dupre.

You're going to do a whole lot more than that.

7

HE'S IN CHARGE

Sam

Feeling Q's eyes caressing her skin, Sam tried not to feel too self-conscious, but it was difficult. While she loved her body, there were always people who didn't, and most of the time she didn't care... but it was hard not to care when a man she wanted to have sex with saw her naked for the first time.

If he didn't like the way she looked that was a problem with him, and logically she knew that, but that didn't always fix what she felt. If Q turned away from her now or said this was all just a joke to get back at her from high school, she would probably run from Stronghold and never come back again.

So, when he walked back in front of her, she couldn't help but peek up at him. Not that he noticed. His gaze was firmly fixed on her exposed breasts. There was nothing in his expression other than admiration and desire. Relief, arousal, and happiness flooded her, allowing her to fully relax. She dropped her gaze, a smile curving her lips, and her spine straightened, pushing her breasts out even more.

"Very nice," Q said, reaching down to cup one of her breasts, his dark fingers stroking her pale skin. The contrast was so pretty, especially when he reached the pale pink nipple and rubbed his thumb over the little bud. It hardened under his touch, and she felt an answering rush of heat between her thighs. If she hadn't been kneeling, she would have tried to press them together. Instead, there was nothing to assuage the ache that was growing between them.

"Thank you, Master Q." She sang out the words, which gave them a very sassy sound. It felt weird calling him Master Q, but she didn't hate it.

He gave her nipple a little pinch, which made her squeal at the sudden, delicious sting.

"Careful, pretty girl, you wouldn't want to be disrespectful." His tone was full of warning.

Sam bit her lip against sassing him since she was already going to be spanked.

"These are very pretty breasts."

Warm palms cupped the undersides while his fingers dug into the soft flesh, thumbs brushing against her nipples as they hardened even further. Sam moaned, her pussy clenching with need. Q crouched down in front of her, giving him a more comfortable position from which to fondle her. Her hands tightened on the back of her neck, fighting back the impulse to touch him as well.

This was one of the things she loved about kink—that she was supposed to stay still, that she didn't always have to think about what to do next, that she could wait for someone to tell her what they wanted her to do. Right now, she wanted to touch him, and it was a struggle to keep herself under control... yet obeying him and fighting against her own instincts turned her on even more.

The way he was touching her, caressing her, made her entire body feel hot. Whimpering, she pushed her breasts toward him, shuddering when he finally pinched her nipples and relieved some of the ache that had been growing there.

"So pretty," he murmured. "I think these would look very nice with some jewelry. Next time, I'll have to bring some."

Sam's nipples pulsed against his fingers for two reasons. First, she loved nipple clamps. Second, he'd said *next time*.

Yes, please.

He might be talking about class, where she'd be in charge of him, but she didn't think so. She was pretty sure he was talking about him dominating her again.

Which she absolutely wanted.

Does this mean we're dating?

Probably not the time to ask.

But I'm going to ask.

Later.

She made the promise to herself, already unsure if she would follow through.

"Okay, pretty girl, up on your feet. I want this skirt off, then you over the spanking bench."

Disappointment warred with anticipation as he released her breasts and held his hand out to help her up. Sam took it and got to her feet, trying not to feel too vulnerable when she saw there were a few voyeurs watching them. One of the hardest parts about kink had been getting used to people seeing her naked. Lots of people.

There were lots of other people in Stronghold's dungeon getting naked who came in all shapes, sizes, and ages. It was the least judgmental place she'd ever been to, and she sure wasn't going to let the dregs of her body hang-ups screw her out of a scene with Q.

Q's hungry gaze roamed over her, clearly enjoying the sight as her skirt dropped to the floor. He wasn't turned off by rolls or cellulite. He was looking at her thighs as hungrily as he had her breasts. Feeling cheeky, Sam shifted a little to show off the curve of her ass, and his gaze dutifully followed.

She was wearing her favorite pair of underwear—the stars had definitely aligned tonight. Red and lacy, they were almost like boy shorts, but they didn't cover nearly enough to be called that. The bottom of her cheeks hung out from beneath them, the scalloped lace clinging to her curves. She found them to be a lot more comfortable than a thong while still leaving plenty of her ass exposed.

"See something you like?" she asked sassily, and Q chuckled.

"Yes, I do, and I'll like it even better once you're over the bench like you're supposed to be."

Sam squealed as his hand snaked out, smacking against the butt cheek closest to him with enough force to sting.

It was going to sting a lot more in a minute, yet she still eagerly laid herself over the bench. Made of wood with padded leather, the bench had two knee supports for her to kneel on before bending over the main portion of it. Reaching down, she took hold of the grips that were there to help keep her in place. The position squashed her breasts a little, making it harder to breathe—or maybe that was just her excitement.

She couldn't decide if she was disappointed Q hadn't taken her underwear off.

That seemed to indicate no sex, which was disappointing, but on the other hand, jumping straight into sex when they'd just barely called a truce didn't seem like the smartest idea. While sex was on the table, after the negotiations during class, she knew she wouldn't be jumping right into it when she was in charge. But she still kinda wished that he had.

Really? You want your first time with Q to be in the middle of Stronghold's dungeon with a bunch of people watching?

Okay, maybe not. She had a tiny exhibitionist streak, but it didn't usually extend to actually having sex in front of people. She was just blinded by lust.

Q's warm palm rested on the curve of her ass and rubbed a slow circle on her right cheek. She gripped the handholds a little harder as she waited for the first smack.

"I have wanted to do this from the moment I saw you again," he murmured, and his hand lifted.

Smack!

The sting wasn't overwhelming, but it sure as heck wasn't small. It was right on the edge of being too much. She didn't have much time to register the pain before his hand came down again on the opposite cheek. Sam gasped and rocked forward on the bench, which rubbed the front of her mound against it, sending a sizzle of pleasure straight through her core.

His hand came down again and again and again, leaving stinging hot flashes of pain over the entire expanse of her ass. Sam shuddered and rocked against the bench, but the little bit of stimulation she could get wasn't nearly enough. Moaning, she lifted her hips up to meet Q's hand as he rained down swats on her upturned ass.

Q

Fucking beautiful.

The temptation to spank Sam until her cheeks were as red as her underwear was definitely there, but he wouldn't go that far tonight. He had a sadistic streak, but he wasn't really a sadist. His cock throbbed as he laid his palm down on her sit spot, causing her ass to ripple, and she cried out from the pain.

Not that it was all pain. He could see the wet spot growing on the gusset of her underwear where her arousal was working its way through the tightly stretched fabric as he spanked her. The outline of her swollen pussy lips was visible through the underwear. Pausing for a moment to stroke his fingers over her panties, a thrill ran up his body both at the touch and the sound she made when he did so.

"Good girl," he murmured before going back to spanking her again.

Her pink bottom was slowly darkening, and he was aiming for a rosy pink before he stopped. Where this scene was going, he wasn't sure. He hadn't planned to be doing this tonight, so he was playing it by ear. Spanking her gave him some time to think about what he wanted to do next.

Or, well, what he was *going* to do next.

What he *wanted* to do was rip those pretty lacy panties off of her and plunge into her from behind. He'd left her underwear on as a barrier to keep him from doing exactly that. While he'd fantasized about spanking her, fantasized about getting his hands all over her, he'd had very specific fantasies about fucking her, and none of them included an audience. He didn't mind people watching, but it did nothing for him, either.

With Sam, he wanted it to be private. Special.

Granted, if she decided to take a ride during their class together, he wouldn't protest. But when he was in charge, he had his own plans... which did not include sex tonight.

Unfortunately.

Shit, he wished he'd been better prepared.

It wasn't like he'd known this was going to happen.

He was never coming to Stronghold without his toy bag again, that was for sure. Lesson learned.

"How are you feeling, Sam? Give me a color."

"Green, Sir." The answer came immediately with happy sigh that made him grin. Yeah, she was feeling good, and he was about to make her feel even better. While he might not be able to do everything he wanted to her right now, he could definitely give her an orgasm.

"Good girl." Shifting his position slightly so he could grip both of her dark pink ass cheeks, he squeezed the soft flesh, digging his fingers in as she moaned. Dipping one hand farther down, his fingers traced over the damp fabric of her underwear, stroking and caressing the pouting folds. Sam moaned, her hips lifting up to meet his touch, while Q pressed his other hand against the bulge at the front of his pants to relieve some of his own ache.

It only took him a moment to reach where her clit was and pressed down, rubbing his fingers in a slow, sensuous circle against the little bud. She cried out, shuddering as she pushed back against his touch.

"That's it," he murmured, slowly increasing the speed of his movements, rubbing the bundle of nerves harder as her breathing sped up and so did her movements. She was pressing back against him, greedy for all the stimulation he could give her. "Come for me, pretty girl."

As though his words gave her the permission, or the push, she needed, Sam's cry peaked, and her entire body tensed as she came apart.

Q only had two regrets—that he wasn't buried inside her and that he couldn't see her face.

8

AFTERCARE

Sam

Ecstasy flooded through her body as Q's clever fingers found the right spot to push, then all the built-up sexual tension inside her released. The painful heat from her spanking morphed, changing into pure pleasure as the waves of sexual bliss rolled through her. Panting and limp, she slumped over the bench, her empty inner muscles still clenching.

Wow.

She didn't know how long she lay there, panting and slowly coming back to herself. It could haven't been more than a few minutes, but it felt like forever. The whole time, Q was rubbing her lower back in broad, soft strokes, petting her. It felt really nice.

"Okay, pretty girl, let's get you up and over to aftercare."

Q's deep voice penetrated the haze around her brain and she sighed, pushing herself up. She was still warm and tingly all over, and her knees wobbled a little. Immediately, Q was at her side, wrapping his arm around her to steady her. She shrieked when she suddenly felt him lift her, one arm behind her back, the other coming up under her knees as if she was the heroine of a romance novel. Except she didn't look like any of those women on the covers... she was a lot bigger.

"Don't! I'm too heavy!"

He snorted, carefully stepping around the spanking bench while she clung to his neck.

"You're not too heavy to go twenty feet to the couch," he responded, his voice slightly strained by the effort of talking and carrying her. Sam pressed her lips together, her arm around his neck, doing her best to help distribute her weight more evenly.

She'd always wondered what it would be like to be carried like this. The truth was... not that comfortable. It wasn't just Q carrying her. She had tightened her stomach muscles and was working to keep a firm hold on his shoulders so she didn't end up being dead weight.

"Does that mean I don't have to be impressed that you literally swept me off my feet?" she teased, enjoying the way he scowled at her before lowering them onto the couch.

"Well, when you put it that way..." he drawled, making her giggle again as she snuggled in next to him.

The same subbie who had been cleaning the spanking bench appeared before them, giving her a wink as she put Sam's corset and skirt on the couch beside them before disappearing to clean the bench again. It was the kind of service people traded for discounted memberships. Sam had started doing it about a month ago to help with the cost of her membership.

But she wouldn't think about that right now. She was going to enjoy being snuggled up on Q's lap, her hot bottom pressed against his hard thighs, while his hand stroked up and down her bare back. It was an incredibly sweet, intimate moment, and she refused to let her money worries ruin it.

"It'll be better next time," Q said suddenly, making her blink with surprise. She did like the sound of that 'next time' again but wasn't really sure what he was talking about.

"What do you mean 'better?'" she asked, leaning back a little and lifting her head so she could see his expression. A wry smile twisted the corner of his lips.

"I mean, more planned out. Something more exciting than just a spanking and an orgasm."

"Hey, now." Sam poked him in the chest. "Don't go knocking a good spanking and orgasm combo. Just because we're in a kink club doesn't mean we have to go crazy. I like being spanked, I like having orgasms, and I really like it when those things are paired." Though she got what he was saying. It wasn't as if they were competing with the others around them, but what they had just done was incredibly simple compared to some of the possibilities.

Q chuckled, shifting slightly to make himself more comfortable.

"I liked it, too, but would have liked it better if I'd planned things out more. Maybe gotten a private room instead of having to do every-thing on the fly. Spontaneity has its place but... I can do better." He said it with a firm resolve that she recognized from high school.

She nearly laughed. It wasn't as though they were being graded on how good a scene they could create, but she had a feeling he was grading himself in his head, based on who knows what criteria.

"Making big plans... do I get dinner first at least?" she teased. The words were out of her mouth before she could take them back, and she stilled. Scening didn't mean he was interested in dating. "Just kidding."

"I would love to take you out to dinner," he said, right over top of her attempt to pretend she'd been joking. He smiled, but it didn't quite reach his eyes. "As long as you actually show up."

Feeling like shit, she sagged against him.

"Sorry, I just didn't want you to feel like I was trying to push you into something you don't want."

Q laughed, and the reservation in his expression disappeared.

"Trust me, pretty girl, I rarely do anything I don't want to do. And I definitely want to take you to dinner."

"Then I would love to go have dinner with you. I promise to show up. We're not in high school anymore." She didn't have to worry about getting distracted by him and not meeting the necessary GPA anymore. "If I can't do something, I'll let you know ahead of time, and I'll tell you why."

"That works for me." Q grinned. "Now, what do you want to do for the rest of tonight?"

As much as she wanted to stay right where she was...

"I should probably get back upstairs," she said reluctantly. "I came with Noelle, and I don't want her to feel like I ditched her."

"Mmm... alright then, let's get you back upstairs."

Q

Truthfully, Q wasn't sure what he was going to do when he returned Sam to her friends. He didn't really want to hang out with that particular group, but he didn't want to leave Sam's side.

It turned out he didn't have to make that decision. The group Sam had been sitting with had dissipated, and now only Morgan and Amy were there, chatting with a Dom he vaguely recognized—Master Zach, who was Master Kincaid's boyfriend but who also platonically scened with Amy, who was engaged. Q perked up. He'd wanted to talk to Zach since he was a Switch, even if he only submitted to Kincaid.

"Hey, where'd everyone go?" Sam asked with a laugh as she and Q walked up, catching their attention. Everyone smiled up at them, and Q gave a little wave as he sat down in one of the comfy Lounge chairs, pulling Sam onto his lap with him. She squeaked delightfully but didn't fight him. Not that it would be easy with the blanket she still had wrapped around her.

Q was holding onto her clothes, which he tucked between him and the arm of the chair. She didn't need them back yet.

"Marissa decided to go home because she has to be up early tomorrow for a flight, Caroline went to scene with Master Ryan, and Noelle with Master Trey." Morgan rattled off everyone's whereabouts without the slightest hint of envy, and she didn't seem at all bothered not to have been chosen.

"Oh good, I'm glad Noelle is getting to scene," Sam said with a sigh of relief. Q wondered if she was feeling a little guilty about having left Noelle on her own, even if she'd been with other subs. Well, if she had been, hopefully she wouldn't now.

"You two looked like you had fun." Amy smiled at Sam with understanding.

"We did. Since she's going to be in charge of me during class, it was nice to get a turn being in charge here," Q joked, winking at Sam when she glanced at him. She stuck her tongue out, and he chuckled.

"So, you're both switches?" Amy asked curiously, peeking at Zach before focusing on them.

"Seems that way," Q said easily. He also had one eye on Zach, curious about the other man's take on things. Q didn't know anyone else in the club who was a Switch other than him and Sam. "I guess I'll find out at the end of the class, but I knew after the Dom class I wanted to try the other side."

Amy looked at Zach. Lounging in his chair, the switchy-Dom pretty much only had eyes for the petite blonde.

"Is that how it was for you?" The curiosity in her voice had thickened, and it seemed like she'd been waiting for the opportunity to bring it up. Which was good for Q. He'd have to thank Amy later for asking for him because that was exactly what he wanted to know but wouldn't have felt comfortable enough to ask.

Since Zach and Amy scened together regularly, they obviously had a different relationship, but she must not have asked him about this before. Zach ran his hand through his dark hair and let out a sigh, taking a moment to think before he finally answered her.

"Not really." Zach shrugged one shoulder. Looking away from Amy, he turned his gaze toward the ceiling while she remained intently focused on him. "I took the class, but I didn't feel like I was missing anything afterward. I'm pretty sure my interest in submitting is Kincaid-specific."

As was his interest in men, though he was silent about that. Q knew from club gossip that Zach had considered himself straight before he and Kincaid had gotten together, whereas Kincaid had always been openly bisexual. Even if Zach's interest in submission was person-specific, Q was still curious.

After all, he couldn't imagine submitting to just anyone, either. Even with Sam, his desire to dominate *her* warred with his interest in what it would be like to have her dominate him. He had fantasized about a faceless woman dominating him when he'd first started thinking about the other side of things, so even without Sam, he would have been interested.

Now, though, he was having trouble picturing anyone other than her.

Try not to fall in too deep right away, Romeo.

"I guess that means you're never going to let me turn the tables on you, huh?" Amy teased.

"Absolutely not, naughty girl," Zach said, flashing her a smile that was silky with erotic threat.

If Q didn't know that Amy had a fiancé and Zach had a boyfriend, he might have thought they were flirting, but he knew little about playing platonically outside of a class. The two of them had been scening together for a while, so it made sense there would be a level of intimacy.

Though it did make him wonder if maybe he and Sam were only feeling intimacy because of the scene they'd just done... or if they were pushing something that wasn't really there because they knew they'd be working together. It had been a fast turnaround for both of them, but he also knew he'd been holding onto a high school grudge, and she had, too.

Maybe if he hadn't been so quick to snap at her when she'd shown up to the Dominance class, there wouldn't have been any friction between them. Or they could have jumped straight to the good kind of friction like they had tonight.

He shifted her on his lap again, aware her plush bottom was pressing against his erection and making it difficult for him to think about anything but sex with her... and that was not happening right now.

"Hey, there you are!" A heavy hand clapped down on Q's shoulder, making him jump. He looked up to see Asad grinning down at him. "And the beautiful Samantha. I can understand why you ditched us."

"I didn't ditch you," Q said, holding one hand up for Asad to shake, followed by Connor. He noticed Sam didn't protest at Asad's use of her full name.

Charming fucker.

"We would have understood if you had," Connor said, smiling as he sat down next to Morgan, who immediately perked up and smiled back at him. Rather than finding his own seat, Asad perched on the arm of Morgan's chair, planting himself directly between her and Amy and giving both of them his best grin. Amy smiled back at him, and Zach frowned.

Sam giggled and snuggled in closer on Q's lap.

It was an odd mix of people, but they ended up having a good time talking. Caroline didn't return, but eventually, Noelle did. Trey gave Zach a nod as he dropped her off. She didn't have quite the same happy, satisfied appearance Sam did, but she was grinning and perfectly pleasant, so Q figured she'd had a good time. He was able to relax as long as she didn't bring up Iris or anything else that might cause an issue.

Of course, her presence meant he didn't get to walk Sam to her car all on his own, but he could live with that. After all, there was definitely going to be a next time.

9

CLASS IS IN SESSION

_Q_

"Knees farther apart." The crop that smacked his inner thigh wasn't gentle, and Q gritted his teeth while Sam covered her mouth with her hand, watching Mistress Julie correct his position. Her eyes were dancing with mirth.

As far as classes went, this was not as sexy as he'd been picturing it. He'd forgotten that the initial classes for the Dom group had been a lot more about function than anything else. The sub classes were turning out to be the same. His only saving grace was that Mistress Julie, not Law, was keeping an eye on him and Sam tonight.

She and Law seemed to have split the class, so Law didn't have to spend time correcting him or Noelle, though for very different reasons. Q preferred it this way. He wasn't sure how he would react to his friend smacking him with a crop.

It was easier to take instruction from Mistress Julie, even if it stung like a bitch whenever she wielded that crop of hers. He also understood why Law wouldn't want to be in charge of Noelle, considering she was an ex-friend of his current girlfriend and submissive. So far, she was behaving perfectly for Mistress Julie, though he did see her looking over where Law was working with Steve, Emerson, and Cassidy more than once.

She might just be curious.

Not my business.

"Better," Mistress Julie said, giving him an approving nod. She turned away to check on Noelle, allowing Sam to step back into place.

"Did you like the crop?" Sam asked, tapping the one she was holding against the knee-high boot on her right foot. Those boots were sexy as hell, and Q had a perfect view of them from his current position. Being on his knees also gave him a delightful perspective of her very short skirt.

"Yes, Mistress Sam," he said truthfully, cocking his head at her. On his knees, with the backs of his hands resting on his thighs, even though he was wearing shorts, he felt incredibly vulnerable and far more submissive than he usually did. There really was something to be said about the body helping with the mindset.

Sam walked around him, the flat leather on the end of the crop tapping gently against his pec and then tracing over his shoulder and upper back as she moved. It lifted, and he only had a moment before it landed with a stinging smack against his ass.

Ow.

Also... *hot.*

No, he wasn't much of a masochist, but Sam hadn't put much force behind the blow. Q was far more turned on by the way she was pacing around him, making him wait for whatever it was she wanted to do to him. Already his erection—which had deflated a bit during the more boring part of learning about the kneeling position and the various options for how to place one's hands—was thickening with interest again.

This was more of an honor bondage kind of situation. He stayed in position while she touched him however she wanted. Part of the eroticism came from the choice to submit.

As if his thought had echoed around the room, he heard Steve speaking up with a question.

"So, what if I stand up, even though I'm supposed to be kneeling?"

It was clear from Steve's tone that he wasn't trying to be a brat. He was just curious.

"It depends on your Dom and what you negotiated beforehand," Law said. "Some might punish you. Some might consider the scene over. Some might want to talk to you about why you felt the need to stand."

"What if we don't want to be punished?" That was Noelle. Unlike Steve, her tone was more like she was challenging what Master Law was saying, but he wasn't the one who answered her.

"Then don't stand up." Mistress Julie's sadistic chuckle was echoed by Law's. "When it comes down to it, the submissives have the power. You safe word if something goes beyond what you're comfortable with. Your Dom can't really force you to do anything you really don't want to do. And if they do, they aren't a Dom, they're an abuser."

Though she didn't look at Cassidy, Q felt like her words were directed at the quiet submissive. The one who'd had a Dom who not only pushed her past her limits but had ignored her safeword. That had been a whole thing, which had ended when the douche canoe deliberately rammed Law's car after getting kicked out of Stronghold.

So far, Law hadn't pressed charges, but he had a year to decide to do so, and he'd had friends in the prosecutor's office who were happy to follow his lead. It gave Cassidy some breathing room because if douche canoe bothered her again, Law was going to come after him with the full force of, well, the law. Hopefully, by the time the year was up, her ex would have forgotten about her.

Hopefully.

"Doms will sometimes push your soft limits, but any stretching of any limits should be discussed beforehand, and you don't have to agree to them pushing you. You also can stretch your hard limits, but only if you want to. You give the Doms the lines, they color within those boundaries." Law looked around the room sternly.

"What if you have trouble telling them no?" Emerson asked, sounding a bit worried. Q looked over to see they were looking at Cassidy, whose head was down as she stared at the floor. He didn't know how much experience Emerson had with kink, but clearly, they knew something about Cassidy's situation.

"You can always come find one of us, and we'll tell them for you." Mistress Julie's smile was as cold as a shark's. "Grab a Dungeon Monitor, an instructor, a Dom you're comfortable with, or Law's submissive, and they'll take care of the problem for you."

Law pinched the bridge of his nose but didn't protest the idea that they go to Iris. Considering Iris was the one who had originally rescued Cassidy, it would be hard to make that argument, though Law clearly wanted to. He hadn't been happy about Iris jumping in rather than getting a Dungeon Monitor.

***

*S*AM

Glancing down at Q, she saw him shaking his head, a little smile on his lips at Mistress Julie's speech. She didn't really know Iris or Cassidy, but she'd heard the story. Poor Cassidy. Sam could only imagine how difficult it was to be in a club where everyone knew your business.

On the other hand, Cassidy was hardly the only one people talked about. Sometimes it seemed like Stronghold and Marquis ran on gossip. Granted, they didn't always get things right, and it never seemed like malicious gossip, but it was part of the community.

"Okay, everyone, that's it for tonight," Master Law said, giving Mistress Julie a look that didn't seem to faze her in the least.

Sam wondered if she'd ever be as unfazed by a Dom giving her a hard look or if that was something that would always affect her because she had a strong subbie side. She aspired to be more like Mistress Julie with her indifference to Master Law's annoyance.

"Thanks for coming, and we'll see the subs next week. Doms, you get the week off, but be back the week after and ready for some hands-on interaction." Master Law grinned, his gaze falling to rest on Q.

Getting to his feet, Q appeared to either not notice or was ignoring the look Master Law had given him.

"Wanna go downstairs and get a drink?" he asked, his gaze solidly fixed on Sam.

"Sure."

She'd kind of been hoping he'd ask. Which confused her even as she was relieved that he had. If she was the Dominant one, shouldn't she ask? It was easier to let him do the asking when it came to anything outside of the class.

Was she being a bad Dominant?

Q slipped his hand in hers, distracting her, and she smiled. She'd dressed a little more conservatively today, no longer feeling like she needed to armor up around him. The dress she was wearing was still sexy and made her feel like a boss bitch, but it wasn't a corset, and she could easily go straight downstairs to the Marquis bar without standing out. Which she'd planned on in case she and Q went down there after class.

She turned slightly to wave to the others. Noelle was busy talking to Master Leo, who she'd been paired with, but Emerson and Steve waved back to her. Since Noelle was deep in conversation with her class partner, Sam didn't take it personally that the other woman didn't see her.

"Have a good rest of the weekend?" Q asked as they walked downstairs. Sam stepped carefully. The heels on her boots were higher than she normally wore, and she didn't want to trip and fall.

"I did. Got all the laundry done and everything."

"Now that *is* an accomplishment."

Sam giggled as they made their way through the hall into the restaurant portion. As usual it wasn't too busy at this time on a Monday night, so they headed for what she was already starting to think of as 'their' corner of the bar. Shane came right over to take their drink order before making himself scarce.

"So..." The way Q said it made the single word a complete sentence.

"So..." Sam didn't really know what else to say, either. She ran her finger around the top of her glass, tilting her head so she could see his face. A bit of a blush began to creep into her cheeks.

She was trying really hard not to think about Saturday night and how it had felt to be spanked, then cuddled. Or how it had felt to have him on his knees before her upstairs. Sure, it had been for class, but it wasn't that hard to picture him in the same position somewhere they'd have more privacy... like her bedroom. Or even one of the private rooms upstairs.

It was a little embarrassing how much she was looking forward to when the class moved to the private rooms. She'd had a lot of fun in those rooms during her previous classes, sometimes with sex and sometimes without, but she hadn't been interested in any of her partners the way she was with Q. Okay, maybe a small crush on Kincaid, but she'd sensed from the beginning that he didn't feel the same way about her, so that had died down pretty quickly.

With Q, it was obvious he was just as attracted to her as she was to him. Not only that, but he liked her—*like* liked her—which made her feel like they were back in high school, except way better because they weren't.

"Was my pose really that bad or what?" he asked.

"Or what." Sam grinned at him. "Mistress Julie is a stickler for the positions. I thought you were fine. Though I didn't mind seeing her give you a hard time."

"At least it wasn't Law. That's what I kept telling myself."

She laughed.

"Yeah, I can see where that would be pretty weird. You guys are pretty good friends?" She let her voice lilt up, turning it into a question. From what she knew about Q, he'd started coming to Stronghold and Marquis because of his friend Angel, but Sam saw him hanging out mostly with Law, Connor, and Asad.

"We're getting there." Q smiled, reaching out with his left hand to rest it on her knee.

It felt nice. Kind of possessive but without making her feel uncomfortable. Mostly, she wanted him to move it higher.

"It's been good getting to know him, Connor, and Asad. My friend

Angel was the one who convinced me to come to Stronghold, but she's busy with her husband Adam and their baby. I'm friends with all of her friends who are also members, but they're all in serious relationships, if they aren't already engaged or married."

"You feel like the odd man out?"

"Yeah. Not because they mean to make me feel that way, and all of them are great to hang out with even when they're being all couple-y, but it's been nice having a few single friends to hang out with. Especially since Connor is also pretty new to all this."

That made sense. Sam envied him the ease with which he talked about his friends. She'd felt like the odd woman out of the entire club for a while, which was probably how she'd ended up being friends with Morgan since they were both the odd woman out. Both were new to the scene, and poor Morgan had had even less idea of how to make friends than Sam had.

Q's words made her wonder if he was intent on remaining single... though Law now had a girlfriend and as far as she could tell, he and Iris were serious. She didn't know for sure since it wasn't like she and Iris were friends. Iris had been picked up and added to a little group with two of the other submissives who had been in the first class Sam had taken, the one where she'd met Morgan. Rae and Domi had been nice, but kept to themselves, which had left her and Morgan to make friends.

Why they'd suddenly decided to start reaching out *after* the class and made friends with Avery, another submissive, and Iris, she had no idea. It had hurt to know that, for some reason, she hadn't made the cut, but she tried to take Morgan's lead in not caring.

"I get that. Especially here. I'm sure it can be disconcerting knowing your friends are going off to have sex." She laughed when he made a face.

"Or knowing you could go watch them if you wanted." Q shook his head. "That's something I'm still getting used to."

"Not into public sex?"

"It doesn't bother me, but it doesn't do much for me, either," he confessed. "Not really one of my kinks. What about you?"

"Pretty much the same." She shrugged. "If given the choice, I'd rather be private."

Q's fingers squeezed her knee, sending a sizzle of awareness through her as he caressed the sensitive inside of her leg. That one small touch heated up all her senses.

"Speaking of being more private, are you planning on going to Stronghold or Marquis this weekend?" he asked, angling his body a little more toward hers. Sam's heart pitter-pattered with excitement as she realized he was going to ask her to scene again.

Unfortunately...

"I'm helping Morgan move on Saturday," she replied regretfully. "We're getting an early start and I'll probably be exhausted at the end, so I actually hadn't planned to go this weekend."

"Ah. I'd offer to come help, but I already have plans for Saturday afternoon... maybe we could get together for dinner afterward?"

If her heart had pitter-pattered before, now it did a happy little jump in her chest.

"Like on a date?" The question popped out before she really thought it through. She wanted to groan because she sounded so desperate. Q just smiled, not at all put off by her over eagerness.

He leaned in, lowering his voice to a seductive croon.

"Exactly like a date."

Excitement pulsed through her.

"I'd love that."

This time, when he walked her to her car, he kissed her before letting her get in. A toe-curling, panty-wetting kiss that left her panting for more, hot all over despite the cold night air.

Holy crap, I have a date!

10

DATE PREP

Sam

"A date with Q? That's so exciting!" Morgan beamed at her, bouncing between the boxes of her stuff that had been packed up. As always, she looked flawless.

Even though they were doing nothing more than spending the day moving boxes, Morgan was wearing a full face of makeup, and her hair was curled and pulled back in a messy bun that somehow managed to look deliberate. She was wearing form-fitting yoga pants and a top that showed off her midriff and clung to every inch of her body. Looking at her, you'd think it was the middle of summer, not very late fall. It was forty-five degrees out!

Dressed more appropriately for the weather in a long-sleeve t-shirt and jeans, with no makeup, and a ponytail that did her hair no favors, Sam felt positively frumpy next to Morgan. At least she wasn't the only one. After hearing that Morgan was moving, Noelle had insisted on coming to help. Morgan seemed as delighted as Sam felt about making a new girlfriend and had gratefully accepted. Noelle was dressed more like Sam. Her expression when she'd first arrived at the door and gotten a look at Morgan had been pretty hilarious.

If she kept hanging around Morgan, she'd learn.

Morgan loved clothes, makeup, and doing her hair, unlike Sam who would put in the effort but only when she had to. She was pretty sure if she showed up tomorrow morning, unexpected, Morgan would look as flawless as ever.

Actually, that would definitely be true now that Morgan was moving in with Brian. They weren't together, but Morgan had once told Sam that she didn't allow men to see her without her 'face.' Granted, Sam had never seen Morgan without a full face of makeup either, so it wasn't necessarily a gender thing, but she would definitely be fully made up while living with a man, even if they were just friends.

"They've also had drinks after class for two weeks in a row now," Noelle said. There was something in her voice that made Sam look at her, wondering if Noelle disapproved for some reason, but when their gazes met, Noelle smiled at her. Maybe she was reading too much into things.

"Maybe we could do drinks all together after class this Monday," she offered. If she wasn't seeing Q tonight, she might have wanted to keep the after-class connection going, but it wouldn't hurt to include the others.

Especially if Noelle felt left out.

"Oh, that would be great!" Noelle beamed at her. Maybe she hadn't imagined the tone of Noelle's voice. There was a definite difference between how she sounded now and how she'd sounded a minute ago.

"You could come join us, too," Sam offered to Morgan, who smiled at her.

"Maybe! I'll probably still be unpacking. I also don't know what Master Brian is going to want us to do during the week."

"I think Brian is probably going to want you to make your own decision," Sam reminded her gently, making sure to leave off the BDSM honorific out loud, even though she did tend to use them in her head. Crap. Was Morgan moving in with a man, and a Dom, really the best idea?

No, it should be fine. Master Brian wouldn't let her bury her own needs or make him make all her decisions. He was a Daddy Dom and a caretaker, and part of that would be pushing her to be her own person.

Morgan blinked owlishly, then shook her head.

"Right, of course, but I'll probably be busy unpacking. There's going to be a lot to do. I need to get my ASMR room set up." She shook her head again. "I should stay home. Maybe some other time."

"Great." Sam smiled encouragingly at her, aware of Noelle watching them closely and with some confusion. She would not say anything, though. Morgan would share the details of her past with Noelle when she was ready. Sam was pretty sure she didn't know everything, though she'd found out an awful lot through the dribbles of information Morgan would sometimes drop. "And you're probably right, you're going to be exhausted."

"Who's going to be exhausted?" Master Mitch appeared in the doorway of Morgan's bedroom. "Cuz it's not me. These guns can go all day." He flexed his bicep, making all of them crack up. With the sweatshirt he was wearing, they couldn't even see his muscles. Blond-haired, blue-eyed, and perpetually joking around, he didn't seem like a Dom until he turned on his Dom attitude, which he could flip like a switch.

He was newly engaged to Domi, but he'd always been friendly with Sam and Morgan. When he'd heard Morgan was moving, he'd insisted on coming to help with the big furniture and brought Master Zach with him. Master Kincaid was helping Master Brian move things around Brian's house to make room for Morgan.

"Good, here's a box." Sam picked up the heaviest one, the one that she'd been about to do herself, and thrust it at him.

Mitch took it with his usual grin.

"Got it. Hey, slackers, come get some boxes. We're almost done!" He turned and retreated from the doorway. Sam, Noelle, and Morgan looked at each other. They were almost done?

She'd thought Mitch was coming to check on them. The guys had been clearing out the furniture and boxes from the main room. Morgan didn't have a ton of stuff, but she'd had most of the basics and a few things her old roommate had left for her. Grabbing another box, which wasn't nearly as heavy as the one she'd given Mitch, Sam followed him down the hallway.

Her mouth dropped open when they reached the living room. Holy crap! It was basically empty. She didn't realize that she and the others had been talking for so long.

"Wow. We're going to be done so much faster than I thought!" Morgan said from behind her, sounding thrilled.

Sam wasn't disappointed. She'd much rather have more time to get ready and more energy than she'd originally planned for her date.

She still didn't know what she and Q were doing or where they were going. She'd left it up to him. Maybe they'd go to Marquis... which she wouldn't hate, but at the same time, she'd like to feel like what was going on between them wasn't *all* about sex.

Q

A peal of laughter from Law's basement made Q wonder what was going on down there. It also made Q think of Sam, knowing she was hanging out with her girlfriends today.

"They sound like they're having fun," Asad said, cocking his head toward the basement door and grinning. "Think they'd like some company?"

"Leave them alone. You're supposed to be here to hang out with me," Law replied with a pointed look. Asad just chuckled. They were gathered around Law's kitchen table—Asad and Law across from each other while Connor sat across from Q. There was food, though Q privately thought the ladies had taken the better snacks downstairs with them.

"It's not my fault they sound like they're having more fun." Even as he spoke, another round of laughter made its way up the stairs.

Law rolled his eyes. "We're not here to have fun. We're here to talk about my proposal to Iris."

"Which you decided to do while she's downstairs, rather than waiting until she's not at home." Connor raised his eyebrows, lifting his water to take a sip.

"She wanted to have girl time, and I figured it would be a good time to talk to you all since she was the one who suggested it." Law rubbed his fingers together. "This way, she won't be suspicious."

The guy looked more nervous than Q had ever seen him. He was contemplating proposing to a woman who he'd been with for less than a year, even if they had moved in together. That would likely make anyone nervous, especially since Iris had only moved in because circumstances—aka her ex-roommate Noelle—hadn't left her with a ton of choices.

It had made sense at the time, and she and Law were doing so well, they'd decided to make the arrangement permanent, but it couldn't be denied that they were moving fast. Hell, who was Q to talk? He'd never had a relationship he'd thought might end in marriage.

"I don't think she's going to be suspicious, considering how fast you're moving," Asad said, echoing Q's thoughts.

Law's fingers stopped.

"Do you think it's too fast?" He nervously rubbed his hand over his bald head, swiping over the crown and around the back before seeming to realize what he was doing. Snatching it back down, a moment later, his hand drifted back up to rub nervously at his goatee.

"I think the more important question is whether you and Iris think it's too fast," Connor said.

"Yes," Asad said at the same time. "Ow!" From the way he jumped, then shot a look at Connor, Q guessed that he'd been kicked under the table.

"Don't listen to him. Asad would think ten years is too fast to get engaged." When Asad opened his mouth, presumably to argue, Connor shot him a look, and he closed it again. "Everyone moves at their own pace. So, do you think it's too fast?"

"Not for me, but I'm a little worried it might be for her." Law was rubbing at his goatee again, his nerves overcoming his self-awareness. "I am older than her."

"Okay, Grandpa." Asad rolled his eyes, grinning when Law glared at him. "I'm just saying. Age doesn't necessarily have anything to do with it."

Pressing his lips together, Law looked at Q, raising his eyebrows as if to ask his opinion. Yeesh. Talk about pressure.

"Have you asked her friends? I think you'd do better to talk to them than us." Way back when Angel as one of his roommates, Q had it drilled into his head never to assume anything, and if you needed to be sneaky, ask the best friend.

Law made a face.

"I will, eventually, but I was hoping I could rely on my friends first."

"Of course, you can always rely on us." Asad held his hand over his heart, his expression too solemn to be genuine. It looked odd on him since, unless he was in his Dom headspace, he was normally smiling or smirking. "I think Q has the right of it, and you should talk to Iris' friends."

"You're all useless," Law groaned. "I need friends who have already been through this."

"I have friends who have already been through this. Want me to make some introductions?" Q grinned. "You could also ask Olivia. You're friends with her."

"I'm still not exactly sure what you're asking us for. Permission? Help with picking out the ring?" Connor shrugged one massive shoulder. "I think you two are good together and will end up married to her, so why not sooner rather than later?"

"Not everyone is as eager to jump into a lifelong relationship as you are," Asad drawled.

Connor blushed. Well, that was interesting. Q hadn't known Connor's thoughts were trending that way. He didn't seem to be dating anyone.

"I agree with Connor," Q said, taking some of the attention off the other man. "As long as you've at least talked to Iris about it. Or did you want to do a big surprise?"

"We've talked about it," Law confirmed, which didn't surprise Q.

Law was a methodical planner that rarely made a decision without thinking it all the way through. Chances were, in this case, he was overthinking things because of that.

"In a general kind of way. Like, saying 'when we're married' or 'in a few years' or talking about how we'd want to raise our kids."

Asad shuddered dramatically. The rest of them ignored him.

"Sounds like you're ready," Q said, Connor nodding to back him up. "If I was talking that way with a woman, I know I'd be figuring out when to propose."

"Hey, you might be closer than you think," Asad teased, glancing at Q before looking at Law. "You missed seeing him and Sam all cuddled up at Stronghold last week."

Heat suffused Q's cheeks. Before he could deny it, Law was already chuckling and answering.

"Oh, trust me, I'm not missing anything. I get to see them in class on Mondays. They have more chemistry than anyone else in the room, except maybe Steve and Master Eric." Law's grin widened as Q sank back in his chair a little. Thankfully, his skin never showed much of a blush, but he still felt it. "I thought I might have to worry about you two, but things seem to be going well."

"They are. I'm actually taking her out on a date tonight."

All the guys lit up and congratulated him. Law and Asad reached over to give him a clap on the shoulder of encouragement. Q grinned, unable to keep the smile off his face.

"Now, for Q it's definitely *too* early to be thinking of proposing," Connor joked, pointing his finger at Q and making them all laugh.

"On the other hand, at our age, why bother spending a lot of time on someone you can't see as a possibility to spend the rest of your life with?" Q caught the horrified expression on Asad's face. "Assuming that a life partner is what you want."

"We're not that old," Law complained.

"Especially if we act young." Asad lifted his water glass in the air like he was toasting. "Long live the Persian Excursions."

No one else lifted their glass.

"I am not toasting to that." Connor shook his head. "That's like making a toast to your dick."

"My dick deserves to be toasted... wait, that came out wrong." Asad frowned as they all cracked up again. "Toasted with champagne, not like, with a toaster. That is not the kind of fire play I'm into."

Q laughed harder than ever, though one hand automatically cupped his crotch at the idea of sticking his dick in a toaster. Ouch.

11

LOOKING GOOD

Sam

Master Brian's house was really nice. Damn. Maybe Sam should have tried to find a roommate instead of living in a studio, but she liked her privacy. She also hadn't liked the idea of living with a stranger. Morgan had lucked out, needing a new place to live right when Brian needed a roommate. She bet he would be pretty easy to live with, even if he was a Dom. Though when she thought about living with him herself, she immediately rejected the notion. Nope.

Living with a roommate in college had sucked. Not because her roommate had, but because Sam had needed her own space to decompress and hang out. She never wanted to share a bedroom, much less a communal space, ever again until she was in a romantic relationship, and they agreed to live together.

Even then, she was probably going to want somewhere in the space to call her own.

"Wow, this room is huge." Noelle looked around Morgan's new bedroom, echoing Sam's thoughts. Even though they'd brought Morgan's bed, dresser, vanity, and all her boxes into the room, there was still a lot of space leftover. Morgan looked nervous but excited. "I need to find myself a Sugar Daddy."

Sam bristled, but Morgan spoke before she could muster a response, and unlike Sam she didn't appear bothered by Noelle's assumption.

"Oh, no, Master Brian is a Daddy Dom, not a Sugar Daddy, totally different." Morgan frowned, putting her hands on her hips and turning in a slow circle. "Though, now that I'm here, I do think he might be undercharging me for rent."

"What's the difference?" Noelle asked, sounding honestly confused, which helped unruffle Sam's feathers. Noelle didn't know and probably wasn't the first person to be confused by the difference.

"Sugar daddies pay for everything and expect sexual favors in return... I think." Morgan glanced at Sam, who shrugged. It wasn't like she knew anything about sugar daddies, but as far as she knew, Morgan had it right. "Daddy Doms... well, sometimes they do age play, sometimes they just like to be called Daddy, but they all tend to be caregivers. Like service Doms, but in a slightly different way. It's not really my kink."

"Huh." Noelle didn't seem convinced. "So... he'll still be charging you rent and stuff?"

"Yeah. I should probably get my vanity sent up first, so I can get back to earning money." Morgan glanced at the boxes that had been set around that particular piece of furniture.

"What's ASMR again exactly?" Noelle asked.

"Autonomous Sensory Meridian Response."

"Brain tingles," Sam added when Noelle blinked in confusion. "Things that you hear or see that makes your brain feel fuzzy and nice."

"It's not for everyone, but I like it and I've found I'm pretty good at it." Morgan shrugged. "It's something I don't need a diploma for."

"You didn't graduate high school?" Noelle held up her hands when Sam shot her a look. "Sorry, I didn't mean for that to come out sounding so judgmental. I was just surprised."

"I'm not sure. I was home-schooled, and I thought I had but my mom wouldn't give me any of the information I needed to prove it." Morgan's tone was matter of fact, making Noelle's mouth drop open.

She glanced at Sam who just shrugged. If Noelle was going to be around for a while, she was eventually going to hear the details of Morgan's life. It would make a heck of a movie except that if it was a movie, people would probably complain that it was too far-fetched. "ASMR and makeup are two things I can do without needing a diploma."

"She does amazing makeup," Sam said.

"Oooh, speaking of, I should grab that so I can do it for your date tonight," Morgan said, turning and picking up one of the boxes marked 'makeup.'

"You don't have to do that."

"I know, but I want to. No payment either. You're my best friend, so it's free."

Morgan beamed at Sam right as her words hit Sam right in the chest. Holy crap. She hadn't realized Morgan thought of her that way. Tears threatened, and she cleared her throat.

"Thank you." She couldn't put everything she was feeling into words, so she tried to put it into her tone. Morgan smiled back, apparently pleased, but that was also typical Morgan.

"Wow, okay." Noelle huffed, startling both of them. Morgan actually jumped as they turned to look at her in surprise. Sam wasn't sure why Noelle was upset. They'd just met her, after all. As she took in their reactions, Noelle's expression crumbled, and she slumped. "I'm so sorry, I... I'm being unreasonable, I know. I'm just extra sensitive about the whole best friend thing after losing mine."

She sniffled, and Sam's heart went out to her.

"Oh, I'm sorry," Morgan said, putting her hands on her chest. "That was insensitive of me. I'm always doing that. I'm still learning."

"No, no, you're fine, it's me." Noelle reached up to wipe away a tear before Sam could reassure Morgan she had done nothing wrong. At least, she hadn't in Sam's eyes. It wasn't as though they could know everything that would set Noelle off, and she'd mentioned losing her best friend in sub class, but not in front of Morgan that Sam knew about. "One day, I'll have a new best friend."

Feeling sympathy surge inside her—Sam knew how difficult it

could be to make friends—she stepped up to put her arm around Noelle's shoulders.

"That's the great thing about friendships," she said. "They keep growing. Morgan and I didn't start out as best friends or anything. We just started hanging out. We'll get there."

"Thanks." Noelle's eyes filled with tears as Morgan slid next to her on the other side. "It's just a lot. I used to do Iris' makeup for dates, and then knowing that you two are besties and I lost my best friend, and I still don't even really know *why* she ditched me... It's been hard."

"Oh, I'm so sorry." Morgan turned slightly to give Noelle a tight squeeze and Sam turned to wrap her arms around both of them. "That sucks."

"It totally sucks," Sam agreed. She couldn't help but wonder if maybe Iris had ditched Noelle for her new friends because they were kinky, and Noelle wasn't. That might be why she was taking the classes now, even though she didn't seem to be super into them.

She also might just have some misconceptions about kink. Morgan had as well, and she'd been in the lifestyle—a very specific, very narrow portion of the lifestyle—for years. Misconceptions could happen for all sorts of reasons. If she wasn't into kink and was only in the class to understand Iris better, Sam had to admire how far she was willing to go.

"Food's here!" One of the guys called from downstairs. Sam thought it might be Brian, but she wasn't sure. They'd said they were going to order pizza for lunch.

Sam squeezed a little tighter, then let go.

"Come on, let's go get lunch."

They trooped downstairs to where the guys were sitting around the kitchen table. Pizza boxes lined the counters, along with a big bowl of salad Sam knew was for Morgan. She wished she liked vegetables the way Morgan did. Morgan was the weirdest picky eater she'd ever met.

"Thanks for getting us lunch." Sam went over to where plates were set out next to the food.

"Thanks for helping us out today," Brian replied cheerfully, lifting a piece of pizza to toast her. "Things go a lot faster with good help, and that should be rewarded."

"Thank you," Morgan repeated, going over to press a kiss on the top of Brian's head before following Sam to the food.

"Thanks," Noelle echoed. Her eyes darted around, taking in everything from the casual kiss Morgan had given Brian, where all the guys were seated, and the boxes lined up along the kitchen wall. Probably those with her dishes. Morgan had been ruthlessly organized in how she'd packed, with every box clearly labeled.

The dining room table was meant for a lot of company with lots of chairs around it. Brian sat at the head and Mitch at the 'foot' with Kincaid and Zach on one side, leaving the other side for Noelle, Morgan, and Sam. One of the chairs on their side had clearly been dragged in from the kitchen, but there was still plenty of elbow room.

"No pizza?" Noelle asked, blinking in surprise when Morgan loaded her plate up with salad and didn't even glance at the boxes. "Yeah, I guess you'd need to eat super light to look like you do. I'd rather have pizza."

"I just don't like pizza, but I love salad." Morgan smiled breezily, taking her plate over to the table.

Sam noticed that all the men were now watching Noelle warily, like they weren't sure whether to speak up. It wouldn't be obvious by their expressions to most people, but after taking a kink class where all of them served as instructors, she'd gotten to know them all well. She could tell when they went into what she called 'watch mode.' It happened a lot during class when they weren't sure if they were pushing too far with a newbie.

It reminded her, as much as she liked them, Mitch was engaged to Domi who was now friends with Iris and so all of them hung out with Iris fairly regularly.

Then again, they might just be wary because they were protective of Morgan.

Stop looking for trouble.

Sam grabbed half a plate of salad as well as two pieces of pizza.

Unlike Morgan, she liked both and knew none of the guys here would be judgmental or rude about her eating choices. Sadly, not something that was universal, but she was in a safe space here, which meant a lot to her. Coming up behind her, Noelle quietly did the same and then followed her to the table. Morgan had sat down next to Mitch, so Sam sat down next to Brian, leaving the spot in the middle for Noelle.

"Are you planning to go out tonight?" Brian asked, looking down the table at Morgan.

She shook her head. "I was going to stay in and unpack, but I have to do Sam's makeup first." Morgan looked up from her food and turned her head to beam at Mitch. "She has a date with Q."

The guys sat up a little, and Sam groaned even as her insides warmed. They'd just gone into 'protective' mode. She'd seen it frequently directed at Morgan but never at herself. She'd never wanted it directed at her, yet seeing them get all frowny and protective over her gave her unexpected warm fuzzies.

"A date-date? I thought you two... didn't get along," Kincaid said, obviously changing up what he had planned to say mid-sentence.

"You're topping him for the class, right? So, that puts *her* in the power position," Mitch pointed out before Sam could answer.

"Yeah, but he's a Switch, and he's already done the Dom stuff." Zach frowned, his gaze focusing on Sam. "I thought you two were just trying scening at the club because of the class. I didn't realize it went beyond that."

"They scened at the club?" Brian jumped on that part of Zach's statement.

"Who was in charge for that?" Mitch's question came out as a demand.

"He was," Zach answered for her.

"Where's he taking you tonight?" Kincaid's attention was laser focused on Sam, making her want to squirm in her seat.

Dammit. She was supposed to have a Dominant side to call on, but it was a little hard to feel it when she had not one but *four* Doms getting all bossy with her. If only she could channel her inner Olivia.

Olivia would never put up with being ignored when the topic of conversation was her own life.

Sam sat up a little straighter and deliberately took a bite of her pizza, chewing slowly as she stared back at Kincaid. Inside, she was quelling, her stomach doing somersaults one after the other, but she didn't think her nerves showed on the surface. She hoped they didn't.

To her amazement, Kincaid stared back at her, opened his mouth, then closed it without saying anything. He looked at Zach, Zach looked at Brian, who looked at Mitch.

Mitch looked at her.

She took another bite of pizza, staring back at him and doing her best to channel her inner Olivia.

Holding up his hands in a gesture of surrender, Mitch shook his head.

"Guess it's not really our business. I'm sure you have him handled."

Holy crap, it worked, and she hadn't even had to say a thing.

"I knew you weren't a sub," Morgan said happily, taking another bite of her salad. Sam had to laugh. It really was one of the first things Morgan had said to her, and she'd been insulted at the time, but Morgan had been right.

Sam was grateful. She wasn't sure she would have figured it out without Morgan.

"All hail Mistress Samantha," Mitch said with a grin.

"So, what does it take to be a Switch?" Noelle asked.

Relieved that the attention was off her, Sam joined in with her two cents, answering Noelle, along with Zach and color commentary from the other guys. All in all, it was a fun way to pass the time before her date.

12

———————

TWO SIDES TO EVERY STORY

Q

"Hey, Iris... so, I have a kind of personal question to ask you, and it's totally okay if you don't want to answer."

Iris blinked at him.

Q hadn't exactly cornered her when she and the others had come upstairs and joined the guys, but she'd stepped over to the fridge to get something, and he'd followed. It was the most private he could get without following her to the bathroom, and he definitely wasn't doing that. He had kept his voice low, though, and no one else seemed to have noticed or heard him.

"Um, okay."

"Why did you and Noelle stop being friends?" When her lips pursed, Q rushed on, so she didn't think he was just being nosy. "She's in the new subs class with me, and she's been making friends with Sam, and some of the things I've heard her say... Well, I just wanted to make sure I had both sides of the story."

"Oh..." Iris blinked again, her eyelashes fluttering so quickly it almost looked like she was batting them. "Um, well, mostly because when we were living together, she decided to end our lease with the apartment building and didn't tell me until after she'd already done it."

It was Q's turn to blink in surprise. Noelle sure as hell hadn't mentioned anything about that when he'd been within hearing. Granted, he hadn't talked to her much directly, but the impression he'd gotten was that Iris had ended the friendship, not Noelle.

"Oh my God, are y'all talking about Cunt Rag?" Rae appeared at Q's elbow, practically quivering with angry energy.

Iris face palmed, her shoulders shaking with suppressed laughter. Rae's words, not spoken quietly, had drawn the attention from everyone else in the room. Quick as a flash, Domi was on the other side of the island, across from him and Iris, while the others ambled over more slowly. The scowl on Rae's face made her look like a small, mean faerie.

"Do I even dare ask who 'Cunt Rag' is?" Asad wondered aloud, positioning himself next to Domi and leaning on the island. Law had moved in beside him, putting him closest to where Q, Rae, and Domi were. Avery and Connor ended up on the other side of Domi, and Connor's lips turned down in a frown.

"Noelle," Rae said at the same time Law spoke.

"Someone they should not be calling that." Law gave Rae a stern look. She looked away from him, shrugging, but she didn't appear particularly repentant.

"We're not at either of the clubs," Rae said, more than a hint of sass in her voice. Q had known she was a brat, but damn.

Still, he'd heard similar from Olivia, who called Jared's ex, Marissa, "Truck Stop." He wasn't sure what that actually meant and didn't think she really had a definition either, but it sure as hell sounded bad. Cunt Rag felt like it was in the same league, except he knew exactly what it was, with no ambivalence about its meaning.

"Don't even try saying she's not that bad," Domi said, pointing a finger across the counter at Iris. Iris closed her mouth and the refrigerator door at the same time, shooting an apologetic look at Q. He really hadn't meant to draw everyone's attention, but he wasn't upset that he had.

It sounded like he was about to get all the tea, but not from Iris. She looked both uncomfortable with and relieved by Domi's order.

"I was surprised to see her in the submissive class." Q made it a statement rather than a question. Clearly, he'd hit on a sensitive topic, and he wanted to know more, but he also didn't want to put Iris on the spot with an audience. It was one thing to have a private conversation, but now everyone was involved.

Domi and Rae made identical faces, and even Avery, who he tended to think was the chillest out of the bunch of them, frowned. Iris' expression was carefully blank—something he recognized as a 'bad sign' from having lived with a woman for years.

"I'm not." Rae snorted. "I bet she expected Iris to come chasing after her, full of apologies, even though Noelle basically kicked her out of her own apartment. When she realized Iris was moving on with her life, she couldn't handle it."

"She is *not* a nice person," Domi chimed in. "She seems like she is. She acts like she is. But as soon as Iris was out of the room, Noelle started talking shit about her, even though they were supposedly best friends. She acted like she was joking, but she was definitely waiting to see if we would join in."

"Noelle can be abrasive. And kind of needy. She's the kind of person who will talk shit about others to feel better about herself, but it's mostly because she's insecure," Iris said, her tone defensive.

"Which doesn't excuse the bad behavior. People can be insecure without being assholes." Rae's uncompromising tone was ruthless.

It was also making him worried.

If he hadn't already known something had gone down between Noelle and Iris, he wouldn't have been wary of her and would have probably been drawn in and believed everything she said. The way Sam did. Now, he also had to worry that these women would be at odds with Sam because she was becoming friends with Noelle.

"She's not always that bad." Iris threw her hands up.

Q didn't question why she was still defending her ex-friend. He'd seen this before with his friend Leigh and her ex, Michael. He hadn't gotten it until he'd talked about it with Angel, who was also Leigh's best friend.

Michael had been toxic and emotionally abusive. A big part of that was making Leigh feel as though she was the one being unreasonable—that she had done something wrong, that she could have tried harder. Now, Leigh could look back with clear eyes and had told him that part of her hadn't wanted to admit that everyone was right about Michael and how he'd treated her.

She hadn't wanted to admit how badly he'd made her feel because then, she would have had to admit she'd stayed with someone when she shouldn't have. Would have had to admit that all of her friends were right about him.

That was especially hard because it's not like people were bad all the time. Michael could be really great to Leigh. He'd especially loved the grand gestures that made him look good to other people. Heck, if Q hadn't been living with Angel and heard the girls talking about him, he would have thought Michael was a pretty amazing boyfriend.

"Nobody's bad all the time, people are complex," Avery said, chiming in for the first time. "If she was bad all the time, it would have been easy to end the friendship. If she was bad all the time, you wouldn't feel guilt over it. If she was bad all the time, no one would want to be her friend. It's not like toxic people are always toxic, which is actually what makes them even more toxic."

"That hurt my head," Asad complained, rubbing his forehead and making everyone snicker, which helped lessen the tension in the room.

"She's right, though." Rae gave Iris a hard look. "Just because she wasn't always a crap person, didn't mean you have to put up with her crap. I still think it's bullshit that she's being allowed in the club."

"As long as she leaves Iris alone." Domi crossed her arms over her chest. "There's no way she suddenly decided she was into kink and ended up at Marquis. It wouldn't surprise me if she even knew Law was teaching the class."

"I did tell her that he teaches the classes," Iris admitted. "And no, she never seemed interested in kink before, but... I don't know." She threw her hands up in the air. "I don't even know why I'm trying to defend her. I just don't want to say something that gets back to her and makes her pissed off. I am so tired of the drama."

"Because you know she'll make drama." Rae scowled. "If she does, I'm taking her down. I don't care if I get kicked out of the clubs."

"No one is taking her down and none of you are getting kicked out of the clubs," Law interjected firmly, his stern gaze sweeping over everyone. "She is being given the same chance as everyone else, but if *she* does something that causes an issue, she will be removed from the club. In the meantime, if she's interested in learning about kink, she'll have the same chance to do so in a safe space, just like the rest of you."

Rae made a rude noise while Domi did the thumbs down gesture, and Q had to do his best to hide his laugh—made even more difficult when he happened to catch Asad's eye and realized the other man was doing the same thing. While neither Rae nor Domi was being particularly nice about Noelle, after hearing what they had to say, he couldn't blame them either.

Noelle was telling a very different story from what they were, and he was inclined to believe them over her. Maybe because he knew them better, but it didn't really matter why.

He was going to be keeping a much closer eye on Noelle.

"She really doesn't seem to be causing any trouble in the class," Connor offered. "She seems sincere about learning."

Q kept his mouth shut. Connor hadn't heard everything Noelle had told the other subs about Iris, and he didn't want the ladies more irate than they already were. It was better to let Connor share his experience with adding any commentary.

"Of course, she does, because if she doesn't suck you into her web, she can't drink your blood," Rae retorted.

"You should write that down for one of your books," Domi told her. "That was good."

"Noted." Rae pulled out her phone and started tapping on the screen, making Avery laugh.

"Books?" Q asked.

"Rae's an author," Domi said proudly when Rae didn't answer right away.

"I've written *one* book. I'm working on the second one." Rae's shoulders hunched a little, and he was pretty sure she was blushing, though it was hard to tell with her dark skin and her face half-hidden. "Sometimes, I use things either my friends or I say."

"Oh, really?" Asad leaned toward her, flexing his biceps, despite the fact he was wearing a long-sleeve shirt that covered most of the show. Grinning at her, he winked. "I have a great idea for a sexy hero who's known as the Persian Excursion."

"Trust me, I already have that one written down." Rae smirked at him. "I haven't used it yet because I'm worried readers will think it's too ridiculous to be realistic."

"You know she writes romance, right?" Law asked with amusement. "That means a fictional Persian Excursion would end up in a committed relationship."

"The key word being 'fictional,'" Asad smirked. Then he frowned at Rae. "And I am not too ridiculous to be real."

"Real life is stranger than fiction," Avery quipped. "Things that happen in real life are often things that people don't believe when in fiction. Like, did you know that Tiffany was a popular name in medieval times? But historical romance authors can't use it because so many people think that it's a contemporary name, and they get all up in arms about it being used in books set before the 1960s."

"Really?" Connor actually looked interested, but then, he collected odd bits of knowledge. "How do you know that?"

"Saw it on social media and looked it up to see if it was true."

"Story of my life," Rae muttered.

"You want truth that's stranger than fiction? Q and Sam went to the same high school, hated each other, then years later ended up at the same sex club, where they're paired off for a class and now, they're going on a date."

"We didn't hate each other," Q protested, as all the ladies perked up, their interest zeroing in on him. Not because they were more interested than the guys, but because this was news to them. "We just... we were always competing for the top spot."

"Oooh, second chance, former rivals to lovers," Rae said, her eyes lighting up, and she started swiping more words onto her phone. Q scowled, but she didn't seem to notice. "That's good, got anything else?"

"He asked her to prom, and she said yes, then changed her mind the next day," Asad said.

Q threw his hands up in the air and glared at Asad.

"That's hardly important."

"No, no, that's back story, that's good. So, rivals but crushes and now second chance lovers... I like that." Rae grinned and Q shook his head.

"As long as somebody's happy," he said sarcastically.

"So, what are you doing for the date?" Avery asked, propping her chin up on her hands, elbows resting on the counter.

"Taking her to pub trivia. Do you think that sounds like a good date?" Getting the feminine perspective was always a good thing, in his experience. Angel had approved, but a second opinion never hurt.

Avery looked at the others, who looked back at her. An odd expression of guilt settled on Domi and Rae's features.

"We don't really know her well enough, and that's a pretty niche date," Domi said after a moment. "You two were rivals in high school? For like, valedictorian and stuff?"

He nodded, looking back and forth between them. Only Rae and Domi appeared to feel guilty about something and he couldn't imagine what.

"Then it sounds like something she would like. Might be fun to be on the same team now." Iris grinned at him encouragingly. "I don't really know her either, but I think it sounds like a unique first date."

Unique was good, right?

"Didn't you two take the sub class with her?" Law asked, frowning at Domi and Rae. The guilt in their expressions increased, and they exchanged glances. Rae sighed.

"We did, but we weren't really good about branching out and

making new friends." She glanced apologetically at Q. "Sam seemed nice, but... we were kinda doing our own thing."

"Nothing wrong with that," Q replied, a little curious about why she and Domi seemed to feel so bad about it, but he didn't mind reassuring her. It wasn't like the whole world had to be friends with each other. "You two already knew each other."

"Yeah, but it was pointed out to us that we could be less insular." Domi smiled at Avery and Iris. "And making new friends has actually been really great. I just wish we'd worked on it sooner. Maybe we'll get the chance to get to know her better now that you're dating her."

Q nodded, but he could feel a little niggle of anxiety curling in his stomach. Everything suddenly felt a lot more complicated than it had yesterday.

13

DRESS CASUAL

Dress casual.

She wasn't really sure what that meant.

Thank goodness for Morgan and Noelle, who had ended up coming over to help her get ready. She'd asked Q what she should wear tonight, and he'd responded with that direction. Eventually, they decided on jeans that hugged her curves and a sweater that was tight and low-cut over her boobs and loose around her mid-section.

Noelle did her hair, curling the blonde locks and then brushing them out into loose waves that cascaded around her shoulders. The makeup was perfect too, not that she expected anything less from Morgan, making her eyes look huge and her lips even poutier than normal without being a full on 'glam' look.

"I need to have you two come over to do me up every day," she joked, peering into the mirror and flipping her hair back and forth.

"You get up too early." Morgan giggled as she put her brushes away.

"What time do you get up?" Noelle asked.

"Six thirty, so I can get to work on time. Morgan just sleeps too late."

"Because I work the night shift. Oooh, do you want some glitter on you? We could make your boobs sparkle."

"Nope, keep that shit away from me." Sam lifted her hands, crossing her fingers in front of her as if to ward the evil away. She knew Morgan was joking, but she wasn't taking any chances. "My boobs are already fabulous. They don't need any sparkle and neither does the rest of my apartment."

Noelle laughed, sliding out of Sam's tiny bathroom and giving herself a little shake. Sam knew how she felt. It was crowded in the small room. She shifted to the side as well, ceding the room to Morgan while she stood right outside the door, so they weren't abandoning Morgan to her clean-up, but they also weren't so cramped.

"Maybe we could do a girls' night sometime and get ready together?" Noelle asked brightly. "I could do both of your hair, Morgan could do my and Sam's makeup..."

"I am not as good at doing hair as you are." Sam reached up to twist one of the curls around her fingers. She could do basic stuff, but she'd never gotten the hang of curls—which was why Noelle had done them for her. "I can do like a French twist and a few braids. Do you want your hair up?" She'd noticed that Noelle seemed to wear it down most of the time.

Making a face, Noelle shook her head.

"Well, I can do my own hair then."

"I would want to do my own makeup, but that sounds like fun," Morgan said brightly, then glanced at Sam. "No offense, Sam. You're good at makeup..."

"But you're better, and I wouldn't do nearly as good a job on your own makeup. No offense taken." Sam grinned. No offense taken for the bald truth. Morgan was getting better about not stating things so bluntly, something Sam didn't comment on since Noelle was there.

If Morgan wanted to ask Noelle to help her figure out how to soften some of her statements, she would. In the meantime, Sam wasn't going to open up Morgan's private business in front of someone else.

She also wasn't going to insist on paying Morgan. How could she after Morgan had called her 'best friend?' Makeup was the kind of thing best friends did for each other. If Morgan ever needed occasional help from Sam, she knew she wouldn't charge her, but she was also determined to find some way to show her appreciation.

Finishing cleaning up, Morgan picked up her phone and glanced at the display.

"Oops, time for us to get going. Q should be here soon!" Picking up her makeup case, she made a shooing motion for Sam and Noelle would get out of her way and give her space to get into the hallway.

Nerves rose inside of Sam. Q should be picking her up in about ten minutes. How had the time flown so fast?

This is why I don't *do my hair and makeup every morning... I'd rather sleep than get up even earlier to have the time to do it.*

"Have fun!" Morgan said, giving Sam a hug as she passed her.

"Let us know how it goes!" Noelle followed Morgan to the front door. "I want to hear everything!"

"I'll text you both later." Having their support made her feel a little less anxious, though the butterflies in her stomach were even more fluttery once they left her all alone. She closed the door behind them, putting her hand over her stomach to quell the sensation. Of course, it didn't work.

Dammit.

She was a grown woman going on a date, not a teenager going to prom. Even though that's exactly what Q made her feel like.

Was dating him a smart idea?

Not only did they have a past, even if it had been high school stuff, but they were doing the sub class together, which could also complicate matters. Sub frenzy, where a submissive became attached to any Dominant who they felt a connection with, was a real thing. That was why the class usually switched instructors around, which had been easy enough when the entire class had happened to be full of straight male Doms and straight female submissives. That wasn't the case with this class.

Sam wandered to the mirror by the front door and stared at herself.

She looked like herself but different. Like a grown-up version of herself who was far more put together and far more confident than she actually was. Somehow who knew what she was doing.

Yet she was going on a date with the boy from high school.

A second chance to get it right.

Not that she was sure she'd done the wrong thing when she'd changed her mind about prom, but there was a part of her that still wondered.

The doorbell rang, and she jumped, startled, her cheeks blushing hot with color at her reaction.

Shit! He's here!

Time to see what happened next.

Q

He'd seen Sam in high school. He'd seen Sam all grown up. He'd seen Sam in the fetware she wore to Stronghold and Marquis... but he hadn't ever quite seen Sam like this. Casual and comfortable, yet sexy as hell. While he was really looking forward to one day seeing her completely comfortable, in pajamas with her hair up and no makeup, he had to admit that he really liked this side of her.

"Damn. You look amazing." His gaze traveled from the soft curls framing her face to eyes that seemed even bigger than usual to her cheeks pink and down to her exposed cleavage, framed by the light blue sweater she was wearing, and the jeans hugging her hips and thighs.

He'd kept his own clothing casual as well, though he'd put a beige jacket on over his "May the (mass x acceleration) be with you" t-shirt to dress himself up a little since it *was* a date. Sam's eyes dropped to the writing on his shirt, and he parted the front of the jacket so that she could see the whole thing, and she laughed.

"Why am I not surprised?" She grinned at him, eyes sparkling with amusement. Their gazes caught and the chemistry between them sizzled in the air. The impulse to step forward and kiss her was strong, but he knew they'd never make it on their date if he did that.

He really wanted to take her on a date.

Dropping the sides of his jacket so they fell back over his chest, he held out his hand.

"Milady." He bowed his head—not nearly enough to be a full-on bow, but enough to give the impression. Laughing, she took his hand, and the sizzle between them flared when her fingers touched his. Attempting to alleviate some of the heat, he turned and tucked her hand into the crook of his arm. "Your chariot awaits."

"Is this when you finally tell me where we're going?"

"And ruin the surprise?" Even as he winked at her, his stomach turned over again with nerves. Hopefully, it would be a good surprise. He really, really, really hoped so.

"Okay then, let's go." She blew out a breath.

Q realized that she was just as nervous as he was, which made him feel a little better.

On the way to the restaurant, they chatted about general things—the latest superhero movie, the Lord of the Rings show, finding out all the things they still had in common. The biggest difference was Q was still immersed in all the media, he had to be for his job, whereas she got to enjoy it as a consumer.

By the time they reached the pub door, with the Trivia sign on the front of it, they had both relaxed. Mostly. There was still tension between them, but Q considered that to be sexual chemistry, not actual tension.

"Oh my God... Trivia night?" Sam's eyes sparkled when she turned to him, pointing at the sign on the door. She lit up from within and was practically bouncing on her toes, as though too much energy had bubbled up inside her for her to fully contain.

Jackpot. He'd chosen correctly.

"Trivia night," he confirmed, stepping forward to push open the door.

It didn't matter that they were a two-person team, they appropri-ately named themselves One Team to Rule Them All, and they *domi-*

nated. The only round they fell down a bit on was the sports round, and even there they held their own since Q collected random trivia in his brain, regardless of the topic, and Sam had a thing for watching the Olympics.

"The final question of the night. Category: Science Fiction Books." The announcer grinned as several people in the audience groaned.

Q and Sam's eyes met over their mostly finished plates.

"Isaac Asimov," they whispered simultaneously, then both erupted into laughter. A nearby table of exceedingly stressed looking forty-sometimes shushed them. Sam put her hand over her mouth, trying to stifle her giggles. Valiantly, Q swallowed his own laughter.

The other possibility was a Hitchhiker's Guide to the Galaxy reference, but that one had worked its way into pop culture thanks to the movie and now too many people knew the answer to life, the universe, and everything for it to be a good final question for trivia. Ninety-nine percent of the time, when trivia brought up science fiction, the answer was either Isaac Asimov or his Foundation series.

"What classic science fiction author helped lay the *foundation* for future science fiction authors and is often known as the Father of Science Fiction?"

Nailed it.

Sam was already scribbling their answer down while Q leaned back and picked up another French fry. More for something to do than because he was hungry. This was so much more fun with Sam than anyone else he'd gone with. His other friends didn't take trivia as seriously as he did, which was fine, but it took the edge off some of his enjoyment when he couldn't be competitive. Or when they scolded him for being 'too' competitive.

What was the point in competing if you weren't trying to win?

But Sam got him. She felt the same way.

The fact that both of them had a hoard of trivia knowledge stowed away in their brains made them one hell of a formidable team.

"Taking this up." Sam jumped up without a backward glance,

making him laugh. She wanted to win just as much as he did. He was pretty sure they had it in the bag, and she was as well, from the way she practically sashayed up to the organizer.

When she turned and headed back to him, she was still bouncing. The table who had shushed them glared at him, but he ignored them. He didn't need to rub in their loss. Truthfully, Q didn't want to win to make other people lose... their loss was just a byproduct of his winning.

It felt nice to win with Samantha after all those years as rivals in high school. He was honest enough to know that part of the reason for their rivalry had been because it was the only way he could get her to pay attention to him. Something he understood much better now that he knew what had been driving her.

"We've so got this," she said, holding out her hand for him to high five.

Q did so, then used it to pull her over to his side of the table. Laughing, she let him maneuver her so she was sitting in the chair beside him instead of across from him. He slung his arm along the back, feeling the heat of her body against his skin where he'd rolled up his sleeves.

"We've definitely got this," he said, curling his fingers around her shoulder as she leaned into him and rested her head on his shoulder. Suddenly, winning the trivia competition didn't matter nearly as much as it had a moment ago.

14

———

CUP OF COFFEE?

Sam

"Want to come inside for some coffee or something to drink?"

It was the most cliché question in the history of dating, but who cared? Sam didn't even care that it was their first date instead of their third, fifth, or whatever arbitrary number she was supposedly supposed to make him wait for. They'd known each other long enough, she didn't feel like playing that game.

Besides, he'd already spanked her and gotten her off at Stronghold. They'd also be doing much more intimate things in class.

Why not invite him in? They'd kicked ass at trivia, had the best first date ever, and she wasn't ready for the night to end.

Q flashed her a smile, his dark eyes sparkling with amusement as if he could read her thoughts.

"I'd love to come in."

It didn't escape her notice that he didn't say a thing about getting a drink. Pressing her lips together to hide her smile, she tried to ignore the way her heart had started pitter-pattering in her chest at high speed and unlocked the door. Thankfully, she usually kept things pretty neat in her apartment, and she'd straightened up a little more before Morgan and Noelle had come over to help her get ready, so she didn't have to worry about that.

Shrugging off her coat, she turned to take his as well, hanging them up on the hook beside the door. By the time she turned back, he was well into her apartment and looking around, making her wonder if he was searching for something specific.

The little studio wasn't anything special. The main room was shaped like an L with her bed tucked into the shorter branch so that it wasn't immediately visible from the door. She was lucky enough to have a very small galley kitchen that was separate from the main room, making it feel a little less cramped and less like a regular efficiency. The bathroom and closet were tucked between where her bed was and the kitchen. Getting to the bathroom meant walking through her closet—which was currently in pretty good shape since Noelle had put all of Sam's clothes back in place while Morgan was doing her makeup.

Most of her furniture were freebies she'd picked up from online or things she'd found at yard sales. The queen bed was a hand-me-down that she'd gotten from her aunt, and she'd saved up to buy the new mattress after moving in. The most expensive thing in the whole apartment was her loveseat, which she had instead of a regular couch, and she'd gotten it on sale from a discount store for a couple hundred bucks.

It was the perfect size for two people, not that she ever had much of an opportunity to share it with anyone. Her diploma hung in a place of honor above the love seat. Her dad had been so proud, he'd gone and gotten it professionally framed, despite the expense.

"Nice." Q turned slowly in a circle taking in the whole room. "It's like a studio but with a kitchen."

"It is a studio, just shaped a little different," she said. "And, like you said, the kitchen."

"Kind of convenient having the bed in the same room as everyone else." He turned back to face her, the glint in his eye sparkling brighter than ever. Sam felt a rush of heat flow through her, her anticipation ratcheting higher as her instincts kicked into high gear.

"Yes, I suppose it is. Can I get you some water or start making some coffee?" she asked, though she didn't make a move toward the kitchen. Her feet were firmly rooted to the floor just beyond her closed door.

She didn't really want to get him a drink and chat and wait to see what happened next.

She wanted to get right to the good stuff. She wanted to celebrate their win. She wanted him to take her to bed, or her to take him, she wasn't sure it really mattered.

"I'm not particularly thirsty." Q took a step toward her as she took one toward him, leaving them less than a foot away from each other.

Sam tilted her head.

"Then why did you come in for a drink?" Her words came out more breathlessly than she intended, making her sound extra flirtatious, which was more than fine.

His smile widened, and he reached for her. Sam stepped into his arms, pressing her hands against his chest, her curves flattening against hard muscles. One of his hands flattened against her lower back and the other slid up to the back of her neck. Fingers curved around her neck, his thumb gently sweeping the side, lips hovering just over hers.

"I didn't. I came in for you."

Yes, please.

Their lips met and parted in a rush of need, their tongues tangling with passionate fervor. Sam's body tingled all over, the ache between her thighs tightening her inner muscles. The kiss deepened as Q's fingers tightened slightly on the back of her neck while his hand slipped between her sweater and her jeans, caressing the skin and making all the littles hairs on her arms stand up.

Heat and need coiled through her, her nipples tightening as her breasts were pressed flat against his hard chest. Rocking her hips as one of his legs wedged between hers, Sam moaned, but the sound was muffled by his kiss. She ran her hands up his chest to his shoulders, wrapping them around him, and kissing him back fiercely as pleasure pulsed through her.

She rocked against his leg, rubbing herself on his thigh, the thick fabric of their jeans keeping them apart yet stimulating her clit, thanks to the seam's ridge against her pussy.

"Fuck." He tore his mouth away from hers, his eyes wild as their gazes met. Sam's lips felt swollen from his kiss, and she shuddered, her thighs squeezing his, holding herself still from pure willpower. Staring back at her, he tilted his chin up challengingly. "Who's going to be in charge?"

Licking her lips, she stared back at him, and something inside her rose like a cobra that had been challenged. She wasn't feeling particularly submissive right now.

"I guess we're going to find out."

Q

Fuck, that shouldn't be so hot. Maybe this was why he was a Switch and not a Dom—he didn't find her words or demeanor at all bratty. They were a turn-on. Q loved seeing a woman who knew what she wanted and wasn't afraid to take it... sometimes. Sometimes, he wanted to be the one to tie her up and tell her that she would take what he gave her. Right now, he wasn't sure what he wanted and felt as though he could really go either direction, but the way Sam was looking at him was making him feel like she might want to be in charge.

Which... yeah, he was down for, yet he couldn't help but push back.

Chuckling, he spun her around so he could back her toward the bed, re-engaging in their kiss but not until after he'd peeled her sweater up over her head. His suit jacket hit the floor next as she shoved it off his shoulders. They left a small trail of clothes between them and the bed.

It really was convenient having the bed in the main room.

Sam swiveled them around, so she could push him up against the bed. When she dropped to her knees in front of him as she yanked his pants down, Q decided it was probably the best idea he'd ever heard.

"Fuck." Her fingers wrapped around his cock, sliding over the length of his shaft, and his hips rocked forward at the contact. Need pulsed through him, tightening his balls as his pleasure climbed. It took a bit of maneuvering to get his shoes off so she could finish taking his pants off, but it gave him the opportunity to get her turned around.

When he pushed her back against the bed, he lifted her slightly, enough to get her feet off the ground, so she was sitting on the bed instead of being trapped between it and his hip. She was still basically trapped, with her knees spread just enough to admit his body and her ass right on the edge.

"I feel like there's a power imbalance here, with me completely naked and you still wearing too many clothes." He'd gotten her down to her bra and underwear, but as far as he was concerned, that was still too much. He wanted her naked.

Sam leaned back, resting her weight on her hands, the position elongating her body and pushing her breasts up, the soft curves of her breasts resting against each other. Sliding his hands over them, he explored her pale, satiny skin while his gaze remained locked with hers.

Her lips curved up in a mischievous smile, and her hazel eyes twinkled with repressed mirth.

"Are you saying there's a disturbance in the force?"

All movement ground to a halt as his brain assimilated the fact she'd just made a Star Wars pun during sex.

Fuck. If he hadn't been turned on before... His dick throbbed as he leaned into her, pressing his length along the wet seam of her underwear, rubbing against her through the thin fabric. He didn't know whether to crack up or just tip her back and fuck her hard.

"Disturbance isn't the right word. More like protuberance." That might have been the least sexy way to describe his dick, but he knew she'd appreciate it.

Sam cracked up, and Q had to grin as she shook her head. Her breasts shook as well, jiggling within their bra cups, and he took the opportunity to slide one hand behind her back and pop the clasp open. That got her attention, and she stopped laughing. Her lips made a small 'o' as the bra's support disappeared.

"Holy crap!" Her hands went to her breasts.

"Uh-uh, pretty girl. Don't you dare cover up." Q tugged the straps of her bra down and off while she sighed and lifted her hands to let him. "I could spend all day playing with these pretty tits."

Moaning when he touched her, Sam arched her back toward him as he filled his hands with the soft mounds in question, and her pebbled nipples rubbed against his thumbs.

"I might just let you," she murmured.

Q smiled as he lowered his mouth to her skin. Moaning again, she leaned back and gave him full access to her body as his lips and tongue moved over her skin. He rocked his hips forward, rubbing his cock against her, feeling the wetness that had seeped through her underwear gliding along the underside.

It was impossible to tell who was in charge.

While her hands were on the bed rather than on him, one could argue that she was mostly immobilized, but in truth, she could reach up at any time. She was the one being pleasured. Caressed. Catered to. Q worshiped her with his mouth, his lips finding her nipple and sucking hard while his fingers toyed with its twin. She tasted delicious. Even more so when she moaned and shuddered at his touch, sending his own need soaring higher.

As much as he wanted to push her onto her back and slide into the welcoming haven of her body, he didn't want to stop... he wanted to hear her beg him or order him to fuck her.

Sam

Whimpering as Q's clever fingers pinched and tugged on her nipple, his teeth nibbling on the other, Sam squirmed against the hard ridge of his erection where it pressed against her pussy. Stupid underwear. Without it, she could have him inside her in a heartbeat... yet the tease was almost satisfying enough on its own.

Especially when she looked into his eyes and saw the heat burning there—the heat was singeing him, too.

When he straightened, his lips left her breast to be replaced by his hand. Caressing. Stroking. Pinching. The hot sting of pain interspersed with the pleasure made her pussy pulse, clenching in need. She loved having her nipples pinched, tugged, played with. The sensitive nubs were on fire from Q's handling. Her breasts ached, feeling heavy and swollen with arousal. He squeezed them hard enough to make her whimper, the soft flesh spilling out between his fingers.

"These would look so pretty with some clamps on them," he said, pinching her nipples again. Clearly, he'd noticed how much she'd enjoyed the sensation.

Opening her eyes, Sam smiled.

"Funny you should say that," she murmured, tilting her head to the nightstand next to her bed, shooting a significant glance in its direction.

"Is that an invitation to search your toy drawer?" Releasing her breasts, he reached for it before she'd even answered. He paused, fingers waiting on the knob, and looked at her, waiting for her consent.

"Yes."

Body humming with anticipation, she watched him open the drawer, and smiled. There wasn't a ton in her toy drawer, but there was more than there used to be. The nipple clamps, butt plug, lube, and leather cuffs were all added after she'd started taking the introduction class at Marquis. The vibrator and condoms were from before that. The cuffs had never been used since she wasn't going to cuff herself just to masturbate and risk not being able to get out. The condoms... well, she hadn't used any of those in a while, either. Something she was thrilled was about to change.

"Well, well, well," Q said, holding up the cuffs and turning his head back to look at her with a wicked glint in his eyes.

Truthfully, Sam didn't feel like being helpless tonight. She wanted to be more active. And she knew how to spot a good bargain. Q wanted to put the clamps on her nipples, which sounded good to her, but...

"I'll let you clamp my nipples if you let me cuff you to my bed," she purred.

15

A BARGAIN IS MADE

She wasn't sure how Q would react to the offer of being restrained in exchange for clamping her nipples, but his expression lit up with interest. His lips spread in a slow, seductive smile, and he nodded.

A trade for a trade.

Who would really be in control? She wasn't sure. On the other hand, she wasn't sure it mattered. One of the things that had been drummed into her head during the classes was there was no one right way to kink. Everyone had to work out what worked for them.

Maybe with her and Q there wouldn't always need to be a clear person in charge. There were times when she would probably want him to be and times when she would want to be. Right now, she wasn't feeling the push to dominate strongly enough to reject the clamps.

Especially if she got to cuff him and play with him after.

Dropping the cuffs on the bed, Q picked up the nipple clamps. They were a standard pair with rubber tips, a little screw on each that made them adjustable, and a chain dangling between them. Sam kept them on the tightest setting now, though at the beginning she'd found it too painful.

Now, she liked the painful grip of a tight squeeze, enhancing her pleasure by the contrast. Her nipples tingled at the sight of them, a physiological response from knowing exactly how it was going to feel.

"Offer your breasts to me, pretty girl," Q said, moving to stand between her knees again. The edges of his lips were still curved into a smile, but his expression had turned more serious, more intense, his gaze hot with lust.

Heat surged through her, washing over her, and Sam straightened, arching her back and thrusting her breasts forward. Her hands cupped the soft mounds, lifting them.

"Yes, Sir," she said cheekily, even as she obeyed. Q chuckled, apparently amused by her sassy tone.

"Good girl."

Heat flushed through her and she would have pressed her legs together if he hadn't been between them. Moaning, Sam closed her eyes as he rubbed his thumb over her right nipple, teasing the little bud to further hardness.

Then the rubber tip of the clamp closed around it, and she hissed with the sharp prick of pain that stabbed through her breast. Somehow having clamps put on her was very different from putting them on herself. It wasn't that it hurt more, exactly, but the lack of control made it less predictable.

The cold metal of the chain bounced against her stomach as Q moved to her other breast, rubbing his thumb over that nipple before applying the clamp. The twin points of pain throbbed on her breasts as her tightly compressed nipples protested the treatment, even as her pussy creamed. The dichotomy of erotic pain—it hurt so good.

"Just as pretty as I thought it would be," Q murmured, brushing his fingers over the tips of her nipples where they protruded from the clamps.

They were even more sensitive with the clamps on. Gasping, she shuddered and let her head fall back as the sensations went through her. Q tugged on the chain, tormenting her with the pleasure-pain, and making her want to writhe.

Taking a deep, shuddering breath, she opened her eyes and met his gaze. She dropped her hands away from her breasts, letting them fall. The slight bounce made the chain jiggle and tug on her nipples, though with much lighter force than when Q had been pulling.

Lifting her gaze to his, she grinned.

"My turn."

Q

Flat on his back in the middle of Sam's bed, Q was perfectly happy lifting his hands so Sam could secure them to her headboard. First of all, he was curious to see what it would be like to have Sam in control outside of class. Second, because she'd decided to straddle his chest while she was securing his hands.

He was looking at the undersides of her breasts, watching the hypnotic sway of the chain as it hung from her nipples. While some of her weight rested on his chest, if she moved a bit farther up, he'd be able to get his mouth on her pussy. Instead, he couldn't touch anything with his hands or mouth, but the visual feast was a tease of the highest order.

The already soft leather of the cuffs was lined with even softer fur, adding to the sensations already arousing him.

As soon as she sat back, releasing his wrists, he tugged to test the cuffs. They were tight enough he wouldn't be able to pull his hands through them, but loose enough that they didn't hurt or squeeze. No need to worry about losing circulation.

His heart rate kicked up when she wriggled her down, so she was straddling his hips instead of his chest. With her hands planted on either side of his chest, her breasts hung down beneath her, the hard nipples turning darker and darker pink, and the chain between the clamps brushed against his skin, cool on his heated flesh.

Lifting her hips, Sam shifted, so she came down atop his erection.

Q groaned, and his hips surging upward, hands jerking uselessly on his restraints. The hot weight of her pressing down on his dick sent pure pleasure rocketing through him, and it was a hell of a tease.

The thin fabric separating her pussy from his dick was wetter than before, and with her on top, he could feel her a lot more acutely.

"Fuck, Sam."

"That's Ma'am or Mistress Samantha, to you," she teased, her tone only half-serious.

Moving her hands to the tops of his shoulders, she curled her fingers so she could drag her nails across his skin, from his shoulders over his chest, barely avoiding his sensitive nipples. Her nails dug in just enough to scrape and sting, but not truly hurt. His nipples ached from the lack of attention as she went around them rather than touching them.

"Fuck me, Ma'am." Panting as he tensed underneath her, a shiver went down his spine when her nails dragged over his stomach.

Sam laughed softly, and Q grinned up at her.

She looked fucking hot, straddling him, silvery clamps dangling from her red nipples, curls falling about her shoulders. If in high school, Q knew he'd end up here one day, he would have happily traded away prom night for this moment. However, high school Q hadn't had this wild imagination.

Sometimes, truth really was stranger than fiction.

"Take off your panties, ma'am." Though his tone was perfectly respectful, it came out as an order. It didn't matter that he was restrained on his back, beneath her, and calling her ma'am. He saw her reaction, the way her lips parted on a quick intake of breath, breasts heaving, pupils dilating.

He might be on the bottom, but he could still boss her around as long as she was willing.

"Pretty sure I'm the one in charge," she said, but even as she said the words, she got to her feet, so she was standing over him. The soft surface of the bed made her wobble a little, and Q spared a moment wondering what it would be like if she fell down atop him.

I would be smothered in boob.

Yup, I volunteer as tribute.

Sam shimmied out of her underwear, which was really just as good as being smothered in boob. The incredible view of her pussy with her legs spread above his body showed off the glistening folds, wet with her arousal. She bent her knees, smoothly dropping back down onto them with her thighs pressed against his sides.

Leaning forward, she reached for the drawer. The stretch of her movement brought the chain between her clamps dangling over his face, and Q took the opportunity to lift his head up, taking the metal firmly between his teeth, and tugging. Sam gasped, and the hand not reaching for the drawer came down on his shoulder and dug in, making him buck beneath her.

Fluttering her eyelashes, she took a moment to compose herself, then glared down at him, her gaze glancing off where the chain was still between his teeth.

"If I wasn't so turned on, I might be really pissed off right now," she said matter-of-factly.

Laughing, Q released the chain, and Sam finished stretching out to grab a condom from the drawer. His cock throbbed in anticipation, but her nipples were looking very dark red, and they'd been in the clamps for a while. As much as he wanted to fuck her, he wanted that taken care of first.

"Take the clamps off, gorgeous girl," he said, jerking his chin up at them. "Then let me kiss those pretty nipples and make them feel all better."

Sam paused, condom in her hand, and for a moment, he thought she was going to do exactly as he said... then she shook her head, and her lips curved into a smile.

"You are awfully bossy for being the one tied up."

He grinned back at her wolfishly, tugging gently on the cuffs.

"Doesn't hurt to ask for what I want."

Rocking back onto her heels, Sam's body pressed down on his groin again as the chain gently tapped against her belly. Q thrust his hips up, rubbing the underside of his cock along the wet lips of her pussy. He groaned at the fantastic wet heat that coated the length of his dick. It was a hot flash of pleasure that promised ecstasy once he was buried inside her.

"I suppose it doesn't." She wriggled atop him, grinding on him as she ripped open the condom wrapper. "But I'm the one in charge right now. When you're on top, you can do things your way."

Q bit his lip against telling her he was perfectly happy with doing things her way, considering the direction she was going. She knew her limits better than he did, had taken more of the classes, and knew the dangers of leaving clamps on for too long. If she felt she was still in the safe zone, he wouldn't try to convince her otherwise.

Especially during a moment like this when she really was the boss.

Shifting back a little more, Sam placed the condom on the tip of his cock and rolled it down. Feeling her fingers brushing against his shaft, Q groaned and thrust his hips, helping her push the rubber over his length.

When she reached the base, Sam wrapped her fingers around the root of his cock and tilted it toward her pussy. Q tried to push upward again, his body straining toward hers, but she was holding him in place. He had to wait as she ran the tip of his cock up and down the folds of her pussy, teasing him, before finally sinking down on him. The wet heat of her pussy wrapped around him, the muscles clenching, then releasing, massaging his cock as she took him in.

He tugged uselessly at the cuffs again, his body demanding to be free to touch her, to hold her, to tease her the way she was teasing him... but he couldn't. There was nothing he could do except lie back and let her have her way with him.

It was fucking hot as hell.

---

*S*AM

Fuck.

Q was *big.* Thick enough her fingers barely touched and long enough she was a little worried he might be *too* big as she sank down atop him. Granted, being on top also made her a little tighter than usual, her muscles tensing as she lowered herself, no matter how wet and ready she was.

Her nipples throbbed in the tight confines of the clamps. They would need to come off very soon, but she'd wanted to establish that she was currently in charge. Plus, she liked the feeling of the chain swaying, tugging gently on the tortured buds, while she worked herself up and down on Q's cock, taking him a little deeper with every stroke.

She moaned and shuddered, her muscles clenching around him as she sank onto him until her swollen pussy lips and clit finally rested against his groin. It was though she could barely take a breath as her body adjusted. Squirming, she rubbed her sensitive folds and nub on his body, making him groan and jerk inside her.

Reaching up to her breasts, she opened the clamps and whimpered as the blood rushed into the crushed nubs. Leaning forward, she let her breasts hang down over Q's face, shifting the angle so her nipple reached his lips. Immediately, he opened and sucked the tortured bud into his mouth, his tongue laving over its throbbing surface as it plumped. The warm heat of his mouth helped soothe some of the sting.

Sam rocked her hips, rubbing herself against him, squeezing his cock, before pulling her nipple free and offering him the other one. When she glanced down, his gaze met hers, hot and full of need. He gave her nipple a final suck before releasing it.

"Fuck me, Sam," he ordered.

This time, she didn't protest his bossiness. She was too aroused. Too needy. And she enjoyed hearing him boss her around, even liked that he was restrained, and she was on top when he did it. The exchange of power flowing back and forth between them was ticking all of her boxes.

Pressing her hands to his chest, her thigh muscles flexed, and she rose and fell atop him. Pleasure spiraled through her, the friction of his cock moving inside her pulsing hot waves of need across her body.

"Fuck." That was no order. It was a hoarse exclamation of passion as Q arched beneath her, his hips thrusting up to meet her fall, filling her over and over again while she rode him.

Leaning forward, she let her oversensitized nipples brush against his chest, the coarse hairs abrading the tiny buds. The change in position pressed her clit more firmly against his pubic bone, so she rubbed against him every time she fell, grinding her most sensitive bits on his body. Each new sensation piled atop the previous one, tightening her muscles, pushing her closer and closer to climax.

The sound of metal against wood preceded the creaking of the bed as Q strained beneath her, his groans of pleasure nearly drowning out the other sounds. Sam pushed down against him, her nipples pressed to his chest, her hips moving as she worked herself back and forth on his cock, rubbing herself against him... using him for her pleasure.

He cried out, his voice filling her ears, as he thrust upward. She could feel him pulsing inside her, even as her body throbbed around him. Ecstasy spiraled out of control, bursting inside her and swamping her senses with pure erotic bliss until she collapsed atop him, replete and humming with satisfaction.

16

MORNING AFTER

Q

The sound of a door closing woke Q. It took him a moment to realize the door was out in the hall because he was in an apartment building and not at home. Not just any apartment building—Sam's apartment building. After she'd uncuffed him, he'd taken care of the condom before getting back into bed to cuddle with her. He'd meant it to be just that, some cuddling before he left, but at some point, when they'd been murmuring to each other, he'd fallen asleep instead.

Now, he was wrapped around a soft, warm woman with one hand on her breast and his cock nestled against her ass, and he was hard as a rock. This was a hell of a lot better than waking up at home alone.

Pressing a kiss to the back of Sam's neck, he squeezed her breast again, and she murmured sleepily and incoherently. Chuckling, Q gently rubbed his fingers over her hard nipple, and she moaned, pushing her ass back against him and making his cock throb.

"Good morning, gorgeous," he whispered, dropping more kisses along her shoulder as he fondled her breast. She sucked in a deep breath, her ass rubbing against the length of his cock as she squirmed.

"Well, good morning to you too... ouch." He'd plucked her nipple, gently but apparently, they were still sore from the clamp's last night.

Chuckling, Q shifted so he could roll her onto her back, then went up on his knees between her legs. Sam blinked sleepily up at him. Her blonde hair was spread out across the pillow, and mascara circled under her eyes. He loved getting to see her like this. There was an intimacy to seeing a woman first thing in the morning, makeup remnants on her face, hair unbrushed... She was showing him a part of her not everyone got to see. A vulnerable part, at that.

"What are you doing?" she asked, the corners of her lips tipping up with amusement as he spread her knees apart.

"Getting breakfast."

Q lowered his mouth to her pussy, enjoying her gasp of surprise and pleasure. This morning, he was feeling decidedly Dominant, and she must have been feeling pretty submissive because she didn't challenge him as he feasted on her, licking her to her first orgasm, then pinning her wrists beside her head with his hands, holding her in place while he fucked her to her second climax.

Unfortunately, they couldn't spend the day together. He had things to do around the house, and she had errands to run, but it was one hell of a morning after.

She walked him out to his car, and he claimed one last kiss and a promise they would have another date later in the week. Sure, they had class tomorrow, but he didn't want to leave anything to chance.

Being home alone all day was enough to make him feel antsy. He'd gotten used to living with other people and had been okay when they'd moved out, but now, he wished he was spending time with Sam instead of knocking about on his own. There were also questions bubbling up they hadn't talked about last night, probably because it was too soon.

Were they dating? They'd gone on a date. Was she seeing anyone else? He hadn't asked. He wasn't. He didn't plan to. Fuck, he hoped she didn't either, but he needed to talk to her about it before he made assumptions or demands.

Were they even at a point where they could talk exclusivity?

He was getting so up in his head, it was almost a relief when Angel called.

"So, how did it go?" she asked the second he picked up. Q had to laugh and shake his head, which made some of the tension hounding him melt away.

"You don't even want to try to pretend you're not nosy?" he teased, putting the phone on speaker, so he could keep chopping vegetables for his dinner while he talked to her.

"I have an almost one year old. I don't have time for small talk or pretense anymore, so just jump straight to the good stuff."

Q chuckled.

"A gentleman never kisses and tells."

"Oh, wow, so you fucked already!"

"Angel!"

"I'm just saying. If nothing happened, you'd tell me."

That was a hard point to argue. He made a mental note for later consideration. Unless he wanted Angel all up in his business, he would need to find better ways to misdirect or redirect her.

On the other hand, he also wanted to use her.

"How early is too early to ask for an exclusive relationship?" Since they were getting straight to the point, Q went all in, and only got silence in return. "Angel?"

"Do you think it's too soon?" she asked.

He hated it when she did that.

"I think I don't want her to think it's too soon." That sounded really weak when he said it out loud.

"But you want to be exclusive with her." It was more of a statement than a question. He could practically hear her brain working as she processed out loud. "You two have been dancing around each other for weeks, but last night was your first date, so I can see why you'd be worried it's too soon. On the other hand, there's no such thing as 'too soon,' only what you are both comfortable with, and you can't know that without talking to her."

Which was what he'd known she was going to say, yet he'd wanted to hear it out loud, anyway.

"Boo talking," he replied, making her laugh in turn. "I don't like talking and feelings. Can't we just magically turn her into my girlfriend?"

"Aw, Q is going to have a girlfriend. That's so cute."

He wrinkled his nose. Somehow, having a girlfriend sounded very high school, but there wasn't really a better word for it. Though considering the 'girl' in question was Sam, maybe it fit better than he wanted it to.

"She liked the trivia night. We won."

"Of course, you did. I'm glad she liked it." There was a smile in Angel's voice even if he couldn't see it. "I bet you two made a spectacular team. Remind me never to play against you. Alright, I have to go. I had five minutes free, and I've used them all up. You're still coming to Friendsgiving next weekend, right? Invite Sam. She's more than welcome to join us."

"I will, but I'm not going to push her to come if she's uncomfortable. She's not even officially my girlfriend yet," he warned her. "Friendsgiving would be a *lot*."

"What, you don't want to throw your new girlfriend in the middle of the loudest, most invasive group of people you know?" Angel laughed. "Don't worry, I know we're a lot. As long as you come!"

"I'll be there, and I'll definitely invite her."

"Awesome. Talk to you later, hun. Bye!"

"Bye, Angel." Shaking his head in bemusement, Q hung up the phone and got back to making dinner.

He loved Angel and enjoyed hanging out with her friends, but they were her *best* friends, whereas they were his friends. Asad, Law, and Connor had become his closest friends in the past few months.

As if the thought of them had summoned the text, his phone buzzed, and he glanced over. Connor was checking in to see how last night with Sam had gone, and his phone buzzed again twice more as Asad and Law also made their interest known. Grinning, Q sent off a quick text to let them know it had gone well... then wondered if Sam was doing the same with her friends.

<u>SAM</u>

Running errands while having a text conversation with her friends made everything take twice as long, but she didn't care. She was grinning from ear to ear while she walked around the grocery store, aware of the way her sore nipples pressed against her padded bra, and the delightful ache between her legs.

She'd freaked out a little when she'd gotten a look at herself in the mirror before she and Q had taken a shower together, but he hadn't seemed to mind her snarled hair and makeup still clinging to her face. Today she looked much more like herself—hair up in a ponytail with no makeup, and he hadn't looked at her any differently when she'd walked him out to his car as he had last night when she'd been all dolled up.

Okay, well, he'd admired the effort she'd put forth yesterday, but he didn't act like how she looked this morning was a disappointment or a turnoff. Going by the early morning sexy times, it might even have been a turn-on.

Her phone buzzed again, and she realized she was standing and staring at a bunch of zucchinis in the produce aisle. Talk about a Freudian slip.

Noelle: *We're getting together before class tomorrow to talk, right?*

Sam: *Yeah! Looking forward to it.*

Morgan: *Yay!*

She couldn't blame them for wanting the in-person update. Although she'd told them that the date had gone really well and Q had unexpectedly spent the night, which was why she hadn't texted until today, she hadn't felt comfortable putting more detail than that in text messages.

To be perfectly honest, she wasn't sure how much detail she'd be comfortable sharing in person, but she knew it would be a little more than she was willing to do by text.

Finishing her errands, she went home... and the whole space felt bigger and lonelier without Q. She liked her 'me' time, but she would have liked more time with him.

Don't be clingy.

With that thought in her head, she got her dinner ready and didn't allow herself to text him. That would be too soon, right? Ugh. She hadn't dated in far too long and was pretty sure some of what was in her head were arbitrary rules made up by movies. At the same time, she didn't want him to think she was pushing him or anything like that.

They'd had a really nice night together, and he wanted to see her again. She should be happy with that. She also was afraid to rock the boat. Relationships weren't something she was good at, whether it was friendship or dating.

It already felt different with Q. Easier. Which was ironic, considering how they'd started out, but it was true.

She didn't want to rock the boat.

So, when she was sitting down to binge watch HGTV and dream about the kind of house she'd like to have one day, she was pleasantly shocked when her phone started to ring. She knew it was Q because his was the only ringtone she *hadn't* changed after he'd sabotaged her phone by making all her ringtones music from Lord of the Rings. She'd had pretty mixed feelings when he'd done it.

She loved the music, but she'd hated the reminder of kids calling her Samwise in high school. Even then, she'd known Q hadn't meant it in a derogatory way the way some of the others did. They called her the fat hobbit.

But Samwise Gamgee was Q's favorite character.

Part of her had wanted to kick him for bringing up those memories, but she'd already retaliated for the ringtone thing. Angel and Lexie had helped her Post-it note his car. They'd covered it completely.

So, really, it was a wash.

She picked up the phone.

"Hello?"

Until he responded, there was a part of her that thought it was probably a butt dial and not a legitimate call.

"Hey, Sam. I hope I'm not interrupting dinner or anything."

"Nope, but you are interrupting *Married to Real Estate*, so make it quick," she teased. She'd already told him about her home improvement show addiction, though she hadn't told him *why* she was so obsessed with the shows.

"Oh, I see where I stand now." He laughed so she knew he wasn't insulted. "I just wanted to call and see how the rest of your day went."

A rush of pleasure surged through her. She'd figured he was calling for a specific reason, not just to talk.

"Good. Ran my errands. Raspberries were on sale at the grocery store."

Q laughed.

"It's amazing the things we find exciting as adults, huh?"

"Like naps and spankings?" she quipped, making him laugh again. Snuggling deeper into her love seat, she wished he was there with her but was happy he'd called. Happy that he seemed just as interested in her as she was in him.

"Hey, so I was talking to Angel today, and she reminded me that she's having Friendsgiving next weekend, and she told me to invite you."

"She did?" Surprise made Sam reply with complete honesty, which was shock that Angel would invite her. Not that Angel was unfriendly or anything—she was very friendly—but she also had her own group of friends already.

They were, like, friendly acquaintances. Not the kind of friendship that would warrant an invitation to a holiday event.

Then Sam realized that the invitation wasn't really to her. It was to Q's...

What?

Girlfriend?

That was the kind of thing that was offered to significant others, right?

Was it too soon?

"She did," Q confirmed, his voice splintering her thoughts and the insecurities that were bubbling up and threatening to take over. "Angel likes you a lot, you know, and she's thrilled that we're... dating."

There was a slight hesitation before he said 'dating,' like he wasn't exactly sure what to call what they were doing, which made her feel a little better. They hadn't talked about their relationship in any firm terms, but if Angel was inviting her to Friendsgiving and Q wasn't taking anyone else, that seemed like a good sign for her hopeful little heart.

"You don't have to come if you don't want to. I told her it might be too soon." His words were a little rushed, and Sam realized he was nervous, which made her feel better about being anxious. "Plus, it's next Saturday evening, and you might already have plans."

She didn't.

"I can come." She didn't want to let him down. Plus, this *was* what she wanted—a real relationship with someone who was kinky. Someone who got her.

Yeah, it was a little mind boggling that person was Q, her high school nemesis and crush, but the universe worked in mysterious ways. Maybe she was due some good karma.

"Great!" The joy and relief in his voice made her relax even more. He was glad she was going. It hadn't been a pity invite.

She had new friends, a new guy she was dating who was acting like he wanted to get serious, and she'd had the best sex of her life... twice in twenty-four hours. Things were looking up.

Now, if only she could win the lottery. With the way her luck was running, maybe she should buy a ticket.

17

———————

DISTRACTED STUDENT

Sam

"That sounds like an amazing weekend. Damn." Noelle fanned herself with her hand, keeping her voice low. "I'm so jealous! I hope I meet someone like that."

Even though it was Monday, the bar at Marquis was a lot busier before class than it was when she'd hang out with Q after class. Busy enough, she was grateful Noelle and Morgan were keeping their voices low, even though they'd claimed a booth rather than seats at the bar.

Chances were, no one was listening, but she still didn't want her private business spread around. She glanced at the wooden bar where Shane was serving drinks, not far away.

Especially now that she knew at least one of the sources of Marquis' gossip train. She bet people let spill all kinds of things in front of Shane, which wasn't his fault, and she didn't blame him, but she'd made a mental note to be careful of what she said in front of the bartenders. All of them reported to Olivia, after all.

"Are you guys hanging out tonight after class?" Morgan asked.

"We didn't say so, but since we have the past couple classes, I'm assuming that's going to be the plan. We didn't really say, though."

"He'd better." Noelle frowned. "That would be awful of him to take you out, have sex, then that's it for Monday nights after class."

An uncertain sick feeling wove its way through Sam's stomach. Yeah, that would suck, but... she didn't think Q would do that.

"I don't think he's the type," Morgan said, shaking her head, which made Sam feel better. "He's been totally hung up on Sam for months, even if he did nothing about it." When Sam looked at her in surprise, Morgan smiled. "He's always watching you."

Morgan had said nothing about it, but then she probably wouldn't, just in case she was wrong. Especially since Sam had told her about their high school days.

"Even if he did, it would be okay. He invited me to Friendsgiving at his friend's house this upcoming weekend." She toyed with her straw wrapper, twisting it round and round over itself. "And he told me he wants to see me again."

"Oh, wow... Friendsgiving. That's kind of serious, isn't it? That's great." Noelle's eyebrows had flown upwards at the news, but she was sincerely encouraging. She might be thinking exactly the same thing Sam had—was it too soon?

"Yeah, one of his good friends, Angel, is hosting, and she told him to invite me." Sam let the crumpled straw wrapper fall to the table's surface. "It is kinda quick, but I'm friendly with Angel and her group of friends, so it's not like I'm a total stranger."

"Shoot, we should get going," Morgan said, glancing up at the clock on the wall above the bar.

Sam turned her head. They had about five minutes to get upstairs, but Morgan got stressed out if she was late and preferred to be a little early. Truthfully, Sam also preferred to be on time or early, but she didn't sweat it the way Morgan did.

Since they'd already paid, there was nothing to do but finish their drinks—since they had class, they'd all had a single glass each—and head to the back of the restaurant. To the diners who weren't in the know, they looked like a group of women headed to the bathroom together. Most of them wouldn't notice when the women didn't return.

A few minutes later, they were in the main room of Marquis. Q was already there, chatting with Law. He turned as she and the others walked in, and Sam raised her hand in greeting, trying not to feel too shy. She shouldn't have worried.

The moment Q saw her, he grinned so wide, she automatically smiled back—and Law had to put his hand on Q's shoulder to get his attention again. Talk about an ego boost.

Q

Class was interesting, but Sam's presence was a constant distraction. Not that he minded. It was just hard to focus on what Law and Mistress Julie were saying when his gorgeous girl was by his side—especially when everyone went to the spanking benches for a demonstration of what it would be like. Q had already done this part in the Dom class, but he wasn't surprised when he liked it a hell of a lot more when Sam did it than he had when it had been Olivia.

Olivia was an attractive woman, but she was also kind of scary, even though she'd softened some since Luke came into her life.

His mind wasn't really on the class or the spanking, which was more educational than erotic, especially with everyone else in class around them. He was thinking about Sam and whether he should invite her over after this or try to get a date for later in the week. He didn't want her to think he was expecting constant sex from her.

Though, of course, he also wouldn't turn it down if she wanted to.

Finally, class was over, and Sam helped him off the bench. Like last week, she was wearing an outfit that was sexy as hell, but not so obviously kink she couldn't wear it downstairs to the bar.

Keeping hold of her hand, he spoke before she could suggest going downstairs.

"Want to come over to my place tonight? Or we can go downstairs. Whatever you're more comfortable with." He tried not to sound too needy.

One of his exes had once told him he had a confusing mix of

'Golden retriever energy' and 'Doberman energy.' Right now, he was feeling that golden retriever energy and trying really hard not to be overeager. All he needed was for Sam to make the same comparison, then ask if he wanted to try out the puppy playroom.

Not his kink.

"Your place sounds great." She smiled almost shyly as he threaded his fingers through hers. "I already had dinner here with Morgan and Noelle, so I wouldn't mind going somewhere else."

"Great." He grinned back at her, trying not to overthink whether she was saying yes because she actually wanted to go to his place or because she wanted to get out of Marquis.

They were turning to go when Noelle suddenly came hurrying up to them, her eyes alight with enthusiasm. Having heard Rae and the others' opinion of her and how she'd treated Iris, he had to hide his reaction to her, which was wary dislike. It might not be fair since he didn't really know her, but unless she'd changed in a very short amount of time, how she'd treated Iris was completely relevant. Not only that, but considering the way *she'd* talked about Iris, he didn't see any signs of remorse from her at all. Not exactly encouraging.

But she was friends with Sam, and he didn't want to rock the boat before he had a chance to talk to Sam about it.

"Hey, you two! Headed downstairs?" She cocked her head at them, something about her manner making Q think not only was she expecting 'yes' for an answer, but she wanted to be invited along. Which... maybe he was projecting or reading too much into things because of what he knew about her, but something about the way she asked made him really uncomfortable.

Although if she was a total stranger, it wouldn't have bothered him, so he tried to mentally shake off his discomfort.

"No, actually, we're going to Q's instead." Sam smiled at Noelle, obviously unbothered by the question because there was no real reason *to* be bothered. He was going to have to watch his reactions to Noelle, at least until he decided whether to talk to Sam about her. Trying to come between friends wasn't something he ever wanted to do, and he wasn't even sure it was the right thing to do.

"Oh! Oh." Noelle blinked, her voice changing between 'ohs.' She grinned at them. "Have fun, you two!" Then she winked.

For Q, it felt way too familiar for someone he didn't actually know, but she was friends with Sam, and he was probably being too sensitive. Thankfully, neither of the women seemed to notice. The last thing he wanted to do was start shit right after Sam had agreed to come over.

"Thanks, I'll talk to you later." Cheerfully, Sam waved her hand, and Q gave Noelle a stilted nod, doing his best to hide his distaste for her. Out of the corner of his eye he could see Law across the room, watching them.

Hopefully, this wasn't going to turn into a thing.

"Drive together or separate?" he asked as they exited into the lobby. Behind the desk, Freddy picked up Samantha's purse and grabbed their jackets. Q was sure that his ears were wide open though, listening for the gossip.

"Separate," she said firmly. The look she gave him was regretful. "I have to get up early to work tomorrow morning, so I can't stay over."

Darn. Well, there went that idea, but at least he knew ahead of time.

"Sure I can't talk you into playing hooky?"

She laughed. Freddy handed everything over, staying completely silent, though he did wink at Q. It felt completely different from when Noelle had done it, seeming supportive instead of invasive. He really would have to watch himself when it came to his reactions to her.

"One hundred percent sure, as much as I wish I could. I'm trying to convince my job to give me a raise. Well, technically, they've already denied me a raise, but I'm trying to convince them it was the wrong decision."

"That sucks." He squeezed her hand as they went down the stairs, keeping his gait matching hers. It was a lot harder to walk downstairs in heels, so she had to move slower and more carefully than he did.

"Tell me about it." She sighed. "I do love my job but it's hard going without even a cost-of-living increase. Sometimes, I think I may need to go get a second job, but I'm not sure what I would have the time and energy to do."

Holy crap, a second job? That was ridiculous. Sam was an OT. That should be a good salary, even if they did live in an expensive area.

"Are you okay with paying for the club?" He had extra money. He'd shared his house for long enough with roommates, he'd saved a lot, and now he made a heck of a lot more than he had ten years ago when he'd first started his job. If Sam needed help, he would talk to Patrick privately about it.

"So far." She smiled at him, though it didn't quite reach her eyes. "Don't worry about it. There are a lot of people who trade jobs at the club for membership discounts, and I'll do that if I have to. I'm already getting one for being one of the volunteer Dominants for this class." There was still worry threading through her voice.

Q knew, while the club gave discounts for people who signed up to help clean, bartend, or DM, it wasn't like it made the membership free.

He was definitely going to talk to Patrick, even though he didn't think Sam would appreciate it. On the other hand, as long as she never knew, it couldn't hurt her pride. Besides, he was doing it for selfish reasons—he had money to spare, and he wanted Sam at the club.

"Okay," he said, giving her hand another squeeze. "Got your phone? I'll give you the directions before we go out into the cold." Directions and help her get her coat on, like the gentleman that he was.

Hobbit in the streets, Aragorn in the sheets.

Or whatever.

18

———

BRINGING HER HOME

Sam

Holy crap. Q lived in a house-house. Like a full-on single-family home with a yard, a driveway, and a garage. The kind of house she dreamed about having one day when she was watching home improvement shows. Sitting in the driveway, she stared up at it, lit up by the lights from the street, hanging over the garage door, and next to the front door.

She couldn't seem to make herself let go of the steering wheel as she stared at the open garage door. The two-car garage only had his car, and it looked like he was getting something before getting out. It occurred to her that she could just drive away.

Back out of the driveway, drive away, and never return.

She'd been relieved when he'd suggested going to his place after class, a chance to save a little money. Clearly, money hadn't been his motivating factor.

How had he wanted to sleep over in her tiny apartment when he had *this* to come home to?

Get out of the car. Take your hands off the steering wheel and get out of the car. You can't just sit here.

The urge to flee swelled again.

She felt like she was in high school all over again, realizing she wouldn't be able to afford a prom dress, much less the rest of it. Like she didn't measure up. Like she wasn't good enough.

Having money doesn't make anyone better than anyone else.

Pressing her lips together, she swallowed hard, trying to ignore the churning anxiety in her stomach. She liked her little apartment. She wasn't a teenager anymore. And if Q didn't like her because he had more money and a better house than she did, that made him a bad person.

Which, he'd seen her place, and he hadn't acted like it mattered to him, so it wasn't something she needed to worry about, anyway. The only person getting in her way right now was her.

It would have been nice if his house didn't step on so many of her deep-seated insecurities, but she shouldn't let it chase her away. She needed to pull on her big girl panties and act like the person she wanted to be, not like the girl she'd been.

When Q's car door opened, she made her fingers release the steering wheel and smile with a confidence she didn't feel. *Fake it 'til you make it.* Taking a deep breath, she grabbed her purse and opened her door. It wasn't as though Q didn't know she had some money troubles. She'd told him earlier about needing the raise. Seen his face.

He hadn't judged, but he'd wanted to help, which had been nearly as bad. He hadn't made a big deal out of it, though, which was reassuring.

It was her turn not to make a big deal.

"It looks like a beautiful house," she said as she walked into the garage, doing her best to keep her envy out of her voice and make it wholly a compliment.

"Thanks. I got it with an inheritance, which was what my grand-father wanted me to do with it." He shrugged nonchalantly, taking her hand when she reached him and turning toward the door inside. "It could probably use someone who loves home improvement shows to give some suggestions on decoration and design." His dark eyes sparkled with amusement.

Sam stuck her tongue out at him, but her heart jumped in her chest at the suggestion. Part of her really liked that idea, but she was pretty sure he was joking. She didn't want to impose, and she wasn't sure how she felt about decorating someone else's house.

"You could try watching them yourself, then you'd know what you like," she retorted, making him chuckle.

"Do you want the grand tour?"

The garage door opened into the kitchen, and Q flipped on the light. It was a very nineties kitchen and Sam's lips twitched as she looked down at the linoleum under her feet. Not that there was anything wrong with linoleum—she'd never grown up in a house without it—but *man* did it make her brain start rolling with possibilities.

Q seriously had her dream house, and part of her wanted to wail about how unfair it was, but she wouldn't. He'd probably rather have his grandfather than the house, and she wasn't going to rub that in. Besides, she'd learned at a young age that life wasn't fair. He was a Black man. His immediate family might not have struggled financially the way hers had, but they would have had to overcome a hell of a lot to get there, and he was still living in a world that would put him at a disadvantage purely because of his skin color.

"You're thinking about all the things you could do to upgrade the kitchen, aren't you?" He grinned at her, squeezing her hand, and Sam smiled back.

"I'm thinking about how damn envious I am, and wondering why you haven't done anything to it," she replied, shaking her head. He laughed and looked around again as though he was seeing it with new eyes.

"I've just gotten used to it. It functions." He shrugged. "Which is pretty much how I feel about the whole house. Besides, I don't know what I would do if I was going to redo it. I wasn't entirely kidding about needing someone to help me."

She bit her lip against offering, too worried that would be over-stepping her bounds. Yeah, they had moved kind of fast into sleep-overs and her being invited to his Friendsgiving, but actually helping him redesign his kitchen... that seemed like *serious* girlfriend territory.

Maybe down the line.

"So, am I getting the grand tour?" Getting out the kitchen would help, plus she really did want to see the rest of the house.

"Absolutely." Q leered at her, winking. "It ends in the master bedroom." He put a bit of emphasis on the word "master," making a kinky pun.

Sam laughed, shaking her head at him.

Q

Showing Sam around his house was a little nerve-wracking, especially because he knew she was into the home improvement stuff. He liked his house and didn't have any problems with it. He hadn't thought twice before inviting her over, but now that she was actually here, he noticed a lot of little things he wished were... different. Not just in terms of cleanliness and clutter.

He wasn't dirty, and he had someone come in once a month to deep clean, but between those deep cleanings, things had a habit of becoming cluttered. That was part of why he'd signed up for the service after his roommates had all moved out. They gave him a reason to do things—like put his laundry away instead of leaving it in piles and clearing off the various surfaces around the house of the things he set on them without thinking.

Unfortunately, he was at about the halfway point between cleanings, which meant he hadn't started picking up stuff yet. He hadn't thought about it until Sam was actually here. Maybe because he was used to it, but now that she was at his side, he was imagining how she was seeing things.

He also noticed all the stuff he hadn't liked about the house when he'd first moved in and had meant to change, eventually, but had never actually gotten around to. Like the linoleum floor in the kitchen, the dark beige carpet on the rest of the first floor, and the light beige color on the walls.

Everything in the house was very beige.

The kitchen lights needed an update, too. So did the bathrooms, for that matter. He was pretty sure all of them were original to the house, which was over thirty years old. Hell, the house was a few years older than he was.

And the only reason he cared now was because he cared a lot more about what Sam thought than he'd realized.

Would have been good to realize that before inviting her over. I could have at least cleaned up a little.

Thankfully, if she noticed anything, she was too polite to say so.

"And this is the master," he said, pushing open the door and letting her in. At least he only had a normal amount of clutter and no weird smells coming from the bathroom.

"It's huge." She gave a small sigh full of envy, and Q was assailed with a new set of doubts. He'd wanted to show off his house to her, even if it was a little messy, because he knew it was a great 'project house.' He'd thought she'd appreciate that, but he hadn't thought about the difference between their homes.

Did she think he was showing off in a bad way? Did she feel like he was rubbing it in her face?

Suddenly, he was second guessing literally everything.

Then she turned to him, smiling.

"Since it's the master bedroom, does that mean you're always going to be in charge? Or can it be a mistress bedroom, too?" Good humor sparkled in her eyes, and Q relaxed.

"It can be whatever you want it to be."

"I think..." She let the moment draw out, making him wait for it. "I think I would like to let go and not be in charge for a bit."

Despite the fact he'd been in class for submission less than half an hour ago, hearing her say that triggered an electric response in his brain. He went from feeling like he could go either way, straight into Dom mode. Sam needed him to take charge. That's what she wanted, that's what she was requesting, and he immediately responded.

"Then it sounds like this is the master bedroom tonight," he said, pulling her to him. Holding her hand, he reached up with the other to cradle her face, the tips of his fingers sliding into her hair. The heels she was wearing put her just below his height, so she only had to tip her lips back a little to be in the perfect position for his kiss.

"I can't stay the night," she said a little breathlessly. "I have to be up really early in the morning."

"Noted. Thank you for telling me." It wouldn't change too much of what he wanted to do with her, but he would be mindful of the timeline and how much energy he took out of her.

Lowering his lips to hers, he took them in a gentle kiss. He felt her tense just before their lips met, then she slowly relaxed. She leaned against him with her hands on his chest as his fingers slipped back into her hair. Feeling the tense muscles in her neck, he massaged them as he deepened the kiss, taking the time to taste her, savor her.

Cherish her.

Sam moaned against his lips. She didn't quite go limp, but her body softened, her posture becoming more supple, and more of her weight leaned on him as he stroked her muscles. Yeah, his pretty girl needed some rest and relaxation.

Sometimes, it was fun to let go of control, but sometimes, people who were the most controlling outside of the bedroom needed the break. He wouldn't be surprised if Sam was feeling that right now. Feeling her relax for him was nearly as satisfying as knowing she was aroused.

Lifting his head, he smiled at her.

"Good girl." She melted a little more, her eyes already a bit hazy with arousal and submission. She was looking at him expectantly, ready to follow wherever he was going to lead her. "I want you to undress. I'm going to get something from my closet, when I get back, I want you totally naked and bent over my bed. Can you do that, gorgeous?"

Her eyes lit up, as though he'd turned on a lightbulb inside her. This was exactly what she wanted. Needed. And Q was going to provide it for her.

"Yes, Sir."

19

NAKED TIME

Getting naked was no hardship. Sam peeled herself out of her clothes eagerly, though she kind of wished Q was there to help her... but he was getting something from the closet. The mystery as much as the anticipation aroused her. She knew something was going to happen, but she didn't know what, and both her mind and her heart were racing as she waited to find out.

Bending over the bed, Sam propped herself up on her forearms, turning her head to watch for Q's return. The mattress felt comfortable, even if the comforter wasn't very inspired. Either Q really liked beige and browns, or he just didn't know what else to do for design.

She really wanted to bring some color into the space... but that was getting ahead of herself. Even if he had mentioned the house needing someone to help it.

Feeling her nipples rub against the soft comforter, she let herself sink into the sensation, veering away from the pesky thoughts threatening her equilibrium. She didn't want to think about the differences in their living situations and their finances. Didn't want to think about how she had to get up so damn early to go to work tomorrow, only to return to her studio apartment.

Nope.

She wanted to lose herself in the push and pull of erotic power play and the sensations of her body.

Q appeared in the doorway of his closet, backlit by the light behind him, holding a box in his hands. It didn't appear to be very heavy, and it wasn't a huge box, but it was big enough to hold all manner of things. He turned off the light in the closet, allowing her to see his expression again, and he smiled.

"Good girl. That's exactly what I wanted to see."

Heady pleasure rushed through her at his words, the sensation a balm on her overactive brain. This was one of the things she really loved about scening—the way her brain finally went quiet as she focused on everything else.

Going to her side, Q set the box on the bed, and Sam lifted her head, trying to see over the edge to what was inside. Chuckling, Q gave her butt a little slap, making her squeal. It stung, though not too badly, and her insides clenched eagerly in reaction.

"Head down on the bed, gorgeous girl, and close your eyes."

Grr. Sighing heavily, Sam did as she was told, and was immediately rewarded with Q's warm palm rubbing over her buttock, right where he'd spanked her. The caress felt good, and she shivered. With her head down, more of her breasts were pressed against the mattress, taking away some of the stimulation for her nipples, but it didn't matter that much. They were still a little sore after the weekend, although she didn't notice most of the time. Now that she was here, she hoped if Q had clamps in the box, they were mild ones.

Two hands began to massage her buttocks, and Sam moaned, lifting her hips in encouragement. It was both relaxing and sexual as he squeezed and kneaded her flesh. She could feel tension slowly sliding away as she sank into her submission, giving herself over to the sensations and to Q's desires.

He would tell her what he wanted her to do, and until he did, all she had to do was remain in place and enjoy what he was doing to her.

Which, so far, was extremely enjoyable.

Q's fingers were magic.

She moaned as he pulled her cheeks apart, the tips of his fingers brushing over her swollen pussy lips and the sensitive crease of her ass. His touch disappeared, and she heard the sound of him rustling in the box. Keeping her eyes closed was difficult but made a little easier by how relaxed she was.

Be a good girl, and keep your eyes closed.

She wanted to know where he was going with this, but opening her eyes would mean she was being naughty and he might change what he was going to do. So far, he seemed more focused on sensual kink, and honestly, that was exactly what she needed tonight, even though she hadn't realized it until he'd gotten started.

"You're being very good, aren't you, gorgeous?" he asked, amusement threaded through his voice. One of his hands gripped her cheek again, holding it firmly but not hard enough to hurt, even when he squeezed a little tighter.

"Yes, Sir." She moaned as his thumb brushed over her anus, teasing the nerve endings there. Was that a hint of what was going to happen next?

Trepidation and excitement rose in equal measure.

She didn't have a lot of experience with anal, and as she'd discovered, Q was *big*. A lot of Doms around the clubs were big into butt stuff though, and she wasn't against it... she just wasn't very used to it. Not to mention it felt very intimate.

There was a little voice in her head that said only bad girls did butt stuff.

Sam wanted to be a good girl, but she also wanted to make Q happy. So, good girls did butt stuff to please their Dom... even though it felt 'bad.' The whole thing about it feeling 'bad' and 'wrong' emotionally, while feeling so good physically turned her on.

As if he could hear her thoughts, Q's thumb pressed more firmly, then pulled away again. Sam moaned as she felt another of his fingers returned, this one slick with lube, and pressed against her hole. It circled and pressed in, opening her. Sam panted as his finger dipped into her most intimate place.

The feeling of being slightly scandalized accompanied the sensation of him sliding deeper, making her feel excessively naughty, even as her body responded with pure heat. Sam moaned again as he pulled back, then pushed a second finger in alongside the first. The stretch made her body ache. Letting him touch her in such a perverse and exhilarating manner made her nerves hum and her pussy clench emptily, as if jealous of the attention.

His fingers moved in and out of her, loosening the tight ring around her entrance. Whimpering, she lifted her hips to meet the thrusts of his digits.

"You are taking my fingers so nicely, gorgeous girl. Now I'm going to plug this pretty ass, then I'm going to flog it." His fingers worked firmly as he spoke.

Her toes curled while she gripped the sheets, her body blossoming with sensation as he fucked her ass with his fingers. Her brain was all fuzzy and hazy, everything but what he was doing to her melting away.

"Yes, please, Sir," she responded happily. A flogging sounded absolutely wonderful right now. She didn't know how he'd twigged onto that she needed sensual kink tonight, but it was everything she was craving.

The fingers inside her slid away, leaving her empty, but only for a moment. Then something harder, thicker pressed against her hole and pushed in. Sam shuddered, clenching before she made herself relax as the slick plug was worked into her. Q was careful, moving it back and forth, fucking her with it the same way he had with his fingers.

Unlike his fingers, the plug was tapered, so it kept getting bigger and bigger the deeper it went, stretching her wider with every centimeter of insertion. She wasn't sure what size plug he was using, but it sure as hell wasn't the smallest. The aching strain of being stretched open was becoming painful, then finally he reached the thickest part.

Sam cried out as the plug slid inside her, panting for breath when the tight ring of her sphincter settled into the notch between the plug's bulb and base. She let out a sigh of relief now that the hardest part was over and the plug was fully embedded inside her. The slight sting of having her hole forced wide open was already fading, only a faint ache left in its wake.

"Very pretty." Q twisted the plug inside her and the slippery rubber slid against her muscles. Shuddering, Sam went up on her toes as the intense sensation ran through her, her body clenching in response, aching from the stimulation. "You look good bent over with a plug in your ass, with this pretty pink pussy wet and shiny for me."

Fingers stroked through her creamy folds and Sam pushed back against them. She wanted to say something back, something as hot and filthy as what he was saying to her, but her mind had gone entirely blank.

"Now hold still while I flog you, gorgeous girl. I'm going to flog you until your ass is as pretty a pink as your pussy, and then I'm going to fuck you until you scream for me."

She wanted to whimper again. He was killing her with the dirty talk, her pussy clenching with need at the images he was painting in her mind.

* * *

Q

Picking up the soft leather flogger he'd chosen from the box, Q hefted it in his hands. The long strands were free flowing, without knots, it was a sensual whip meant more to caress than to sting. Dragging the supple strands down Sam's back, he lightly slapped her ass with the flogger.

She sighed happily, lifting her hips, her body automatically asking for more. Q was happy to oblige.

Focusing his efforts on her creamy cheeks, he swung the flogger in a figure-eight, allowing him to hit the underside, topside, and center of her buttocks, depending on how he angled the whip. His cock throbbed against the front of his jeans, his body reacting to the sight of her submission, to the way she gave herself over to him, to the burgeoning color in her skin.

The flat base of the plug was nestled between her cheeks, bobbing up and down as her insides clenched and released. Beneath it, her pussy lips glistened, swollen and slick with her arousal.

Fucking gorgeous.

Letting the flogger fall over her skin, Q stepped forward to run his hand over her warmed bottom. It wasn't hot yet, not by any means, but there was a bit of warmth emanating from the light pink skin.

"How are you doing, gorgeous girl? Give me a color."

The clubs used a color system for safewords—Green meant go, Yellow meant slow down, and Red meant stop. He was pretty sure she was deep in Green territory but wanted to double check and not let her drift too far. As tired and tense as she was, when she relaxed with the flogger thudding against her skin, it would be very easy for the sensation to become hypnotic.

"Green, Sir."

Every time she called him 'sir,' he swore the front of his pants got a bit tighter.

Giving her ass a pat with his hand, he stepped back and started flogging her again. The thuddy sound of the strands hitting her flesh was like rainfall. The color in her skin slowly turned from a blush to a dark pink under the steady assault.

When he paused and put his hand on her cheek, he could feel the heat against his palm. Sam moaned when he squeezed her tenderized flesh, bucking her hips against his touch.

"What do you think, pretty girl? Should I flog you some more or fuck you?" He would leave it up to her, though his cock was hard as a rock and hopeful for the latter. He wanted to give her what she needed, and if she needed to be flogged more, it would hardly hurt him.

They had time for either option.

Thankfully, her answer came quickly and happened to be what he was hoping for.

"Fuck me, please, Sir." She'd lifted her head to say the words, glancing over her shoulder, to give him a pleading look.

"As you wish."

Whether she got the Princess Bride quote, he couldn't tell, but it didn't really matter. Q quickly shucked his jeans and grabbed a condom from his nightstand, rolling it on over his erection.

As he stood behind her, he paused with his tip right at her pussy, running his hands over the soft flesh of her ass and enjoying the way she hissed and shuddered at his touch. The flogger had done its job well, sensitizing her skin so his touch felt twice as stimulating than it normally would.

"Oh, fuck," she muttered into the bedding, her hands gripping his sheets as he squeezed her ass cheeks. Thrusting, he sank the first few inches of his cock inside her. Her body opening for him was sweet heaven, slick, wet, and ready, and the plug in her ass made for a tighter fit than normal.

Now it was Q's turn to groan as he massaged her ass, pulling out slightly so he could thrust in even deeper. Sam's body rippled beneath his, her hips lifting up to meet his thrust. When he slid all the way home, he could feel the heat from her ass warming his groin.

Fuck that was hot.

He loved knowing he'd done that to her.

Looking down at her pink ass, the hot curves bright against his hands and cock, he watched as he slid out of her, then rammed back in, making both of them cry out. Moving his hands, he cupped them around her hips, using her curves as leverage to fuck her harder.

Unlike the flogging, he didn't intend this to be slow or gentle.

He was going to do exactly what he'd promised—fuck her until she screamed.

<u>S</u>AM

Oh fuck, oh fuck, oh fuck.

The switch from the gentle caress of the flogger to Q's rough hands gripping her hips, his cock pounding relentlessly into her from behind, had her senses rioting. With him pinning her in place, she couldn't do anything but cry out, whimper, and clench as he fucked her at his desired pace. The hard thrusts of his cock rasped along her senses and sent her passion soaring.

"That's it, gorgeous. Take my cock like the good girl you are."

Oh, fuck.

Hot need pulsed through her body as Q spoke, his words coming from between clenched teeth, timed with the thrusts that were rocking her body.

"You're so fucking wet and hot around my cock. I can feel you squeezing every inch of me."

Sam whimpered. The need inside her was tightening, winding around her, spinning and pulling her thinner and thinner until she was about to snap.

"Cum for me, gorgeous girl. I want to feel you cum while I fuck you."

That was all she was needed to push her over the edge. Sam screamed his name as ecstasy flooded her, exactly like he'd promised.

20

CHECK YES OR NO

Q

How did one go about asking a woman to be his girlfriend? That was the question Q pondered as he held Sam's hand on the way to Friendsgiving.

Of course, the other question was, did he even need to?

They'd spent the entire week either talking on the phone or together every evening. She'd gone home on Monday, just like she'd said, but they'd talked on Tuesday, and he'd asked if she wanted to get dinner together on Wednesday. Dinner had turned into another night at her place. He'd noticed she seemed a little skittish about having him back there, so he'd done his best to show how comfortable he was in her apartment without making it into a thing.

It seemed to have worked since she'd let him stay the night again.

Unlike him, she had to get up at the butt crack of dawn for work, but he didn't mind being woken up early if he got to stay over, so that worked for him.

Thursday was another evening on the phone, then she'd come over last night for dinner and a sleepover.

Q had loved every minute of it. It wasn't just that the sex was great —it was. He'd loved being tied up while she had her way with him on

Wednesday as much as he'd enjoyed tying her to his bed last night and returning the favor. He just enjoyed being around her. He didn't want to date anyone else and sure as hell didn't want her dating anyone else either.

At the same time, a week seemed too soon to be talking 'relationship' over dating.

Wasn't it?

His last relationship had taken several months of dating before they'd started using the 'R word.'

Glancing at Sam as he made a turn, he realized they'd been sitting in silence for several long moments. She was staring out the window, one of her legs jiggling nervously. He squeezed her hand.

"Nervous?"

"A little."

"I could say 'don't be,' but I'll be honest. This group of people is a lot all at once. At least you already know most of them from the club. So, you kind of know what to expect." Although she hadn't actually hung out with the whole group of them outside the club, as far as he knew.

It was a lot louder and more rambunctious when they were all packed into one house, without kink protocols and a lot more people. Angel had the habit of inviting whoever she wanted, not just their kinky friends, which meant everyone pretended to be vanilla. He'd already given Sam the heads up that not everyone there would be kinky.

"I guess I'm just nervous what they'll think about me," she said after a moment. "Which is silly, because, like you said, they've already met me. I guess I assumed they didn't have an opinion about me before, or I didn't care if anyone had an opinion. I mean, I cared, but it wasn't like the end of the world if someone didn't like me."

Laughing, Q gave her hand another squeeze.

"It's not the end of the world if someone doesn't like you now. I like you and that's what matters."

This time the look she shot him was a little irritated.

"I still care if they like me... especially if they're your friends and their opinions mean something to you. My friends like you, and if they didn't, I would wonder why and try to decide if there's a good reason for it."

"That's valid," Q said ruefully, thinking back to some of his exes and some of his friends' exes. When they hadn't liked someone's significant other, there had been a good reason. Sure, sometimes people rubbed each other the wrong way, but none of them had disliked anyone for no reason. There was a difference between 'not getting along' and thinking 'you shouldn't be with that person.' "Still, I already know they all like you."

"Yeah, but that was before I was with you. They all liked me when I was just around. They might not like me as your..."

"Girlfriend?" Q suggested, jumping on the chance, even as a little voice in the back of his brain screamed that it was too soon, and he was making a horrible mistake. "I mean, if that's what you want to be."

She giggled and the high, happy sound went straight through his chest, relieving the tension around his heart. That didn't sound like she hated the idea.

"I feel so high school right now, but yes,"—turning to look at him, their gazes caught and held—"I would love to be your girlfriend."

Q grinned back at her, the emotion expanding inside him making him feel warm all over.

The moment hung until the car behind him honked, and he realized the light had turned green.

Releasing Sam's hand just long enough to raise his in apology as he put his foot on the gas pedal, he quickly recaptured her fingers. She made a happy sound as their hands found each other again. Q felt the same way.

SAM

"And you've met my girlfriend, Sam."

That was about the fifth time Q had 'reintroduced' her to

someone she already knew, emphasizing that she was his girlfriend, and it still hadn't gotten old. Pure happiness rushed through her every single time. From the twinkling amusement in Leigh's and Jared's eyes, they thought it was endearing as well.

"We have, I'm so glad we'll have a chance to get to know you better," Leigh said, leaning into Jared's side, her eyes bright with interest. "So, you're official now?"

"As of about thirty minutes ago when we were in the car on the way over." Q was preening and Sam laughed. He looked so darn smug, it was impossible not to take his attitude as a compliment.

"Oh! My baby!"

To Sam's surprise, he suddenly dropped her hand and darted off into the crowd of people, leaving her standing there staring after him with Jared and Leigh.

"Um..."

"Don't worry, he'll be back in a moment," Leigh reassured her, amusement on her face. "Melody just woke up from her nap."

Melody? It took a moment for the name to click in Sam's head— she knew everyone here, but she didn't *know*-know them. Melody was Angel and Adam's almost one year old daughter.

Leigh hadn't lied. Q was back almost as quickly as he'd left, grinning from ear to ear as the baby tugged on one of his ears.

"Coo! Coo!"

"Oh my God. Is that how she says Q?" As if her ovaries weren't already freaking out. She wasn't even sure she wanted kids, but seeing the adorableness of Q holding a grinning baby was enough to make her question the possibility.

Damn, she had it bad.

"Yes, it is. My name was her first word." The smug expression on his face stayed in place when Angel popped up next to him, shaking her head.

"Her first word was 'Mama,' you dingleberry." Angel reached up to push a blonde lock of hair off of Melody's face. Despite the fact Angel was half-Asian, her daughter had ended up with blonde hair and blue eyes, like her father and apparently one of Angel's grandparents, though the rest of her facial features were pure Angel.

"Wow, she looks exactly like you," Sam said, staring. Angel brightened, beaming at Sam as if she'd just said something brilliant.

"Thank you! That's what I keep telling people, but all they see is the hair and eye color and they say she looks like Adam."

"I mean, sure, but she has *your* face." Sam wasn't exaggerating. Other than her coloring, Melody looked like a little 'mini-me.' She could understand how people could be distracted by the hair and eyes, they were striking. Melody was a gorgeous little girl.

"Every kid says 'mamama' when they're learning how to make noises, but that doesn't mean she was actually saying 'Mama,'" Q argued, ignoring Angel and Sam's conversations.

"She said Mama first, Leigh, tell him."

"I am not going to be a part of this argument," Leigh said, laughing and holding her hands up in the gesture of surrender. "I don't even see why it matters, she says both now... and now, she's signing for milk, which means I think she needs Mama."

"Ha." Angel stole her daughter back from Q. Melody reached for her, her chubby little fists squeezing together. "Yes, I see you're hungry, baby. Let's go take care of that. Which is what I meant to do before you were stolen from me." Holding her daughter possessively to her chest, she whisked away from them, heading for the seating on the other side of the room.

Seeing her coming, Patrick immediately jumped up from his seat to let her take it.

"Was Melody using sign language?" Sam was in awe as she watched Angel sit down. The shirt she was wearing had a hidden layer, so it only took Angel a moment to whisk her boob out and pop her nipple into Melody's mouth. The baby reached up to play with one of Angel's curls as she began to feed, while the conversation continued on around them, clearly expanding to include Angel.

"Yeah, she got some Baby Signing Time DVDs. They're amazing. Melody could tell Angel she wanted milk or 'more' before she could talk." Q and Angel acted like siblings, and she could totally hear the pride coming out in his voice, as if he was actually Melody's uncle.

"Wow." Sam knew little about babies, but that sounded pretty cool.

"It's been fun learning with her," Leigh said, grinning. "Kind of handy for kink, too, for when you can't talk." She held both her hands up in the air, twisting her wrists back and forth. "All done."

Sam cracked up and Q laughed while Jared shook his head and shrugged, though his dark eyes were filled with amusement. Taller and broader than all of them, he was like a giant-sized Q, who wasn't exactly a small guy. Jared was a lot quieter than Q, though.

"She's not wrong," he admitted with a slow smile. "Though I like 'more' better."

"That's harder to do one-handed." Leigh pressed the tips of her fingers to her thumbs and tapped them together, like the tips of her fingers were kissing each other. Yeah, that one would be harder to do one handed.

"Oh, hey! Andrew, Kate, Law, and Iris are here!" Q said, straightening up and waving.

A little fission of trepidation fizzed through Sam. She'd never spent time with Iris, and she wasn't sure she wanted to after a lot of the things Noelle had said about her. Especially since it was unlikely Iris didn't know Sam and Noelle had been spending time together. It was a group gathering, though, so Iris would have to be polite even if she was upset about that, right?

"I'm gonna go grab another drink," Leigh said, glancing into her cup, then up at Jared. "Join me?"

"Of course." His big hand splayed over her lower back, guiding her toward where the drinks were set up, which was far away from Q and Sam. She kinda wished she could join them, but she plastered a smile on her face as Law and Iris came over, holding hands, Law slightly in front of her, pushing their way past others who gave them a nod or a wave. Kate and Andrew were waylaid by some of their other friends, leaving Law and Iris to continue on to Q and Sam.

Adam and Angel had a big house, even bigger than Q's, but as more people arrived, the rooms were becoming more crowded. A few people had gone out on the back porch, even though it was a particularly cold day for November. So, Iris and Law slid right into the place Jared and Leigh had just vacated, which was about the only place they *could* stand at this point.

Iris gave Q a hug, which he returned with one hand, his other still in Sam's, before pulling away and everyone greeted each other.

"And you know my girlfriend, Sam."

Yup, still potent enough to make her blush and warm with happiness.

"Sam, whom I've now had in two classes as a student and is volunteering to help with the current one? Yes, I believe we've met before." Law's tone was especially dry, and Sam pressed her lips together to hide her smile as Iris elbowed him in the side. "Oof."

"Ignore him, he gets weird about being called my boyfriend. I'm Iris. I don't think we've met officially." Iris seemed perfectly friendly, though maybe a little nervous, as she reached out her hand for Sam to shake.

"We haven't, but it's nice to meet you." She let go of Q's hand to shake Iris', relieved to see she wasn't the only one a little anxious over this meeting.

"I'm excited Q has a girlfriend now. When I hang out with Law, Q, Connor, and Asad, I always have fun, but the testosterone can get a little out of hand. It'll be nice to have someone else there." Iris smiled, but it didn't quite make it to her eyes, which were pinned anxiously on Sam's face.

"Oh gosh, I can only imagine, especially with the Persian Excursion there," Sam replied, smiling back. Her answer seemed to soothe some of Iris' anxieties, and the other woman relaxed.

Had she been nervous that Sam wouldn't like *her*?

Maybe?

Either way, as they started to chat it became easier to forget the things Noelle had said about her. Iris was perfectly friendly, and Noelle's name never came up. By the time everyone was sitting around the table—which was long enough it went through two rooms so it could fit everyone—Sam was comfortable being across from her and Law, talking with them.

The table was way too big for everyone to talk to each other, so it ended up being segmented with those across from each other. The conversations did shift some, so she also ended up chatting with Angel, who was sitting beside her, and Patrick and Lexie, who were sitting across from Angel, but she spent the most time talking with Iris and Law.

And she enjoyed it.

21

GIRLFRIEND PRIVILEGES

Q

"I ate too much." Q groaned, leaning back against the couch and rubbing his stomach right above where Sam's head rested in his lap. "I feel like I'm going to explode."

"I told you two pieces of pie were too many," she teased, then winced when he poked her stomach. "Hey!"

"You can't tell me you're not feeling it, too."

Yeah, she was. Sam had done a lot of work to be happy with her body and feel okay eating what she wanted to eat, but she may have overdone it a bit today. Everything had just been so *good*. It turned out Angel had done a lot of the desserts, but her friend Justin had done most of the actual cooking. He was as good as a professional chef, and Sam had already been full before the desserts came out.

She hadn't been able to say no to a piece of apple pie, but unlike Q, she had refrained from choosing a second option. Though she had had one bite each of his pecan chocolate chip and the pumpkin.

Girlfriend privileges.

He hadn't even protested.

"I didn't say I wasn't," she retorted, poking him back. He groaned again, rubbing the spot where she'd gotten him, and she giggled.

"Did you have fun?"

"I did." She closed her eyes as his fingers stroked through her hair, spreading it out across the thigh she wasn't resting on. The scalp massage felt good.

"You and Iris seemed to get along well." His tone was cautious. Careful.

"We did." She wasn't sure how much more she wanted to say. Clearly, he'd realized there was cause for possible friction since she was friends with Noelle, but she expected him to be on Iris' side. He'd never been rude to Noelle when they'd interacted, but she wouldn't expect him to be, no matter how he felt personally. "She seems really nice."

Keeping her eyes closed was easier than opening them and studying his expression since she wasn't sure what he would see in hers.

Iris had been really nice, but it was impossible to forget the things Noelle had said and the sadness over the ending of their friendship. She didn't really know what to do about that.

It had been a while since she'd had any close friends, but she was pretty sure befriending a friend's ex-bestie was as big a no-no as dating a friend's ex-boyfriend. Maybe bigger. She would still be polite to Iris when she was around her, and if she enjoyed the other woman's company... well, it wasn't like she was choosing to hang out with her. It was just a side effect of dating Q.

But she did feel just a little guilty.

"I'm glad," Q said. "I wasn't sure how it would go after the things Noelle was saying about her."

Sam's eyes popped open in surprise, looking up at him. It wasn't the best angle, but it gave her a fairly decent view of his expression. He looked more thoughtful than anything else, his gaze meeting hers, and one of his eyebrows lifting questioningly, as if wondering what had startled her.

"Noelle said something to *you*?"

Now that she hadn't known. When had he and Noelle been around each other without her there to hear what Noelle was saying?

She didn't think Noelle had ever said anything about Iris while Q was around.

"The first day of class before you got there." His fingers rubbed over her scalp, and she felt her eyelids drooping back down again. "She said something about losing her best friend because she didn't understand kink and made it sound like Iris had ditched her."

"I didn't realize she'd said something to all of you." Sam blinked. That was kind of ballsy. Noelle hadn't even known any of them yet. That was a heck of a lot to put out in front of strangers, but then, not everyone was as closed-off as Sam was. Some people didn't mind sharing their personal business, and that was fine, even if it wasn't what she would be comfortable with.

But wow.

Q snorted.

"Yeah, I don't think she knew any of us knew Iris, or she wouldn't have said anything. According to Iris, Noelle canceled their rental lease without telling her, which was what ended it fully."

She'd canceled the rental lease without telling Iris? Wow that was... Sam opened her mouth. Closed it.

"Do you know why she did that?" There must have been some reason. Noelle seemed sincerely upset by the end of the friendship... maybe she'd canceled the lease because of something to do with the kink?

Though she hadn't mentioned it.

"No, but it sounded like she and Iris were already on the outs." Q tugged gently on her hair, and Sam opened her eyes. "I wanted to tell you, but I didn't know how to bring it up until now. I know you two are friends and don't expect you to change that based on third-hand information, but... I don't want you to get hurt."

"Thank you," she said after a moment, not sure what else to say. It sounded like Iris and Noelle had their own sides of the story. Which wasn't going to change how she treated either of them, but it was also nice to know that Q was looking out for her.

"Of course, pretty girl." He tugged her hair again. Not in a hard way, it felt really good, adding to the head massage. "Now want to get up here and fuck me?"

Sam groaned. Not because she didn't want to, but because she wasn't sure she could move. He wasn't joking. As he played with her hair, she could feel a bulge slowly growing beside her cheek. If she turned her head, she'd be able to nuzzle it, but she wasn't sure she wanted to encourage him.

"I think I'm too full. You can fuck me if you want to, though."

Now it was Q's turn to groan.

"I'm not sure I can get into a good position for that... what if we just roll onto the floor? I can spoon you or something."

She cracked one eye open and gave him an arch look.

"I have to admit, I thought my first night as your official girlfriend that you would have better moves to wow me," she said, suppressing her laughter when he glared at her.

"Okay, well now you've done it. Prepare for your world to be rocked."

He did just that, with nothing more than his hands, mouth, and cock. Apparently, he had room for a second dessert after all, and Sam was not averse to working off some of the food they'd just eaten with her favorite kind of exercise.

Q

Despite the craziness of the holidays, he and Sam quickly settled into a relationship. Not much really changed. They kept on the way they'd started, spending every other evening together and every other night on the phone. The biggest change was having the official designation and feeling more secure about what they were doing.

For Thanksgiving he went down to North Carolina to visit his grandmother's house while Sam stayed home and celebrated with her dad. He'd thought about inviting her, but figured it was probably too soon for that, especially since he had to travel, and she wanted to spend time with her dad.

Of course, he told his family about her, including his mom. Their tradition was for the whole family—all the aunts, uncles, cousins, and second cousins—to meet at his grandmother's for the holidays. Sam would have been perfectly welcome. There were always a bunch of people there... maybe next year.

It surprised him that he was already thinking that far ahead.

"What did your mom say?" Sam asked while they were on the phone later that evening.

"She wants to meet you, of course, but I don't know when that's supposed to happen. She usually only comes back to Maryland once or twice a year, and I only go out to see her once a year."

"Mmm, yeah. I'm not sure I'd be able to take any time off to travel, even if I could afford the actual traveling."

"I'd pay for your tickets and stuff, you wouldn't have to worry about that," he said immediately, then wanted to bite his tongue off when she made another noncommittal humming noise.

He had no problem spending his money to make her life easier, but he knew she didn't like the idea of it. Some things she was willing to bend on, and he was pretty sure he could talk her around letting him pay for travel to see his side of the family, given enough time.

"Still nothing about a raise from your job?"

"No, I've pretty much given up on that." She sighed. "I think I might put in some applications to other practices after this weekend. December isn't exactly prime hiring time, but at least my resume would be out there. It would make me feel like I'm doing something proactive instead of waiting for something I'm pretty sure isn't coming."

It really sucked because he knew that she liked what she did, and she was otherwise happy where she was, but... she needed to be paid better. Unfortunately, it was a common issue, especially living in their area. There was a reason so many people had housemates and shared spaces.

"That sounds like a good idea. At least then, you know your options."

"That's what I was thinking. Anyway..."

Even though she fell silent, Q could tell she wanted to talk about something else. Anything else. So, he went for the obvious.

"What about your dad? Did you tell him you have a boyfriend?"

"I did." She laughed. "Turns out he had some news for me on that front as well. He has a girlfriend! He was kind of scared to tell me until I told him about you. Apparently, her Christmas tradition is to go on a cruise with her friends, and she invited him to go with her, but he didn't want to say yes until he'd asked me."

"Did you tell him to go?"

"Yeah, I told him he deserves a vacation like that. It's not like we have to celebrate our holiday on the day of. Plus, I was talking to Morgan about the holidays, and she's all alone for them so I figured she and I could spend Christmas together if I didn't have anyone, too."

Well, there went his hope of convincing Sam to come down to meet his family for Christmas.

If it was too soon for Thanksgiving, it's definitely too soon for Christmas, dipshit. Thanksgiving doesn't have the pressure of gifts and everything like that.

It was probably for the best that she had other plans. Otherwise, he'd want to stay with her instead of going to North Carolina again. There was no way his grandma or his mama would be okay with that, especially not for a brand-new girlfriend they hadn't even met yet.

"That sounds like fun." It would also mean Morgan was looked after for the holiday.

"Yeah, Kincaid's going to be there, too. Morgan had already made plans with him because Zach is going out west to see his family and he's not 'out' to them yet about Kincaid."

Well, that sounded... not good. Q wasn't close with Kincaid and Zach, but he knew they had been together for a while. Thanks to the gossip vine at Friendsgiving, he'd heard a few murmurs about Kincaid being out as bi while Zach was only out at the club, which had been causing some friction between them. They made a good couple, though, so he hoped it wasn't the case or that they figured it out.

"That should be a fun group, I'm glad you won't be alone."

"Me, too. I'll miss my dad, and it'll be weird not seeing him on the day of, but he seems really excited about being invited to go with her, and I don't want to stand in his way."

There was an odd note in her voice, but Q wasn't sure if it was because of her dad's new girlfriend, not seeing him on Christmas, or the idea that she was somehow standing in his way.

"Will you get to meet her?"

"Yeah, but things are so crazy for everyone during December, it probably won't happen until after the holidays." She laughed. "Which is probably for the best. It'll give me time to get used to the idea of my dad having a girlfriend. Maybe I can introduce you to him at the same time, and we can make it a whole thing."

Q laughed but didn't hate the idea. That way he could be there for Sam. Even though she was an adult, it couldn't be easy knowing her dad had a new woman in his life.

"I'd like that," he said. "Then we'll just have to figure out a time for you to come meet my family."

"Sounds good." The happiness in her voice made him feel a little better that they'd be apart for Christmas.

They were moving fast, yes, but it wasn't as if they'd just met before they started dating. If anything, this felt like the way things were supposed to have been.

22

───────

REALITY CHECK

Sam

Sam: *I can't make it to dinner tonight, sorry!*

Sending the text message sucked. The reason sucked even more. Sam hated not having money. Part of her was tempted to put dinner on a credit card, but she knew it was far too easy to start putting all sorts of things on the card, and she didn't have the money to pay it off.

She'd been spending too much doing fun things as it was, and while she was a big believer in feeding her soul, at the end of the day, actually feeding herself had to take priority. At least she'd been able to talk to Patrick, who had been happy to let her sign up for some shifts at Marquis and Stronghold, doing the serving/clean-up stuff in exchange for her membership. To her surprise, it wasn't even a discount. He'd said she was completely covered with everything she was doing.

Unfortunately, he didn't have any paying positions, or she would have jumped at the chance for a second job at the clubs.

She'd already spent her lunch hour sending out her resume in a fit of anger and angst.

If she couldn't get a raise, she needed a new job that paid more, or she would have to start changing how she lived, which was already pretty frugal. Going out to eat at Marquis with Noelle and Morgan had basically been a splurge, and even then, she'd been getting the cheapest thing on the menu.

She could look into a new housing situation but moving cost money. She wasn't sure she could afford to move right now, even if it would save her money in the long run. Sure, it was easy to think 'oh I'll find somewhere I can have a roommate and share expenses,' but she'd also need a down payment and rent something to move all her stuff.

Even if she wanted to live with someone else, which she didn't, that idea was out of her reach.

What about living with Q?

Yeah, she wasn't going to let her brain go there, even for a moment. It was way, *way* too soon.

Besides, she didn't want him to think she was using him for his house.

For a moment, her brain entertained a happy little fantasy of being his live-in sex slave before reality intruded. For starters, definitely not her kink. Secondly, she loved her work. She just didn't love her paycheck. And thirdly, she was not going to bang for the roof, or whatever it was called. She wanted her own money.

Needed it, even.

She'd considered asking her dad for help, as a Christmas present, but with him going on a cruise, she didn't want to ask him for anything extra. And heaven forbid he actually canceled the trip in order to help her out. She'd eat nothing but ramen for the month before she let that happen.

Thankfully, her phone buzzed with a responding text, halting her increasingly depressing thought spiral.

Noelle: *Why not? Are you okay?*

Taking a deep breath, she made herself type out the words. There was nothing wrong with not being able to afford it. She did not need to feel ashamed. Repeating the words like a mantra in her head only helped a little with the rising emotions.

Sam: *I can't afford it, low on funds right now and need to be smart with my money.*

There. That was a good way to put it without making herself appear pathetic. Not that she was pathetic, but this was definitely bringing up all sorts of feelings she hadn't had since high school. Feelings she'd been trying to *avoid* since high school.

Morgan: *Aw, I totally get it hun. We can reschedule for later!*

Sam pressed her lips together, relieved Morgan was so supportive but also dreading future conversations that she still couldn't afford it. People tended to be pretty understanding about it around the holidays. Morgan probably assumed she was spending money on gifts or things.

If only.

She and her dad didn't exchange gifts. Their present to each other was sitting and watching Christmas movies together while eating popcorn and ordering Chinese food for dinner, which was what they'd done every Christmas since she was a little girl. As a child, she'd sometimes wished for more, but as she'd gotten older and understood their financial situation, she pretended to love it for her dad's sake. Then one day, she realized it really was all she wanted— time with her dad and a treasured memory from what could have been an even more depressing situation.

He'd really made the best of things for her, and now that she was an adult, it was her job to do the same for him, so he could enjoy his golden years.

Noelle: *Aw, I really wanted to see you two! I can cover you for tonight.*

Sam: *Oh, you don't have to do that.*

Noelle: *I know I don't have to. I want to! I have extra money and want to see you. Don't tell me no!*

Morgan: *I can go in half so it's not all Noelle! I had a great weekend.*

Which meant, in Morgan-speak, she'd raked in a bunch of money on her channel. A moment later, while Sam was still staring at her screen and trying to decide what to say, her phone buzzed again. Another text from Morgan, but this one was directly to Sam instead of to the group message.

Morgan: *You don't have to if you don't want to, but you've done so much for me, and I'd like to do something in return for you! Think about what you would do if the situation was reversed.*

If the situations were reversed and Morgan couldn't afford to go out for dinner, and Sam had extra money, she would have paid for the other woman's dinner in a heartbeat. Sam sighed. Dammit. When Morgan put it that way...

Sam responded to the group text.

Sam: *Okay, I'll let you two pay for me just this once! But next week, you'll come over for dinner at my place.*

She'd find a way to scrounge some money for extra groceries and get everything on sale. That would make two weeks she didn't have to pay for dinner at Marquis. Even though she would be buying more groceries than usual, it would actually be cheaper. Yeah, she could do that.

A rush of warmth and gratitude went through her. She was lucky to have such good friends. Sure, she still needed to figure out the job and money thing, but at least the relationship parts of her life were going well.

***

Q

Something was up with Sam during class, though Q wasn't sure what. Thankfully, the part of class in the main room didn't last long, then they were sent back to the private rooms for some 'hands-on' practice. Something he'd been looking forward to for a while, though he wasn't sure how he felt about the room they'd been assigned.

He'd never been in the 'shoe room' before. It was also known as the foot fetish room. Not something he would think himself into, but as he stood in the center of the room watching Sam—or Mistress Sam, as she was right now—perusing the options lining the walls, he had to admit he didn't hate the idea of seeing her in sexy heels.

"I think... these." Sam picked up a pair of incredibly strappy black high heels and turned around, walking toward him. Her eyes were alight, her chin up, every inch of her screaming that she could take on the world and win. Just holding the shoes had done a complete change in her attitude, and it was one of the sexiest things he'd ever seen, even if he didn't completely understand the why behind the transformation. "On your knees, Q."

Fuck, yes.

Whatever had been on her mind was gone now, and she was completely in the moment.

So was he.

Dropping to his knees, his cock rose as he was going down. He automatically assumed the 'subbie' position—knees apart, spine straight, head dropped. He was a bad sub, though. He peeked to watch her coming closer, his body reacting to the confidence shooting through her.

Stopping in front of him, she paused and slid her feet out of her own shoes—a pair of sensible high heels that were sexy but not in the way that the ones she was holding were. A moment later, she put one bare foot on his thigh and dangled the strappy heels in front of him.

"Put these on me." Excitement tinged her voice, which excited him, too.

Wordlessly, Q took the correct shoe for the foot residing on his leg and helped her into them. While he'd never thought there was anything particularly sexy about helping a woman into her shoes, he'd seen it done before in movies and tv shows. There still might not be something inherently sexy about it, at least not to him, but putting these shoes on Sam was different.

Maybe because she was so clearly enthusiastic about them. Maybe because touching her was always going to be a turn-on for him. Maybe because when she lifted her leg to put her foot up on his thigh, he could see straight up her skirt, almost to her pussy. It was a tantalizing tease and one he greatly appreciated.

His fingers lingered over her skin as he secured the straps. From his position, he had a fantastic view of her legs when they were both on and she stood before him, looking down at her feet and admiring the turn of her calves. Q grinned as he realized something.

Sam raised her eyebrows.

"What?" she asked, a little defensively, and he realized she thought he was laughing at her, which couldn't be farther from the truth.

"I was just thinking, you're now at the perfect height to straddle my face. I could eat your pussy kneeling right here," he responded truthfully.

He loved seeing the way her cheeks went pink and how her eyes went hot and distracted whenever he said something filthy to her. It only took her a moment to recover. Giving herself a little shake, she looked down at him, hot need in her eyes.

"I think that sounds like the perfect idea." Reaching down to her skirt, she lifted it high enough to confirm what Q had guessed when he'd caught the little glimpses under her skirt.

Mistress Samantha wasn't wearing any underwear.

"Yes, Ma'am," he said eagerly, sinking down a little lower on his knees and tipping his head back as she moved forward, one leg on either side of him. She was the *exact* height for her pussy to end up on his mouth.

Sliding his hands up to hold her steady, Q wrapped his arms around the backs of her thighs, his hands curving over the front while his tongue slid between her sweet folds. Sam moaned as her hands went down to rest on the back of his head, pushing him further into her pussy at the same time she gave herself a bit of extra support and balance.

Sam

Oh fuck, oh fuck, oh fuck...

Q's tongue could literally make her forget all her worries and cares. Once he'd put the image of her riding his face in her head, she'd had to make it a reality... and it was even better than she'd imagined it would be. With his arms cradling her lower body, holding her in place and helping keep her upright when her knees went weak from pleasure, she was free to lose herself in ecstasy.

Moving her hips, she let herself fly free, taking everything he offered until she couldn't bear it anymore. Splintering apart against his mouth, she shuddered with the waves of ecstasy.

When she was able to stand on her own, she rewarded him with a nice, thuddy flogging while he was bent over the shoe bench before turning him over and riding him to mutual climaxes. With his freshly flogged back pressed against the leather bench, she was able to watch the heat in his eyes grow while he was caught between erotic pain and pleasure. His cock throbbed inside her, his hips thrusting up to fill her while she used his hands to help balance herself.

They didn't do much with the shoes or her feet, but neither of them minded.

23

———————

A JOB OFFER

Sam

Holy crap, a job offer.

Sam stared in shock at her phone. That was not what she'd been expecting the email to say.

Ignoring the conversation Morgan and Noelle were having, she scanned the email, her heart pounding so loudly in her ears, she wasn't sure she would have been able to hear them, anyway.

Okay, it wasn't exactly a job offer, she still needed to interview, but it sounded like they wanted her. Badly. Badly enough to be offering an equal salary, but... oh. Interesting. It was a multi-location practice, and they didn't want her for Maryland. She'd need to move.

To Ohio?

Her brain froze.

Move?

Leave everything and everyone she'd ever known? She'd just started making friends. She had a boyfriend. Her dad was here, and he had a new woman in his life Sam wanted to meet.

But the cost of living would be so much less, as the recruiter pointed out in her email, and she'd be making the same amount.

"Sam? Are you even listening to me?" Noelle's irritated question finally broke through her whirling thoughts.

Guiltily, Sam jumped in her seat, dropping her phone onto her lap. Talk about rude. She had Noelle and Morgan over for dinner, then got distracted by her phone. She hadn't meant to. She'd figured she'd see the rejection, then get right back to dinner.

"Sorry, sorry. I got an email I needed to see. What were you saying?"

"I was saying that I think there should be some kind of hotline at the club. A phone number people could call if they have questions or concerns they don't feel confident enough to approach someone." Noelle tossed her hair over her shoulder, still looking put out that Sam hadn't been listening to her.

"I think that's a great idea," Sam said honestly. She didn't need to lie to make up for not listening. "I would have loved that, especially if there was also an option to text."

A phone call could be as nerve-wracking as in-person. Going to the classes had helped, but she would have loved a hotline for some of the questions she'd had. Much less intimidating.

Noelle preened.

"See? You should talk to Patrick about it." Morgan grinned, twirling the spaghetti noodles around her fork. They'd been on sale, as had the ground turkey and sauce, which had allowed Sam to make a pretty good spaghetti Bolognese without adding anything to her grocery budget. *And* she'd be able to eat the leftovers for a while. She'd splurged a little, getting fresh veggies for the salad, but everything but the lettuce had been on sale.

Noelle and Morgan seemed happy with the meal, which was a relief. She'd also realized dating Q had started helping her out too— when they had dinner at his house, he cooked enough for an army and always sent her home with leftovers. He claimed after having roommates, he'd never learned to cook for one or two people.

Which made her feel a little guilty, but at the same time, the food was good, and she knew how boring it could be to eat the same leftovers all week. That was the life she lived right now, but if she had the choice, she would love to be in Q's position, where she could give food away, or Noelle and Morgan's position, where they could pay for a friend's meal without thinking twice about it.

One day.

Maybe sooner if I get a new job. In Ohio.

But I won't have any friends there.

Were there any kink clubs in Ohio?

Getting a little ahead of myself here.

She pushed the job thing to the back of her brain.

"Anyway... what are you both up to this week?" Noelle asked, leaning her hand on her chin. "Any fun plans?"

"Same old, same old for me," Sam said.

"I've been talking to Amy about going to some kind of dance class," Morgan said. "She wants to lose some weight before the wedding." That was hardly a new concept, but Sam was surprised when Morgan frowned and stabbed her lettuce with a bit more force than necessary. "I think her fiancé said something to her."

"About her weight?" Noelle's eyes flared. "That's ridiculous. Amy's not overweight."

"No, but she wants to look a certain way in her wedding dress." Morgan shrugged.

Sam took it as a good sign that Morgan realized there was something very wrong with Amy's fiancé saying something to her about her weight, but she also knew on a deeper level, Morgan didn't see it as anything unusual. "We're thinking about doing a pole dancing class. I think it'll be fun if either of you wants to join us."

Sam had always wanted to do pole dancing, but she already knew what her answer had to be.

"I can't," she replied wistfully. "I'm too busy with work and Q. Plus, I asked Patrick for more work at Marquis and Stronghold."

"Oh, that's so cool that you're getting more involved in the clubs," Noelle said, lighting up. "Maybe I should do that."

"You get a discount on your membership if you do it regularly," Morgan told her. "It's a lot of fun and a good way to get to know people."

"I could definitely use a discount. It's really adding up fast." Noelle grinned. "And I would love to meet more people. I don't think I'm really connecting with Master Connor." Her smile slipped a little. "He's friends with Master Law, so I'm sure he's heard all sorts of things about me from Iris. I don't think we're ever going to be friends again."

"I'm sure it's not that," Sam said, reaching over to pat Noelle's hand sympathetically. "Master Connor is really shy. I don't think he connects much with anyone."

"Maybe, but I feel like he doesn't like me. I wouldn't be surprised if Iris and Master Law made sure of it."

"I don't think they'd do that," Sam said automatically, shaking her head. It didn't even occur to her that Noelle might react badly until the other woman sat up straight, glaring at her.

"Why? Because you're dating Q, who's friends with them? So, now you're on her side, too?"

"What? No!" Sam stared across the table at the other woman while Morgan's head whipped back and forth between them, her expression confused and wary. "There are no sides. You're my friend. I saw her at Friendsgiving last month, and she was perfectly nice— she knows we're friends, and she didn't say one thing about you all night."

"Oh." Some of the anger in Noelle's expression cleared. "Well, that's good to know, but that doesn't mean she's not saying it when you're not around. Since she knows you're my friend, she probably wouldn't say anything in front of you."

That hadn't been the vibe Sam had gotten from Iris at all, but she didn't think further defense would make Noelle feel any better. The only person who had said anything at all about Noelle had been Q, and she sure as hell wouldn't say that. Not after seeing how Noelle reacted to being told Iris 'had said nothing about her.'

She didn't want to put her friend and her boyfriend on the outs with her in the middle. Q hadn't said anything that bad, really, but this was not the time to ask Noelle if there was any truth that she'd canceled the lease without telling Iris.

"That's true," Sam agreed, mostly to keep the peace but also because it was true that Iris could be talking about Noelle when Sam wasn't within earshot, knowing Noelle and Sam were friends. She didn't think Iris would, but she didn't actually know her that well and couldn't deny it was a possibility.

She wouldn't deny it, even if she was one hundred percent certain, not with how upset Noelle had gotten over thinking Sam was siding with Iris against her.

"Sorry, I know I'm being overly defensive, it's just... literally anything to do with Iris gets under my skin. I know I need to stop." Noelle reached up to run her fingers through her hair, an aggrieved expression on her face. "I just... I don't want to lose you two, you know?"

Sam and Morgan jumped to reassure her that they weren't going anywhere. Guilt seethed under Sam's skin. She probably shouldn't have said anything or defended Iris. She hadn't been thinking. If she hadn't said anything, the moment would have passed, and they'd have had an entirely different conversation.

Next time, she'd know.

"Don't you two need to get going?" Morgan asked after they had settled Noelle down. Glancing at the clock, Sam looked up and cursed, jumping to her feet.

"Yeah, let me just put these things away." She looked at Noelle. "You can go on ahead if you want, so you're not late."

"Aw, thank you. That's okay, though, I'll help clean up. If one of us is late, we'll both be late." Noelle beamed at her, all traces of her previous upset totally dissipated.

Sam smiled back.

She was lucky to have such good friends. Why did her personal life have to finally start coming together when her professional life might be best served by moving to Ohio?

Q

"Okay, what's going on with you?"

"Hmm?" Sam looked up from where she'd been staring into space. They were on his couch, and he'd been paying attention to the television, but she hadn't. Ever since Monday, she'd been a little distant, though they'd had a very nice scene in the dungeon room during class. Now they had a few weeks off for the upcoming holidays, and he was looking forward to taking her to Marquis for an overnight as a Christmas present.

Shit.

He hoped she wasn't worrying about presents or anything. He knew she was still having an issue with money, which was why he'd talked to Patrick about covering her membership. Patrick had been happy to do so and even promised not to tell Sam that Q was covering the part of her fees her work shifts didn't.

Patrick also warned Q that he would throw Q under the bus in a heartbeat if she found out and was upset that Q was paying part of her membership fees. But he understood Q wanting to and why he didn't want to tell Sam.

Leaning over where her feet were resting on his lap, he grabbed the remote and hit pause.

"I know something's wrong because you're not commenting out loud on which Property Brother is hotter or asking my thoughts on 'twin sandwiches,' so out with it. What's going on?" Resting his hand on her ankle where it was peeking out from under the soft, stretchy pants she was wearing, Q kneaded with his fingers, giving her a little reassuring massage while he waited for her answer.

Sam sighed and dropped her head back against the arm of the couch.

"I don't know. I'm just all in my head right now."

"Anything you want to talk through?" he offered, not sure if she would take him up on it. Sam was a thinker, whereas Q tended to talk things out. He was dying to know what she was thinking about and hoped she'd share, but he wouldn't push her if she wasn't ready.

"Mostly just thinking about the job situation. So far, I only got one bite, and I would still need to do an interview... I don't even know if I want it. What I really want is for my job to give me a cost-of-living raise so that nothing has to change."

She pouted adorably at him, and Q gave her a sympathetic smile, increasing the massaging strokes of his fingers and moving them down toward her feet. With a sigh, she settled back against the couch, losing the pout. "

You can stop doing that never."

He laughed. If a foot massage made her feel better, he was happy to be her masseuse.

"Have you told them you're looking at other places?" he asked. "It's amazing how the budget can suddenly be found when they realize they might lose you."

"I haven't," she admitted quietly after a moment, opening her eyes to lock gazes with him. Her lips tipped up in a half smile. "I'm not always good at advocating for myself. It's what made me think I'm a sub, actually."

Q considered that for a moment because he understood what she was saying. She wasn't very assertive outside the bedroom, though he thoroughly enjoyed every glimpse he got of Mistress Samantha inside it.

"I know some subs who are very good at advocating for themselves outside the bedroom," he said finally. "Angel being the first one to spring to mind. She's bossy as hell, even with Adam, but the second she gets in the bedroom and he takes charge, she melts."

That had been disconcerting to realize. At one point in his life, he'd had a major crush on Angel, though he'd known nothing would ever come of it. So, he'd put his feelings to the side and concentrated on being the best friend he could be. Whether she ever saw him as anything more hadn't mattered. When Adam had come along, he'd fully accepted that was the end of any hopes he might have had in that direction.

It hadn't affected their friendship at all... because he hadn't let it. When some of his guy friends had joked about him being 'friend zoned,' he'd informed them that no, he was her friend. She hadn't promised anything more, ever, and he valued her friendship, regardless. He wasn't her friend just to try to turn it into something more or to have sex with her.

That had shut them up pretty quick and given them something to chew on.

Eventually he'd realized that Angel's bossiness was part of what had attracted him, but she was so much better matched to Adam. He and Angel would have ultimately been a disaster, and a breakup would have definitely ended their friendship. Over time, his feelings had faded, and after he'd found Sam, they'd disappeared entirely. He hadn't even realized how Sam's reappearance in his life had completely obliterated the last shreds of his attraction to Angel, even when he and Sam had been at odds at first.

Thinking about it, he had a feeling part of his attraction to Angel had been how much she reminded him of his high school memories of Sam.

"I want to be Angel when I grow up." Sam sighed again.

Laughing, Q dug his thumbs into the pads of her foot, making her moan.

"I'm very glad you're not, thank you very much," he teased. "I would have to be the boss in the bedroom all the time. I like it when you take charge, and I get to let go."

When their gazes caught, Sam's eyes glowed with happiness. Warmth filled the air between them and sudden emotion caught in Q's throat. It was so much more than attraction, so much more than desire, it caught him off guard.

The TV suddenly blared back to life as it defaulted from the paused recording back to the regular channel, and both of them jumped, then burst out laughing.

But even the laughter couldn't break the tension fully because Q had just realized... he'd fallen in love for the first time in his life.

24

ALMOST HOLIDAY TIME

Q

It was the week before Christmas, and for the first time, Q was kind of wishing he wasn't leaving to see his family for the holiday. Not because he didn't want to see them but because he didn't want to leave Sam's side. Everything was going really well with them, although he still hadn't said the L word. There was something wrong with Sam, and he didn't know what it was.

Most people probably wouldn't have noticed how distracted she was, but Q had made a study of Sam, and her brain was constantly elsewhere.

He couldn't be sure the issue was just one thing, though.

There was her dad and his new girlfriend, and Sam's upcoming holiday alone. Even though she didn't say so, he could tell she felt a little weird about it.

There was Noelle and Iris. She'd mentioned that Noelle had gotten upset with her and was convinced that Iris was telling Connor stories about Noelle. That had been easy for Q to deny. Connor just didn't connect easily with people—which apparently, was what Sam had told Noelle.

Q had bitten his lip against commenting that maybe Noelle was projecting since she had plenty to say about Iris. Sam didn't need any more pressure on her right now, so he was stepping carefully until he figured out what was bothering her.

It could also be her job and the financial stuff, which he really hated. He could help her but he didn't know how to offer her money without it sounding skeevy. He was also pretty sure she wouldn't take it if he did, which was why he'd gone the slightly underhanded route with talking to Patrick about her club membership.

At least tonight, he was able to give her something that she couldn't turn down because it was a Christmas present.

"I know we've been here every week for months now, but this feels different," Sam said as they walked up the stairs. They'd gone in through the rear entrance of Marquis, skipping the restaurant portion, though they could still hear the people in there having dinner.

"Maybe because it's a Friday instead of a Monday, and you're not having dinner with Morgan and Noelle beforehand." Q squeezed her fingers as he made the suggestion, glancing over to meet her gaze.

She laughed.

"There is that. It's a little weird knowing we'll be eating *in* the upstairs room and watching rather than participating... but like, good weird," she quickly tacked on to reassure him, and Q smiled.

He wasn't worried that she'd called it 'weird.' She was right. It felt different, and a little odd to be doing something different but in a good way.

When they reached the top of the steps and moved into the lobby, Q helped her with her coat and barely held back a low whistle. When he'd picked her up, she'd come down from her apartment, all he'd been able to see were her fishnet stockings but her coat had hid the rest of her outfit.

It was worth seeing.

She hadn't worn a corset to class since that first one, but tonight, she was wearing a dark blue one that made her skin and hair glow gold in contrast. Her breasts were pushed up into a tantalizing shelf, the deep cleavage inviting further inspection. Below the corset she had on a tight leather skirt that clung to her curves and ended maybe an inch or two below her ass. The fishnets she was wearing turned out to be thigh highs, and the tops hugged her thighs, leaving several inches of bare skin between the stockings and her skirt.

Whether she was wearing anything under the skirt was up for debate, but she definitely didn't have anything under the corset.

Q's fingers itched to stroke all that smooth, satiny skin.

It didn't matter that they got frisky, one way or another, most nights they spent together. When she was partially covered up and partially exposed, he wanted to touch everywhere that was exposed, then peel off all her clothes so *nothing* was covered.

"Damn girl, you look amazing!"

Turning slightly, Q mock-glared at Freddy for stealing his line. Standing behind the podium, looking especially dapper in a light blue suit that matched his eyes perfectly and made his blond hair appear even blonder, Freddy grinned back at him, unrepentant.

Laughing, Sam twirled in between them, so they could both see all sides of her.

"Thank you," she said to Freddy.

"I was going to say the same thing, but I was struck dumb for a moment," Q complained, making her laugh again.

Pink tinged her cheeks in a blush at the compliment.

"Well, thank you, too," she said, leaning forward to give him a kiss. The heels she was wearing made her just a touch taller than him, which he liked. Put his face closer to her boobs. Definitely not a bad thing.

"I can take your coats and bags. We'll get your bags to your room while you enjoy dinner." Freddy came around the desk to retrieve them, his eyes sparkling with mischief. He winked at Q. "You look pretty amazing, too."

"Uh huh. I'm not going to forget that you stole my thunder." Q handed over the coats, shaking his head as Freddy laughed, and Sam giggled again. "But thank you, anyway."

"You're welcome," Freddy replied cheerfully. "I'm assuming you heard that we have guest performers tonight?"

"Yeah, all the way from Pittsburgh." Sam grinned. "Master Mitch is having a fit about it, last I heard."

"I can't blame him." Q shook his head. "If my parents were kinky, I wouldn't want to know about it, much less having them perform at a club I belonged to." The very thought made him want to scrub his eyeballs with bleach.

"Did you know there is science behind the idea that genetics play a part in whether we're kinky?" Sam asked. Turning away from hanging up their coats, Freddy froze and stared at her. Q felt his jaw drop as he stared at her. She shrugged. "What? I read an article about it."

"I'm pretty sure I could have gone my whole life without knowing that," Freddy said fervently. "As a grown-ass adult, I have accepted that my parents had and probably still have sex, but I have never, ever wanted to think about what kind."

"I would like to scrub that from my brain." Q rubbed his hand over his face as if he might actually be able to scrub away the thoughts now invading his head. He and his dad's very awkward birds and the bees talk when he was a teenager had included a lot of information but definitely nothing about kink. As far as he was concerned, his parents were one hundred percent vanilla, and he didn't even like to think about *that*.

Poor Mitch.

He wouldn't think too much about Mitch because that would remind him that tonight's show was Mitch's parents, which would make him think about his *own* parents...

"They own a club up in Pittsburgh, right?" Sam asked. It took Q a moment to get his head back on straight and realize she was talking about Mitch's parents again.

"Yeah," Freddy answered as he picked up their menus and stepped out from behind the podium to lead them into the main room. "The Outlands. It's undergoing some renovations right now, which is why they're down here visiting. It'll be reopening soon."

"Are there clubs everywhere?" Sam asked curiously, following Freddy through the door into Marquis' proper. They weren't the first to arrive for dinner, but the booths were only about half full at the moment. Not everyone came for dinner beforehand. Some viewers wouldn't arrive until just before the show.

"Oh, yeah, all over. There's an amazing island resort called the Hideaway I've always wanted to go to, and there's some Daddy ranch out in Montana and an actual castle in Ohio—"

"Ohio? A castle?" Sam blinked owlishly, nearly stumbling over her feet. Q moved quickly to catch her. She wasn't looking at him, though, her entire focus on Freddy. He had to admit, a BDSM castle in Ohio sounded pretty out there.

"Yeah, Jessica, Justin, and Chris went there for their honeymoon. You should ask them about it." Freddy smiled as he came to a halt beside one of the tables. "Now, let's get you two seated so I can get back to the front."

Q helped Sam into the booth. She had a rather thoughtful look on her face. He did vaguely remember hearing something about them going to a place called The Castle for their honeymoon, he just hadn't realized it was in Ohio. He'd thought, like, England or somewhere foreign.

Freddy put down their menus and gave them one last smile before striding back out to the lobby.

Once they scooted around to the back of the booth, so they had a clear view of the circular stage in the center of the room, Q leaned back and ran his arm along the top bench behind Sam. He didn't need to look at the menu—it was the same food they served downstairs in the restaurant, and he already knew what he wanted. Instead, he watched Sam looking over the menu, sticking his hand in his suit jacket pocket for the box he had tucked away.

Next to her corset and leather skirt, he felt a little overdressed, but he'd wanted a pocket to carry the box in and... well, she'd once made a comment about how much she enjoyed seeing a man in a well-tailored suit.

Their server came by to take their drink order before whisking away again. One of the things about the Marquis serving staff, they knew to make themselves discreet.

Looking down at the menu again for a long moment, Sam then glanced over her shoulder at him when she realized he still wasn't looking at his menu and smiled.

"Already know what you want?"

"Yes." Q smiled wolfishly at her, turning his answer into an innuendo, and her eyes lit up with appreciation. "Also, what I want for dinner."

Her pink tongue flicked out, swiping across her lower lip as heat filled her eyes.

Yes, this was a dinner date, but the very location of the date made everything feel erotically charged. He wasn't entirely sure what was going to happen after dinner. He'd reserved the Dungeon room for them. It was their favorite, with all the standard kinky dungeon equipment, but he didn't know who would ultimately end up being in charge.

"Naughty." She breathed out the word, letting her hand drop from the menu down to his thigh and squeezing his leg. His cock, which had been half-hard since the moment she'd taken off her coat, swelled with interest at her touch.

"Shh, don't say that too loud or Santa will take me off the nice list." He winked at her, and she laughed.

"I don't think either of us are going to make the nice list this year," she teased, leaning back to snuggle in against him. Shifting toward him on the seat, knee bending, she rested the top of her leg against his. The flirtatious position gave him access that he hadn't had before, and now it was his turn to rest his hand on her thigh, stroking his hands over the bare skin between her stockings and skirt.

Sam's quick intake of breath and the way she shifted her hips toward him gave him all the encouragement he needed. Catching and holding her gaze, he stared into her eyes as his fingers slipped between her skirt and found her bare, wet, and ready for him. His cock throbbed against the front of his pants as he slid his fingers along her pussy lips teasing her.

"Yes, I can see you're very naughty," he murmured, leaning closer to her. Close enough to kiss, yet only teasing her with the promise of one as much as his fingers were teasing her sensitive pussy. "I'm going to help you with that."

"Oh, you are?" Sam raised her eyebrow at him, tilting her head so her lips brushed against his as she moved. Her body shifted again, her breast brushing against his arm in front of her.

"I am." He moved his arm away, reaching into his jacket pocket. "I have a little something here for you."

To his surprise, her expression immediately changed, going from sexually charged and happy to a frown. Q straightened in his seat a little.

"I didn't get you..." she started to say.

He immediately realized what the problem was. Her and her damn pride about money. But he wasn't going to let her turn this down.

"Trust me, pretty girl, this is for me." He smiled, pushing the box at her.

The suspicious look she gave him only made his smile widen. Yes, it was technically a gift for her, but she'd understand once she opened it.

25

A NIGHT AT MARQUIS

Sam

The guilt about not having a gift for Q threatened to overwhelm her. She'd asked her dad for money for Christmas, rather than anything else, and she was waiting to get it before buying Christmas presents. Sure, she'd baked some cookies for him, along with Morgan and Noelle, and even ended up making some for Amy, Marissa, and Carolyn, but that didn't count. Not really.

He was her boyfriend. She was supposed to be able to do more. She *wanted* to do more.

Having him pay for a night at Marquis *and* give her a gift on top of that made her feel as though she was failing. As if she was deficient. She knew that wasn't his intention, which made her feel even guiltier because her emotions were ruining his kind gesture.

Instead of letting herself spiral completely out of control, Sam opened the box he'd handed her. It was a very light box and not very big, but she couldn't even begin to guess what was inside, other than it was probably some kind of sex toy. Since they were at Marquis and he'd said it was also for him, that was the only thing that made sense.

So, when she opened the box and saw red, lacy fabric, her eyebrows went up.

"Go to the bathroom and put them on," Q ordered. The firm tone he used sent an instant stab of lust straight through her.

"Yes, Sir," she replied, with only a little sass.

Scooting around the booth, she paused when their server suddenly appeared again. They put in their orders, then she took off to the bathroom. It didn't take her more than ten seconds of actually handling the underwear to realized there was something in the crotch of them—something hard that had been sewn into the fabric and nestled right against her clit when she put them on.

If these aren't remote controlled, I'm a millionaire.

Suspicion was confirmed the moment she walked out of the bathroom, and she was hit with a blast of vibration directly against her clit. It was hard enough, startling enough, she immediately stopped walking, putting one hand out to catch herself and lean against the wall for support. Almost as soon as her fingers touched the wall, the vibration stopped, and she looked up. She didn't have a perfect view of Q in their booth, but good enough for her to see his slightly guilty but sexually intense expression.

Guilt because she doubted he'd meant to make her stumble, and she knew exactly what the rest of his expression was for. Even though he felt a little bad about it, he still liked that he'd stopped her in her tracks.

Truthfully, she didn't hate it.

Her body was already humming and buzzing from that brief stimulation, as though all of her senses had woken up all at once and were ready to party. As she stared at Q, he lifted one hand and crooked his finger.

Damn if she didn't want to go running to him.

Gathering herself, she straightened and tugged on the hem of her skirt, pulling it down a little, before restarting her walk back to their booth. After a few steps, she felt a low hum in her panties, right where the hard vibrations had hit her before. The much lower stimulation and half-expecting it kept her from stumbling again.

As she made her way across the floor, the vibration slowly increased, though not nearly to the initial level that had blasted her.

Heat swept over her in waves, and by the time she made it to the booth, she was flush with hot need and wouldn't have minded another surge like the first one.

Of course, Q stopped the vibrations entirely, smiling at her the entire time.

Sam glared at him.

"Having fun?" she asked, sliding into the booth beside him and trying not to feel awkward as she scooted. Was there anything less sexy than scooting around a booth in a leather miniskirt and a corset that didn't allow her to bend? She should have thought this through a little better, but she'd been thinking about how good she looked standing.

He lifted his arm so she could scoot up next to him, which she did, despite her sexual frustration. Maybe *because* of her sexual frustration. It turned her on that he was controlling her orgasm, even as it drove her nuts.

"I was going to ask you the same question," he replied, eyes twinkling merrily.

Jerk.

He was saved by their food arriving. Sam stuck her tongue out at him as she shifted back to her spot, so he could have both hands back —which he needed to cut his steak.

Dinner was delicious. Q didn't turn on the remote, so she could eat in peace, which she appreciated. They flirted and bantered and talked about their weeks. The only thing she held back from him was the job stuff. So far, the only place to reach out was the Ohio job, so she'd scheduled the interview.

But she didn't want to tell him about the interview.

She didn't know if she would take the job if it was offered to her, but she felt guilty even considering it. So, she didn't want to talk about it and ruin their night together. Granted, she had a different excuse every night for not bringing it up, but she couldn't make herself say the words.

She wasn't sure he would understand. She was fairly certain he would want to fix things for her. It hadn't escaped her notice that Q paid for as much as he could whenever they were together, which she didn't feel comfortable with, but she tried to remember that it wasn't always about her. Just like with Morgan and Noelle.

If he wanted to do certain things with her, like going out to dinner or ordering in, and was willing and able to pay for it—something she knew she would want to do if their positions were reversed—she did her best not to argue against everything. Though she did prefer it when they weren't spending money or she could pay for herself.

For all that she'd occasionally wished for a Sugar Daddy, she was now living the proof that she would make a terrible Sugar Baby. So, there went that dream.

It wasn't until after dessert was finished that Q put his hand in his suit jacket pocket, and she felt the vibrator hum to life again. Now that she was sitting down, it pressed even more insistently against her swollen clit, and the resurgence of stimulation made her squirm.

"Everything okay?" Q put his arm along the back of the booth and scooted closer, so the sides of their bodies were pressed together.

"Fine. Everything's fine." Jerk. She didn't know why she didn't just admit that he was driving her wild, but something about his smug expression made her want to pretend otherwise. Q's chuckled, which was even more infuriating.

Their server appeared to clear away their dishes and give the table a quick wipe down, and as they were doing so, Q hit another button on the remote and the vibrator pulsed against her clit instead of the steady hum she'd been experiencing.

Sam bit down on her lower lip to keep from moaning, though she didn't know why. No one here was going to judge her, least of all the server who had probably seen a hell of a lot more without batting an eyelash.

But just like when she'd answered she was 'fine,' some part of her balked at showing too much of her reaction.

Her pride was a thing of wonder.

The lights dimmed and Q's smile widened.

"Looks like the show is about to start." His arm shifted to drape over her shoulders, his fingers hanging down so the tips brushed against the top of her breast. Under other circumstances, the barely-there touch might not have even registered or felt ticklish, but with her senses already hyperaware, he might as well have pinched her nipple. It had nearly the same effect.

Sam sucked in a deep breath, which made her breasts lift in the corset, but Q didn't take advantage to touch her more firmly, which was maddening. Pressing her thighs together, she tried to get more stimulation for her poor clit, which was being tortured by the gentle pulsing vibration of the panties.

The room went fully dark, indicating the start of the show, and Sam took another deep breath. Hopefully, the show would give her something else to focus on other than the throbbing need between her legs.

The room lightened just enough to see people moving in the darkness, bringing in equipment. In the center of the stage, she could see two people motionless—one on their knees and the other standing beside them, hand resting on her head. The lights slowly began to come up again, until everything on the stage was clearly visible, including the two people.

Holy shit, Mitch's dad is HOT.

Damn. If that was what Mitch was going to look like in thirty years, good for Domi.

The Dom, Master Gavin as he'd been named in the program, stood in the center of the dais, drawing attention naturally. He was tall, well-muscled, and had a full head and beard of silver hair, sprinkled through with some black. He was bare-chested, showing off the curls of grey on his chest, as well as several tattoos on his arms, and wearing a kilt.

"Do you think he has an accent?" she whispered, without thinking about who she was sitting next to.

She could practically feel Q's frown. His hand lifted and gave the top of her breast a little slap. Simultaneously, the vibrator on her clit went from a steady pulsing to intermittent, so she could no longer anticipate how intense the vibration would be or when it was going to hit.

Oops.

She hadn't meant to make him jealous, but who could resist a Scottish accent?

Kneeling beside him, Mitch's mom, Leah according to the program, was as blonde as Mitch was, very pretty, and appeared to be completely comfortable in her own skin. She was wearing nothing but a sheer slip. Yeah, Sam could understand why Mitch would want to miss this show, but she was glad she was here to watch it.

In the center of the stage was a piece of equipment she'd seen before, but never in a dungeon or sex club. Trust kinksters to pervert an inversion table.

"Up, lass."

Yup, that was a Scottish accent alright. She smiled in the darkness when she heard Q huff. At least he couldn't see her expression, but as if he knew what she was thinking, his hand slid down over her breast, into her corset, and he gave her nipple a sharp pinch, making her gasp.

On stage, the woman got to her feet and stripped off the thin negligee. They didn't go straight into hanging her on the inversion table—they started with Leah facing it and using it for support while Master Gavin flogged her. The thuddy sound of leather against skin made Sam ache with envy, and she almost didn't notice as the vibrations against her clit increasing until her pussy spasmed in response.

Her thighs quivered as she watched the two, her breath coming in short, steady pants — almost in sync with the vibrations rumbling through her. Almost. Her orgasm creeping closer and closer, she suddenly realized she was holding onto the table, her hips moving against the seat, trying to grind down on the vibrator.

Q leaned in, his hot breath sizzling her ear.

"Should I let you come, naughty girl?"

Arousal thrummed through her, sending a soft moan clawing at her throat.

"You chose the show," she gasped and swallowed back her cry as Q once more fiddled with the controls. Not that anyone would have noticed. Not with the sounds coming from the stage as Leah's hips lifted to meet the flogger.

Now, the vibrations came in short, fast bursts, almost too much for her to handle.

"Yes," he whispered, grazing his fingers against the swell of her breasts. "But watching versus knowing that you're hoping to listen to another man's accent because you find it sexy are two very different things. Do you wish I had an accent?"

Fuck.

"No. I like your voice... especially when you're talking dirty to me."

The crack of the flogger sang through the air just moments before a pleasured moan took its place.

Crack. Moan. Crack. Moan. Over and over. Her body moved in time, rocking back and forth, grinding against the unrelenting pulse of the vibrator. She was going to come, and soon... unless Q did something to stop her.

"Like if I told you I love watching you squirm for me? I love that with a touch of a button I can make your pussy hotter and hotter, until I turn it off and leave you hanging, knowing you'll beg me for more."

She almost screamed when he did turn it off, her hips still moving, still seeking culmination. Clenching her jaw against the words that wanted to spill from her mouth, she held herself completely still, throbbing with the need that surged inside her, demanding satisfaction. It was so strong, she could barely breathe.

"How are you doing, pretty girl? Are you ready to beg?"

Asshole. Jerk. Smug fucker.

Thankfully, she was smart enough and had the willpower not to actually call her Dom names while he was torturing her.

She gritted her teeth and pulled her gaze back to the stage where the flogging had finally stopped. Master Gavin turned Leah around to secure her to the inversion table by her ankles. As he captured his wife's lips in a hot kiss, his fingers buried in her hair, Sam felt the vibrations begin again.

Low. So, so low. Enough to tease her swollen, oversensitive flesh, but still not nearly enough to send her over the edge. She swallowed back her sexual frustration as her thighs clenched against the onslaught.

"Let me know when you're ready," Q whispered in her ear, before capturing her earlobe between his teeth.

That slight bite of pain pushed her closer to culmination, and the table creaked in place as she shifted.

Onstage, Master Gavin slowly flipped the table, until Leah's head was hanging down... right at cock height. His kilt dropped to the floor, revealing his erection. Leah opened her mouth to take his cock between her lips, apparently completely comfortable with the upside down sixty-nine. Sam didn't know whether to be awed or aroused... then Q made the decision for her.

Her body rippled as Q's hand slid into the top of her corset, fondling her breast, just as the vibrations pulsed again. They were still too low to allow her to cum, but she couldn't stop herself from grinding against the seat, trying desperately to reach the peak that was so damn close yet so far away.

Sam closed her eyes, moaning as her focus went to her own body and the need that was growing inside her. With her eyes closed, it was as though she could hear so much more. Not just the sounds from the stage, but the more muffled sounds from the booths around her as others enjoyed themselves while watching the show.

"Please," she whispered. Somehow, it was easier with her eyes closed. "Please, Sir, let me cum."

"Good girl." The vibrator roared back to life, and Sam cried out as the intense stimulation hit her, sending her soaring as every muscle in her body locked up and released. She was barely aware of Q's arms around her as she writhed in the booth, waves of ecstasy flooding her system, while he held her in place, supporting her through it.

26

IT'S GETTING HOT IN HERE

Q

The show had been hot, but not nearly as hot as Sam had been when she came apart in his arms. By the time the lights had gone down again, ending the show, she was limp against him, and his cock felt like it was about to burst through his pants. He wanted to be inside her with a need that he could barely articulate.

"Sam... pretty girl... show's over," he murmured when she didn't move. The lights were already coming up to their pre-show brightness, so there was some illumination within the booths as well as the main stage. People were already coming out to clear the equipment. He could also see some of the other patrons moving from their booths, heading either to the door back to the lobby or the door to the hotel.

He and Sam would be going to the latter.

Slowly, she roused, lifting her head and giving it a shake, her eyes a little glassy.

"Fuck. I think I missed the end of the show," she said, her voice hoarse. "That vibrator was..."

Perfect. That's what it had been. He'd enjoyed edging her as much as he'd enjoyed pushing her over it.

"Fucking gorgeous. Watching you cum for me was fucking gorgeous and the only show I was interested in. Now, let's get back to our room, so we can entertain ourselves." He wanted their private room and more time to play. Not only that, but he wanted to see what she made of the current setup, the one he'd requested specifically to run to their tastes.

Sam gave herself a little shake, her eyes clearing, and she smiled at him.

"Yes, let's."

As he and Sam exited the main room, the other booths were empty or had the curtains drawn for privacy, with soft moans coming from behind the velvet. The hall was empty, but they already knew where they were going. Thanks to the classes, they were both intimately familiar with all the private rooms.

When they reached the Dungeon room, Q held the door open for Sam, and she strode in... and came to an abrupt halt when she saw the interior.

The spanking bench and the St. Andrew's cross took up center stage in the room and on either side of them were two tables. One table had an assortment of floggers and toys. The other table did as well, but it also included a strap-on.

She half-turned to look at him, raising her eyebrows.

According to Angel, butt stuff meant 'I love you.' Q couldn't bring himself to say the words yet, even though he felt them, but he could *show* Sam his feelings. Even if she didn't get the entire message, she would understand that he was making himself vulnerable.

If that was what she wanted tonight. Regardless, he would have given her the option.

"If you want, you can take charge for the rest of the night." He gestured to the table with the strap-on resting among the toys. "Or I can top you, and we'll see what goes from there." There was a plug and lube among the toys for her, but he wasn't sure how she'd feel about actual anal sex. It wasn't on her hard limits, but it was on her soft, and he knew it was because she felt it was intimate.

Unlike him, she wasn't an anal virgin, but it also wasn't something she did regularly or with just anyone. It meant something.

Letting go of his hand, Sam prowled around the tables with the bench and frame between them, inspecting them from every angle. Her posture changed subtly as she moved, and Q felt his own attitude shifting in response. He really could have gone either way tonight, but even before she stopped next to the table with the strap-on, he knew what she was going to choose.

Gently running her fingertips over the leather straps of the harness, she looked up at him, the corner of her lip quirking up, eyebrows rising.

"Are you sure you want to let me take control after everything you just put me through?" Her voice was husky. Teasing. Confident. The shift from submissive to Dominant had been subtle but clear.

She wanted to take charge, and Mistress Samantha was already shining through.

He smiled and rather than responding verbally, Q got down on his knees.

---

*S*AM

Sexual power was such an interesting thing. Sometimes, Sam wanted nothing more than to let go and have Q direct everything. Other times, she would fight to be on top because she didn't want to let go at all. And sometimes, like tonight, she could really go either way.

She'd been perfectly happy in her submissive role, despite the edging and the sexual frustration. If they'd come back here and Q had continued to do filthy hot things to her, she would have loved every second of it.

But being given the option, she'd seen the strap-on and realized what she was being offered.

Sam had never pegged anyone. Even with Q being a Switch, she wasn't sure that would be something he would want to do. She knew he was an anal virgin, though he was no stranger to anal *play*. However, those were two very different things.

The moment she realized what he was offering, she wanted it. Badly. Not only because it was something he was giving to her, but because it was something she could give to *him*. He wanted her to be the one to take his virginity.

It was both hot and terrifying, and not something she could turn down. She wanted to give him what he wanted, what he needed, because he'd given her so much. Because she wanted to imprint herself on his memories. Because she was falling for him.

Q on his knees, waiting for her to torment him the way he'd tortured her, was one of the hottest things she'd ever seen. Heat and desire blew through her, along with confidence that always infused her when she was topping.

She couldn't control so much in the world, but she could take control of their shared world for a while. She needed it so badly.

"Good boy." The words had always felt strange in her mouth before Q, as if they were more of an insult than a compliment. Somehow, with him, the connotations changed.

Calling him a 'boy' wasn't demeaning, just as being called a 'good girl' didn't make her feel demeaned. She could see the glow of pleasure in his face, the way he lit up at the compliment, as though it meant the world to him. Sam knew exactly how that felt.

"Back on your feet, Q. You need to get undressed. I want you naked and over the bench while I figure out exactly what I'm going to play with from all these toys you've set out for me."

The plug for sure, to prep him for the strap-on. The dildo currently attached to the harness wasn't huge, but it wasn't small, either. Fairly average sized—Sam would guess about five or six inches long and maybe an inch around. Smaller than Q, which she found amusing.

Apparently, he didn't want to take what he dished out.

Although, he hadn't taken her ass yet, so truthfully, it was more what he would *eventually* dish out. Because Sam accepted it as inevitable with the way their relationship was going. She wanted Q in every way, and this would be part of it. What made their relationship a little different from a lot of her friends was that she was going to get *his* ass as well.

It made her feel both powerful and humble.

Looking over the toys, out of the corner of her eye, she watched Q undress. He wasn't trying to be sexy as he stripped, but watching his clothes drop to the floor would always turn her on. Studying the possibilities on the table he'd set up, in case she wanted to bottom, she picked up the crop.

Looking up, Q sent her a heated look. His cock was thick and erect in front of him, so hard, it practically bounced off his stomach as he walked to the spanking bench.

"A crop, Mistress?" he asked, putting his knees in place and bending over.

Seeing him naked and draped over the bench was almost as much fun as seeing him undress. No matter what he did, he looked like a work of freaking art, carved out of ebony marble.

"Have I been bad?"

"Oh, yes." Sam smiled wickedly, tapping the flat leather tip of the crop against her calf. "I hope you had fun tormenting me during dinner because you're going to pay for it now."

***

Q

Fuck, Mistress Samantha was hot. He watched her saunter over to him from his position over the spanking bench. His cock was pointing straight at the floor, throbbing against the leather padding that pushed his ass up into the air. The position made him feel both vulnerable and aroused.

Submitting wasn't always easy for him, so it made his choice to submit to her even more meaningful than if it had been easy. There was a part of him yelling that a real man didn't do this, but he pushed away that judgmental voice. He'd come to learn what he liked, and he accepted himself as he was.

Leather touched the top of his back, running over his shoulders and making goosebumps tingle on his skin. It swept down the back of his spine to the top of his ass, then lifted. He jumped when it came down again, and a little splotch of pain in the center of his cheek sizzled along his synapses.

Moving around him, Sam lifted the crop again and flicked it against his ass, only the leather tip making an impact. The slight sting was intensified by the small area it covered. It hurt, *and* it made his dick throb...at the same time. Laying the crop down on the table, she picked up the plug he'd set out, along with the tube of lube. His muscles clenched automatically, as if his body was already prepared to fight to keep her out, even though he knew he was going to like it.

Q had struggled with how much he liked it during his Dom training. He'd struggled with the bit of masochism he had, struggled with how much he'd liked having something in his ass, struggled with the part of him that had liked being in the submissive position. Talking to others at the club had helped him accept all the parts of himself.

Probably didn't hurt that the people who had brought him into the scene—Angel and Leigh—were two of the strongest women he knew, and they were submissive. While society might say that was because they were women, all he had to do was look at Freddy or Olivia's boyfriend, Luke, to know gender had nothing to do with it. Freddy was one of the scariest divorce lawyers in D.C., which was saying something, and Luke owned a contracting company and did plenty of construction himself. Luke, especially, was pure Alpha male... until he got on his knees for Olivia.

So, Q had a lot of good examples at how strong personalities could find joy in submission. Especially since he wasn't even submitting all the time, the way they did.

"We're going to start with the plug, then I want you up on the cross so I can use some of these implements you so thoughtfully left out for me," Mistress Samantha said. When she got into her Domme space, her voice became haughtier, which also did something to him.

The slick tip of the plug pressed against his anus, pushing inward slightly. She twisted it, teasing his nerve endings as just the tip moved back and forth, pushing in, then retreating again. Groaning, Q lifted his hips to take more, enjoying the slight burn as it stretched the tight ring of muscle guarding his entrance.

"Fuck." The word fell from his mouth as the plug eased deeper, no longer teasing, now invading. The burn of insertion increased, despite the lube, as his muscles adjusted. His rock-hard cock banged against the spanking bench as his body reacted. That hurt, also in a good way, and he groaned.

A gentle hand rubbed his lower back, moving in slow circles, helping him to relax as the plug went deeper. It hadn't looked that big on the tray, dammit... but it had also been a while since he'd had anything in his ass. Something he probably should have thought about before offering it up tonight.

As least Sam was smart enough to make sure he was prepared, even if he hadn't been because he'd been too excited. He'd forgotten what this felt like. The intimacy. The vulnerability. The pain that accompanied the feeling of fullness before it faded into pure pleasure.

"Relax." Her voice was low, soothing as her fingers caressed him. He took a deep breath in, then let it out, and the plug went in deeper. The same muscles that had been working to keep it out ended up pulling it in farther. He cried out when the thickest part of the bulb moved past the tight ring. Then it was over and the feeling of fullness drowned out the slight ache from the insertion.

"Good boy."

Warmth washed over him at her acknowledgment. Her hands moved over his lower back and his ass, caressing and stroking, and giving him a moment to breathe as his muscles adjusted to the intruder.

Soon, I'm going to let her fuck my ass. Fuck.

His dick throbbed, and he wasn't sure if it was in anticipation or apprehension.

Her hand came down on his ass, giving him a little smack, and his muscles tightened pleasurably around the plug.

"Now, on your feet. I want you up on the cross facing me."

The position would put his entire front, including his cock, at her mercy. He hadn't thought it was possible to get even harder, but it felt as if all the blood in his body was rushing to his groin and leaving none for the rest of him.

Apparently, he really liked living dangerously.

27

DIRTY TALKER

Sam

It was impossible not to feel powerful as she secured Q's wrists to the St. Andrew's cross. Her body brushed against his as his cock bobbed in front of him, rubbing her thighs and stomach. The thick stalk was pointing right at her, the tip purplish with need, and a drop of precum pearled at the tip.

Reaching down, she wrapped her fingers around his shaft, her thumb sweeping over the head to swipe the precum. Groaning, Q thrust his hips forward, and the wooden cross creaked as he pulled on the cuffs around his wrists.

"Fuck that feels good."

Even when he was bottoming, Q couldn't help the dirty talk.

Sam couldn't entirely hide her smile.

Though she could punish him for speaking out of turn, she wasn't that kind of Dominant. She enjoyed hearing what he had to say, especially since she knew it was being said out of pleasure. It might be fun sometime to see if he *could* stay completely silent, but tonight she wanted to give him a reward, not punish him.

Well, not punish him much.

After the way he'd edged her, he definitely deserved a bit of torment, but she didn't feel the need to add to it. Having him tied up and at her mercy, her hand around his cock while he moved his hips, using her hand to pleasure himself... then letting go. Yup. That was the kind of punishment she wanted to give him. Q groaned, his brow wrinkling as he moved his hips, his body automatically seeking more stimulation.

"Spread your legs for me," she ordered, kneeling down. His cock bobbed next to her head, his ball sack hanging loose and low beneath it. As he obeyed, she couldn't resist leaning a little to the left, so her cheek rubbed against the side of his shaft, her hot breath on his sack, and she smiled when she heard him whimper.

Yeah, turnabout was definitely fair play.

Q was now completely immobilized, bound and spread for her pleasure. When she got to her feet, she met his blazing hot gaze, and his eyes were full of desire as he stared back at her.

"Now what, Mistress?" he asked.

Something in his voice made her think he was trying to sound confident, or even challenging, but all she heard was his hunger.

"Now I'm going to do some target practice," she replied coolly. It was a test of her willpower not to laugh out loud when his eyes widened dramatically.

She wasn't going to do anything too bad, but she wanted to give him a night to remember, which meant *not* going straight for his ass. First, she was going to use the crop on him a little, then when he was all heated and caught between pleasure and pain, *then* was she going to peg him.

"Fuck me," he muttered under his breath.

Well, yes. That was the idea. Sam barely managed to keep from cracking a smile.

Picking up the crop, she sauntered to stand in front of him, flicking it out. He winced, but she wasn't actually trying to flick him with it... yet. The leather flap at the end touched his thigh, and she dragged it up his leg, gently brushing against his skin from his ankle to his hip bone. Then she lifted it and brought it down on his inner thigh, hard enough to sting but not too harshly.

Erotic pain versus real pain.

Q hissed and shuddered in his bondage before stilling again, his eyes hot with lust as she repeated the process up his other leg.

This time, he was ready for the small blow, and his cock jerked in reaction.

"How much of a masochist are you, Q?" she asked, running the leather up the base of his cock to the tip. His expression was torn, but his cock jerked, rubbing against the flap, seeking the stimulation.

"Gorgeous, right now I'm not sure there's much you could do to turn me off," he admitted. "Though cock and ball torture has never been my thing."

It wasn't her thing either, but she was getting off on the trepidation wreathed around him. The apprehension. The knowledge she could hurt him... until he used his safeword, knowing *he* didn't know how far she planned to go.

It was a mind fuck, and she was enjoying the hell out of it.

Q

She was fucking with his head.

At least, he was pretty sure she was just fucking with his head, and she didn't actually plan to crop his cock. What would he do if she did?

Cock and ball torture wasn't in his hard limits because he was a little curious about it, but he wasn't ready to go hardcore during his first rodeo. Was he? The unknown was turning him on as much as anything else. His ass clenched around the plug, his muscles squeezing tightly around it.

When the crop lifted and moved, Q tensed, but it slowed just before hitting his cock. The leather still stung where it hit the side of his shaft but not as badly as it could have. She'd pulled the blow at the last second, leaving him panting, his heart racing, and, adrenaline rushing through him, even though she hadn't actually done it.

The leather caressed his shaft up to the sensitive head, and Q thrust, trying to rub his erection along the instrument of torment. He gritted his teeth against a moan as she lifted it just an inch or two and brought the tip down on *his* tip, sending pain flashing through him.

Fuck that hurt.

Yet his dick throbbed even harder in the sting's wake, as if she'd just stroked his cock instead of cropping it.

She lifted the crop again and brought it down on the other side of his shaft. The sting flared and pulsed through him, and Q couldn't bite back the moan of pain.

"Regretting your decision to put yourself at my mercy?" she asked, running the tip of the crop up to his nipples. When she lifted the tip and brought it back down, right on the sensitive bud, Q cried out.

"No," he said honestly, despite the way his nipple was smarting. That hadn't been quite as bad as nipple clamps and over with far more quickly. The sting had also gone straight to his dick, turning his arousal from painful into a warm heat that filled him from the inside out. He also felt a little unbalanced since she'd only tended to one of them, and he wanted her to hit the other one to even him out. "I'm here for your pleasure, Mistress."

It had been the right thing to say. The crop lifted and fell, hitting his other nipple with the same force as the first. Q groaned as she began to flick the crop against his body—his chest, his ribs, his thighs, and a few little flicks against his dick. She was very careful when she used it against the thick mushroom head of his cock, but it honestly didn't matter.

He was so hard, and his cock was so eager for *any* kind of stimulation, he thought he might cum if she *did* hit the tip with more force. Instead, she scattered the pricks of pain all over his body, the crop coming down again and again. His eyes closed as pain and pleasure collided.

At a certain point, sensation became sensation, and his body hummed with the sheer bliss of it, no longer able to differentiate what hurt and what felt good. He was lost in a haze of sensual torture, his body aching for release, even as he drifted in clouds of pleasure.

When he felt her loosening the restraints on his right ankle, he realized she'd stopped cropping him. He hadn't even noticed.

"Sam?" He murmured her name as she got to her feet, and she smiled at him. Oops, he hadn't called her mistress. Or ma'am. Thankfully she didn't seem to mind.

"Do you think you can walk? I want you in the bedroom."

It took a moment for his brain to catch up. The bedroom was the hotel room portion of the suite. He nodded. Somehow, he'd make the trip. He was a little fuzzy on the details, but she got him out of the cuffs and into the bedroom, where he fell back on the bed, with his cock leaking precum onto his stomach.

Fuck, he couldn't remember ever having been more turned on, and she was going to take his ass while he was in this state.

He was so lost in sensation, he didn't even notice her getting undressed or putting the harness on. One moment, he was staring at the ceiling, lying exactly how she'd left him, and the next, she was there, lifting his legs up into position and pulling the plug from his ass. Q groaned as she eased the toy out of his hole, his muscles fluttering around it, then gaping emptily.

It was only a moment before the dildo on the strap-on was taking its place. Sam leaned over him, watching his face as she began to slide the fake cock into him. For some reason, Q had assumed she'd do this in doggy-style position and being face to face as she took his cherry made the moment disturbingly intimate.

Despite the haze he was in, he didn't think he'd forget a moment of this, not for his entire life.

The way the cock felt sliding inside him, invading him. Knowing Sam was the one controlling the toy and that he was giving himself over to her. The way his insides clenched and tingled around the insertion, his body shuddering. The dragging rasp of friction as she pulled out partway before shoving in deep, the toy rubbing over his prostate.

Her hand gripped his cock, pumping as she thrust, filling him, and pleasuring him in every way possible.

Reaching up beside his head to grab onto the sheets, Q arched and cried out with a husky groan as she fucked him. Heat and need slid up and down his spine. His cock thrust into her hand before his hips fell to meet her thrusts, the motions a perfect symphony of sweet bliss.

This was completely different from any of the classes, completely different from the toys and wands he'd tried out in the pursuit of knowing what to do with a sub's ass. The way his prostate throbbed and pulsed inside him matched the rhythm of her hand, and he could feel his orgasm moving toward him like a tidal wave coming in to shore.

"Fuck! Sam!" He writhed, ecstasy pouring through him as the tidal wave hit, dragging him under into the tumult of sweet release. Hot fluid spurted, covering her breasts as she still moved the toy inside him, sending wave after wave of hot rapture pouring out of him.

---

*S*AM

Cock in one hand, the remote to the vibrator inside her was in the other. As Q's climax hit and he began to cum hot jets of seed all over her breasts, Sam squeezed his cock even tighter as she upped the intensity of her vibrator. Watching him moving beneath her, seeing his expressions change, knowing she was the one giving him such inexpressible pleasure, had her quivering with her own need. As he emptied himself on her like a fountain, she pushed in deep, rubbing her swollen clit against the harness while the vibrator inside her reached a fever pitch.

She cried out with him, her body throbbing and pulsing with its own pleasure, panting together as every ounce of ecstasy was wrung from them.

The vibrations quickly became too much, so she shut them off, then slumped over Q, her breasts coated in his cum. The warm liquid dripped off her nipple onto his belly, and she had the strangest urge to bend down and lick it off. Giving in, she smiled when he moaned, both at her movement and watching her actions.

"That might be the hottest thing I've ever seen," he said hoarsely. His head fell back, eyes closing, as she moved away, the strap-on cock sliding from his body.

Watching him while she'd taken his anal virginity had been the hottest thing *she'd* ever seen, but she didn't say so. She didn't trust her voice.

If she tried to speak, she might tell him she was in love with him.

28

IN WHICH EVERYTHING GOES WRONG

Sam

Something about waking up as the big spoon the night after she'd pegged Q was amusing. She smiled before she even opened her eyes. She was holding on tightly to him from behind, his ass nestled in her groin, her breasts flattened against his back. When she moved her hand against his stomach, she felt his cock brush against the back of her hand.

Which was apparently all it took to wake him. He let out a small groan before turning over to face her, a small smile on his face.

"Good morning."

She didn't get a chance to reply before he rolled her onto her back and *showed* her a good morning.

So, to say she was in a good mood when they reached her apartment was an understatement. She'd been satisfied in just about every way she *could* be satisfied. Her body ached pleasantly in all the right ways and the deep-seated contentment settled in her core emanated outwards, like a soothing glow.

"What do you want to do today?" It was a cold, cold Sunday, and she could totally go for some couch snuggling.

"I thought we were watching The Two Towers," Q said, his hand on her back as he followed her into the apartment. They'd watched The Fellowship of the Ring the week before. They'd have to wait two weeks for The Return of the King since he was going to still be in North Carolina with his family next weekend, but that was okay.

"Just making sure. We could always do something before. Or after." She smiled at him over her shoulder, hefting her bag on her shoulder as she headed to her closet to put it down. She'd put the clothes away later, but if she didn't put the bag in her closet, who knew when she would actually get around to unpacking it.

She'd known she would want comfy clothes today, so she was wearing her fuzzy pajama pants and a comfortable hoodie. A far cry from the outfit she'd worn into Marquis, yet Q looked at her the same way—like she was the most gorgeous thing he'd ever seen. He flashed her a grin, then moved toward her kitchen, probably to get something to drink. Just that smile made her weak in the knees.

Fuck, she was so head over heels for him... but it was too soon, wasn't it? How fast did it take to fall in love?

She'd never been in love before, so she had no idea.

While she'd deeply cared about a few of her exes and even loved a few of them, she'd never felt for any of them the way she did about Q. Should she tell him?

No. She was supposed to wait for him to say it first. Right? That was a thing. Maybe. That or it was a Hollywood thing that influenced her brain into thinking she shouldn't be the one to say it first, but she didn't want to come off like a desperate girl.

Putting her bag down just inside her closet, she turned around and came back around the corner into the main room. Q was standing on the other side of the apartment, glass of water in hand, staring down at something on her table...

Oh, wait...

Oh, no...

Oh, *shit*...

Q

Last night and this morning had been utterly perfect. He'd given himself completely to Sam, and she'd given him the night of his life. Everything still ached but in a good way, letting him know he'd had a damn good night. He was looking forward to a day of cuddling with her, away from the cold, in her cozy apartment—which was a lot warmer than his house on days like today.

They'd cuddle under a blanket and watch The Two Towers, then he'd convince her to let him take her grocery shopping, so he could make chili for dinner. He'd secretly make a double batch, so she could have leftovers for the week. She should even be able to freeze some if she wanted.

That way he wouldn't have to worry about her too much while he was away for the week with his family for Christmas.

So, the very last thing he expected to see laid out on the small table, just outside her galley kitchen where they normally ate, was a printout of a job offer in Ohio. Staring at the paper, Sam's question to Freddy about the club in Ohio drifted through his head.

She hadn't been asking because she'd been surprised that Ohio would have a kink club.

She'd been asking because she'd been offered a job in Ohio.

Holy fuck.

"Q... I... it's not what it looks like."

The stammering statement made his head snap up. Anger roiling through him, he very carefully put down the glass he was holding, pulling back on the instinct that said to throw the water over the offensive paperwork.

"It looks like you printed out a job offer from a practice in Ohio." His voice sounded odd to his ears. Flat. Almost robotic. He pressed his hands against his thighs to stop the fine tremor going through them. "The letter says they loved talking to you, so I'm assuming you interviewed with them."

Damn his ability to read so fast. It hadn't taken more than a quick glance at the papers for the words to take shape and convey their meaning in his head.

His heart was beginning to pound harder and faster in his chest, making it difficult for him to breathe and to think. There was a white noise ringing in his ears, but he made himself focus when she turned bright red.

"Okay, so it is kind of what it looks like, but that's not what I meant..." She looked at him helplessly, her expression tugging at his heart strings, but he was too angry to let it affect him.

"So, what did you mean? Because if it's exactly what it looks like, then it looks like you were thinking about taking a job in a completely different state, and you hadn't even mentioned it to me."

Really it was the fact that she hadn't said anything to him. She'd mentioned looking for a new job, but she sure as hell had said nothing about looking so far away or doing an interview.

"Because I wasn't going to take it."

"Then why did you do the interview? Why is the offer printed out? Have you told them no yet?" Q rapped his knuckles against the papers, hard enough to hurt, and he welcomed the physical pain as a distraction to the way his chest was starting to hurt. He tried to take a deep breath, but it was like the air got caught in his throat, making his lungs ache from the lack. When Sam's mouth snapped shut, he knew she hadn't told them no yet. "Were you just going to keep this a secret until I found out you were moving one day? Or had already moved?"

"No, of course not!" She reached up to rub her forehead, her eyes filling with tears as if it was finally hitting home to her how upset he was—and now she was upset too. Good, she should be. He'd just had the rug yanked out from under him, and she'd been the one to do it. Acting innocent, as if she hadn't done anything wrong, was only making him even angrier. "I would never do anything like that."

"All evidence to the contrary. This seems like it's a pattern with you."

"We're not in high school anymore!"

"Then stop acting like it! Why the hell didn't you say anything to me?"

"I told you I was applying to jobs." Her voice wavered, her hands twisting in front of her. She said the words weakly, lacking any force behind them, and the fact she wasn't apologizing and still making excuses made his temper flare.

"You didn't tell me you were thinking about moving out of state for one. You didn't even mention the interview or the job offer. That tells me you didn't want me to know, which means you knew it would be a problem and your solution was to not say a word about it." Fuck, it felt like his chest was caving in on itself, and it took all of his willpower to force his shoulders back. He'd been getting in deeper and deeper—hell, he was fucking in love with her—and she'd been thinking about leaving the state.

Thank God he hadn't said the words to her yet. At least he'd have a little dignity left intact—what little he had left after last night. And he intended to keep it.

He couldn't imagine what her reaction would have been to find out he'd fallen in love with her while she was planning on possibly leaving him.

This was so much worse than high school.

"I have to go."

He started walking toward the door, moving as quickly as he could without running. The small apartment, which had always felt cozy, now felt too small, and the walls were closing in around him. He couldn't breathe properly. Not when he was in such a confined space with her.

He needed to get out before he said something he'd regret.

"Q!"

Hand on the knob, he looked over his shoulder. Sam stared at him, wringing her hands in front of her, tears sliding down her cheeks. The look in her eyes nearly made him turn back around and comfort her... but what the hell would he be comforting her for?

For lying to him? For misleading him? For saying he was her boyfriend, then not actually behaving like they were in a relationship?

He shook his head and turned away.

<u>Sam</u>

When the door slammed behind Q, Sam dropped to her knees, pressing her hands over her heart, which felt like a great, gaping space in her chest. Tears dripped down her cheeks onto her shirt, creating two huge wet splotches, and she barely even cared. It hardly mattered.

Q had just walked out of her life as quickly as he blown into it.

If only she could have found the right words to make him understand, to make him stay, but he'd been so angry, and her brain and her tongue had frozen in place.

Especially because there was some truth to what he had said.

She'd done the interview.

She'd printed out the job offer.

She hadn't rejected it yet.

Sure, she meant to, but part of her hadn't been able to stop thinking about how much they were offering. About how much cheaper housing and living expenses would be. About being able to make enough that she didn't have to depend on anyone else.

About feeling like she was worthy of Q's attention.

Oof.

The realization hit her right in the gut.

Part of the reason the job was so appealing was if she was making that much money, she would feel better about herself. She'd told Q they weren't in high school anymore, yet here she was with the same mindset.

She hadn't told Q about the job for the same reason she hadn't told him why she couldn't go to prom.

She'd been ashamed.

Still felt ashamed because she hadn't been able to equal the amount he spent on her, and she didn't want him to know how badly she was struggling. So, even though she'd told him about the job search, she'd downplayed it. Maybe if she hadn't, he would have been more understanding.

Maybe if she'd been honest, he would have reassured her that he didn't think less of her.

Maybe if she'd been honest, she wouldn't be left all alone in her apartment, instead of cuddling on the couch with him.

The feeling of loneliness intensified as she wiped some of the tears from her face with the back of her arm and got to her feet. Several long minutes had passed. Q wasn't coming back. Sniffling, Sam went to get her phone from her purse.

She'd fucked up.

Q wasn't the only one she hadn't told about the possible job. She hadn't told her friends either. Or her dad. Out of all of them, Q knew the most.

She had wanted to keep it all a secret.

That ended now.

She still didn't know what she was going to do. There was a part of her that really wanted to run away to Ohio. A completely new start, making all the money she'd wanted... and living on her own, comfortably, but with no friends, her dad hours away, and no Q.

What she did know was she didn't have to go through this heartbreak alone. It was time to start letting people in.

"Hello?" Morgan's greeting was full of curiosity, which made sense since Sam rarely called. She always texted.

As the tears welled up again, choking her voice, she wished she'd texted this time.

"Morgan, I fucked up."

Saying the words out loud made them even more real. Sam sat down on the couch as she started crying again.

29

———————

HOME FOR THE HOLIDAYS

Q

"Wow, somebody needs a happy meal."

Q lifted his hand and raised a single figure salute to his cousin Daria. They were the closest in age among the cousins, which had led to them hanging out the most during the various holiday gatherings throughout the years. Back then, she'd been named Darren, but she'd made the transition in her early twenties and nothing had really changed between them except she had better advice than when she was a teenager.

Something he should probably take advantage of, now that he thought about it, but he didn't know if he wanted advice.

It had been two days since his blow-up with Sam.

She'd texted him yesterday asking if they could talk. He'd been on his way down to his grandma's and had texted her back that he was going to concentrate on his family for the next few days, and they could talk after he got back. He still needed time to cool down.

Time and maybe some sense knocked into him because he was already making excuses for her in his head. It was like he wanted to set himself up to be hurt again.

Third time's the charm.

"Okay then, Scrooge." Daria chuckled, sitting down on the porch swing next to him. This part of North Carolina wasn't that much warmer than Maryland, so Q was bundled up in a coat and scarf, his hands stuffed in his pockets.

It was a cold Christmas day.

Or maybe he was just cold without Sam in his life.

"I don't suppose you could take the hint and just let me hang out here on my own for a bit? Wouldn't you rather spend Christmas day with your wife?" Q asked with a sigh, but there was no heat in his words. He wasn't angry at Daria. He wasn't even sure he was mad at Sam.

But he was disappointed. It was making it hard to enjoy Christmas and his family. A stark contrast to Thanksgiving.

"No can do. Unless you want the moms out here next. I'm the compromise. Rashida understands. She's gonna keep them occupied while I hang out here with you."

Shit.

Yeah, he'd much rather have Daria than his mom and aunts.

"I'll have to thank Rashida for her sacrifice." Though, truthfully, it wasn't a huge one. The moms all loved her and the fact she was currently seven months pregnant didn't hurt.

"I've promised to update her later tonight about why you're such a sad sack."

Q snorted, lifting his beer to take a drink. He didn't usually drink at the family gatherings, but today, he'd wanted one. Just to take the edge off. And instead of being in the middle of the kids, he'd gone out to the front porch to wallow.

He'd been hoping not to be missed among all the chaos. He'd waited until after the presents were open to sneak off and thought no one had noticed. He should have known better.

Daria let him sit in silence for a whole thirty seconds before she finally nudged him with her elbow. Except instead of a nudge, it was more like a jab to the ribs, and it hurt.

"Ow. Okay, fine." Q sighed again. "It's like this."

He'd already told her about Sam at Thanksgiving. Daria had

remembered the girl who changed her mind about going to prom with him. She'd been intrigued that he and Sam had found each other again—at a kink club no less. The update on what had happened since then was a lot less fun.

The noise going on in the house behind them reassured him the rest of his family probably wouldn't hear him talking, but he kept his voice low just in case. The last thing he needed was everyone trooping out to give him relationship advice. Or, worse, asking what kink was.

"So, I told her we'd talk when I got back," he finished up wearily. Laying it all out, he still wasn't sure how he felt about everything that had gone down. He'd been right to be upset, but at the same time, he felt like shit about how he'd walked out on her. On the other hand, he wasn't sure that staying would have helped. He didn't know what he might have said if he had. He'd been pissed and lashing out.

"Do you think you might have been leaving her before she left you this time?" Daria asked.

Trust his cousin to get straight to the heart of things. Q winced. He felt the question like a physical blow, which meant there was more than a little truth to it.

"Maybe," he temporized, rather than admitting it. "But the fact she didn't even tell me she interviewed for a job in Ohio shows that we're not on the same page."

"She did say she wasn't planning on taking it."

Q threw up his hands, careful not to slosh his beer.

"Then why even interview?"

"That's something only she can answer." Daria was silent for a moment. "Money changes things, though. I could see Rashida doing something similar when we first got together. Not because she'd want to leave me, but because of the money."

"Money isn't everything."

"Says the person who has it." Daria turned her head, grinning at him, tossing several of her braids over her shoulder as she did so. "It's a lot harder when you're the one struggling, especially if she's had trouble her whole life. Does she want you to be her Sugar Daddy?"

"No."

Taking another sip of beer, Q considered that. Sam had a lot of pride. She'd had it back in high school. She had it still. No, he didn't consider it a big deal that she didn't have money... but that was because he *did*. He didn't mind paying for things for her, but *she* minded, not something he'd really considered.

"Have you told her that you paid for her club fees?" Daria asked.

Another direct hit.

"No."

"So, she's not the only one who was keeping secrets."

He wanted to protest that his secret had been to help her, and it had, but it had also been to help him. It was also the kind of secret that felt good to do but knowing Sam... there was a reason he'd kept it a secret. She would have found it embarrassing. Would have hated knowing he was paying her way into Stronghold and Marquis, even if it was only a tiny portion of her way since she was working off the rest.

Dammit. Life would be simpler if she just let him shower her with everything he had...

But then she wouldn't be Sam.

"I need to talk to her."

"You need to talk to her," Daria confirmed amiably. "Probably regret it if you don't. Maybe come clean about the fact that you were paying for her club fees while she's still feeling guilty about not telling you about the job stuff."

Devious. Q had to laugh. He held out his beer bottle so Daria could clink hers against it in a toast.

"That's the best advice you've had so far."

Sam

Christmas was so much lonelier than she'd expected it to be, even though she was with friends. She missed her dad, but she missed Q even more. Not that he was going to be here, at Morgan's, but she felt his emotional absence even more keenly than his physical. She hadn't heard from him since he'd texted that they'd talk when he got home.

Which meant she was on her own, completely, all week.

"Here, try the eggnog." Morgan shoved a glass of frothy white liquid in front of her gleefully. At least someone was having fun.

Sam made herself smile. She knew Morgan was trying to cheer her up. Morgan and Noelle had been there for her for the past few days, though Noelle was spending today with her own family.

Sam and Kincaid had come over to Morgan's in a kind of lonely-hearts-Christmas gathering, and they'd been surprised to find Amy there as well. Apparently, her plans with her family had fallen through, and she hadn't been able to get a flight to join her fiancé, so Morgan had invited her to join them instead.

If Sam wasn't so down in the dumps about her own situation, she would be pretty entertained watching Kincaid and Amy dance around each other. Neither of them seemed to know quite how to interact with each other when they were outside of the club and Zach wasn't there as a buffer. They were stiltedly polite, pretending to be relaxed.

Meanwhile, Morgan had gone all out for festive cheer. Brian had helped her decorate the house they lived in, and it looked like Christmas had thrown up all over it. The outside was festooned with lights, garlands, and a blow-up snowman family. Inside, the couch cushions were red and green with gold writing, wishing season's greetings upon anyone who entered the living room.

The giant Christmas tree next to the couch was covered in baubles, lights, and a giant star on top. Every single surface in the main rooms had some kind of Christmas decoration on it, whether it was a candle, a nutcracker, a snow globe, or whatever. Santa sat on a sleigh hitched up to eight tiny reindeer on the mantle above the fireplace where the stockings hung down.

It was like a child's dream of what Christmas should look like, and Sam absolutely refused to ruin this for Morgan because she knew that's exactly what this was—the Christmas Morgan had always wanted and never had. She hadn't missed that there were several presents under the tree from 'Santa'—most likely from the Doms at Stronghold and Marquis who had all come together to help Morgan out.

Taking the eggnog from Morgan's hand, Sam took a sip. Eggnog wasn't her favorite, but this one was pretty good. Creamy, cold, and sweet but not overly so

"That's good," she said smiling, glad she could be honest about it. Morgan beamed at her, then turned to serve glasses to Kincaid and Amy. She was dressed up in a sexy Mrs. Claus dress with green and red striped tights. Sam had gone for a red sweater and jeans, while Amy was wearing a sweater with Santa Claus riding a T-Rex for some unknown reason. The T-Rex was also wearing a Santa hat. Kincaid had on a dark green button-down shirt and jeans, which was dressed up for him.

While Morgan was serving their drinks, Sam's phone buzzed, and she was pathetically, desperately quick to check and see who was texting her.

Her heart started pounding in her chest when she saw it was Q.

Q: *Merry Christmas. I hope you're having a good day.*

That was it. That was all it said. She didn't know if she was relieved or wanted to throw her phone across the room. What the hell did it *mean?!* He was wishing her Merry Christmas but there was no indication of how he was feeling. Was he doing it to be polite? Because he missed her? Because he felt guilty that he was going to dump her in a few days?

"You okay, honey?" The couch shifted as Amy sat down next to her, concern all over her expression. Sam couldn't help but wonder if part of the reason Amy had made the move was because she was trying to put some space between her and Kincaid, but Sam appreciated the support.

"Yeah… I mean, no… sorta… not really."

"She and Q are having trouble because Sam interviewed for a job in Ohio without telling him." Morgan's matter-of-fact tone didn't make Sam sound any better than she felt.

"I wasn't going to take it."

"Then why interview for it?" Kincaid asked, frowning at her. She knew he didn't mean to make her feel worse, but if she could have gotten away with kicking him, she would have.

"I don't know." She'd been thinking about it ever since her argument with Q. Why? Why, why, why? "I guess I just wanted to see if I could even get it. The cost of living is so much lower and... if I hadn't started dating Q, I might have considered taking it. No, that's a lie, I think I would have taken it."

Even though she loved having friends, she was used to being alone. Starting over and having to make new friends wouldn't have been the worst thing in the world. It would have sucked, and she would have missed them, but since having close friends was new to her, it wasn't as though she would be doing something she'd never done before.

"So, you're not going to take it now?" Amy asked, reaching out to take Sam's hand. It felt supportive. Non-judgmental. Amy was good at being a sympathetic ear, and right now, Sam needed one. She kept her gaze averted from Kincaid, who was still frowning contemplatively.

"I haven't told them no yet. It might depend on what happens with me and Q. We're supposed to talk when he gets back from seeing his family later this week. That text was him wishing me Merry Christmas, so I guess he doesn't hate me, even though I didn't tell him about the job thing."

"I would miss you, but I'm not mad at you for not telling me," Morgan said, perching on the arm of the chair Kincaid was sitting in. He reached up to rub her back, the movement completely platonic despite how sexy Morgan was.

"You're not dating her, sweetheart. It's easier to keep a long-distance friendship going than a long-distance relationship. Q's pretty firmly established here. I don't know that he'd be willing to uproot himself."

"I would never have asked him to," Sam said quickly. Now she couldn't avoid Kincaid's gaze, and his eyebrows went up.

"You might not have asked, but what if he offered?"

No. She would have told him no because she wouldn't have wanted him to leave everything behind. She wasn't worth that. She was also smart enough not to say that out loud in front of a Dom. It sounded bad.

It sounds bad because it is bad. It sounds like you don't value yourself the way you should... because you don't.

Ouch.

"What does that expression mean?" Morgan asked, leaning forward. "You look like you just bit into something sour. Is something wrong with the eggnog?"

"The eggnog is delicious. I just realized something about myself that I don't like very much." Sam looked down at the eggnog to avoid having to look at anyone else. "I think I might need to work on my self-worth. I just realized I don't feel worthy of Q."

"Oh, honey. There's no such thing as being 'worthy' of someone else. Is he not worthy of having the woman he's chosen?" Amy's voice was all sympathy, but her words were almost brutal in their impact.

More ouch.

"Yeah but... it's just hard. He's a lot more well off than me. I'm struggling." There. She'd admitted it out loud, and it wasn't as hard as it would have been a week ago. Maybe because she was also struggling from the loss of Q, and she'd rather lose her pride than him. "A job that pays more in an area that costs less, where I wouldn't have to worry about money all the time... it sounds amazing. I just want to be his equal."

"Not making as much money as him doesn't mean you're not equal." Morgan's voice was full of sympathy as well, but it was also matter of fact in the way she got when she was repeating something from therapy. "Everyone brings something different to the relationship. Unless he's holding financial stuff over your head."

"No. He would never do that. He likes to pay for things, but he never makes me feel bad about it." She did that all on her own. Sighing, she rubbed her forehead. "I meant I don't want him taking care of me."

"Why not?" Morgan frowned, confused. "Everyone takes care of me. It's nice. It means they care about me."

Sam opened her mouth. Closed it. Everyone was looking at her expectantly. Amy raised her eyebrows.

She couldn't think of a single thing to say to counter Morgan's argument that wouldn't sound abhorrently bitchy. Because Morgan was right. Everyone took care of her. And Morgan accepted it happily because for so long no one had cared about her.

What did it say about Sam that she had so many people who cared, and she wouldn't accept help from any of them?

30

FRIENDSMAS

Sam

The music for the end of Love Actually played, and Morgan sighed with happiness.

"I love this movie." Her voice was dreamy, as though she was imagining being in the movie—or, at least, being one of the happy couples in the movie.

It amazed Sam how Morgan could stay so optimistic despite everything she'd been through. She still wanted to find love. She gracefully accepted help. She'd been ground down into the dirt, yet she was willing to put herself out there again. Whereas Sam hadn't even texted Q back because she was too wrapped up in trying to figure out if there was any hidden subtext to his message.

"I think I need to be more like you." The words popped out of her mouth before she really thought about them.

Sitting on the floor between Kincaid's knees, Morgan twisted around to give Sam a surprised look.

"Like me?" There was real shock in her voice. Amy and Kincaid, who were on either side of her, were also looking at her, though without Morgan's surprise. She avoided meeting their gazes as heat filled her cheeks, almost wishing she hadn't said anything... except she knew her words would mean a lot to Morgan.

"Yeah, like you. I wish I was better at accepting help and at looking at the positive side of things. I don't mean to be a Debbie downer, but it keeps happening anyway." She rubbed her hands on her thighs. She didn't felt like a Debbie downer or that she was negative most of the time. She thought she was being realistic, but hanging out with Morgan made her look that way in contrast.

Morgan reached out to take Sam's hand.

"You have a choice, though. I didn't. Not really. I either had to accept help or end up out on the street. I had no idea how to function in the real world. You do. I want to be more like you."

Staring back at her, Sam shook her head.

"What, bitter at the world and scared of being in a real relationship?" She tried to make it into a joke, but the same bitterness she was referencing had worked its way into her voice. Amy shifted on the other side of her, wrapping her arm around Sam's shoulders.

"Oh, honey. You're just very down to earth, and that's not necessarily a bad thing." Amy grinned. "Q has his head in the clouds, so he needs someone to bring him back down to earth, while you've got your feet firmly on the ground and need someone to lift you up. You two balance each other."

He hadn't been very head-in-the-clouds during their argument, but Sam understood what Amy was saying, and she wasn't wrong. Sam hadn't really thought about it that way. Q did have a tendency to jump straight into things. Always had. Sam had always taken more time and been more deliberate about her decisions. She'd envied his fearlessness, but at the same time she'd seen how leaping before one looked could be a detriment.

Maybe that was why she'd needed to do the job interview and hadn't told them no yet. She'd needed to know that all her options were open. She'd needed to know what all her options *were*. How could she consider something if she didn't know if it was actually on the table?

"That doesn't sound so bad," she admitted. Now that she knew the 'why,' she'd be able to explain it to him. Hopefully.

"It would also probably help to let him help you," Kincaid finally spoke up. "Tell him what you can accept help with. It sucks when your partner is floundering and you feel helpless, especially if you can see ways to help them, and they won't let you."

Amy made a small noise of sympathy, staring at Kincaid from Sam's other side. She had the urge to scrunch herself smaller and get out of their way. There were some serious vibes going back and forth between the two of them.

Sam didn't know what to make of their dynamic. Talk about complicated. Amy playing platonically with Zach, who was Kincaid's boyfriend, while she was engaged to a totally vanilla guy, but *they* didn't actually have a relationship together...

Yeah, things with Q didn't seem so difficult by comparison.

"He'll come around," Amy said sympathetically after a moment. "It's just hard for him."

Kincaid gave her a tight smile that did absolutely nothing to relieve the growing tension in the room.

"I hope so."

"So, who wants dessert?" Morgan asked, bouncing to her feet. The movement, along with her cheery question, *did* break the tension, which Sam was pretty sure had been her intention. "I've got a choco-late yule log and candy cane ice cream."

"That sounds amazing." Kincaid stood up as well, obviously to help her serve. He glanced down at Sam and Amy on the couch. "Ladies?"

"Yes, please."

"None for me." Amy shook her head, patting her stomach. "I've already eaten too much—don't look at me like that, Kincaid. I'm not talking badly about myself. I've just been dieting and exercising and still gaining weight, and I have a wedding dress to fit into in the spring." She sighed. "I don't know what to do, but I know eating extra dessert isn't going to help if I'm gaining weight on salad while working out five days a week. I've already splurged enough on my calories today."

Now Kincaid was really frowning, and so was Sam.

"Have you been to see a doctor?" she asked before Kincaid could say anything. "If you're doing all that and gaining weight, you should be checked out. It could be your thyroid or any number of things."

Amy had started to wrinkle her nose, but her eyes widened at Sam's last sentence.

"Wait, really? I haven't been because I figured they'd just tell me more diet and exercise, but I'm already doing that."

"You should get checked out," Sam said firmly. "Request bloodwork. If they tell you no or say you need to diet and exercise, even though you already have been, tell them to write down in your file that you requested tests and were refused and require them to write it in front of you."

Unfortunately, Sam had all too much experience with needing to take such measures. Her doctor now was great, but some of the ones in the past had seen her size and her weight and discounted literally everything else about her. Didn't matter what the actual problem was, they thought 'lose weight' was the solution.

"I can give you my doctor's information if you want. She'll take you seriously." Just in case Amy's usual doctor didn't.

"I might take you up on that." Amy's smile was a little tremulous. She looked up at Morgan and Kincaid. "I'll take a tiny piece of yule log and a half scoop of ice cream. They do sound good."

As Morgan and Kincaid moved to the kitchen, chatting about their favorite parts of the movie, Sam pulled her phone out of her pocket.

"Are you going to text him back?" Amy asked in a low voice. "I think you'll regret it if you don't."

"Yeah, I am." She stared at her phone screen for a long moment.

Sam: *Merry Christmas Q. I hope you're having a good one.*

Less than thirty seconds later, her phone buzzed again, and when Sam saw the attached picture, she burst out laughing. Which, of course made Amy want to look and had Morgan and Kincaid hustling back. Turning the phone screen, she showed them the picture of Q on all fours, reindeer antlers on his head, with a little kid wearing a Santa hat on his back.

Maybe they would be alright.

Q

Marquis was still beautiful decorated for Christmas when Q walked in, even though it was a few days after. Making his way to the bar, Q almost stumbled when he saw Law there, talking with Shane and Freddy. He'd come because he hadn't been ready to call Sam yet, despite the texts they'd exchanged the past couple days, but his empty house had felt way too cold and lonely after coming home from his grandmother's. He hadn't wanted to go to Stronghold where so many of their friends would be. Possibly even Sam herself. Marquis had seemed like the safest option for somewhere he felt like he was home but wouldn't have to talk to anyone.

So much for that.

He wanted to know what Law was doing down at the bar. It had been years since Law had touched a drink, but he was a recovering alcoholic. While he sometimes hung out around the tables at Stronghold that were near the bar because his friends were, Q had never seen him at an actual bar before.

From the dark frown on his face, he appeared to be upset about something. For the first time all week, concern for something other than his own situation pierced Q.

"Everything okay?" he asked, coming up to the bar table where Freddy and Law were talking fiercely in low tones.

Freddy was wearing a flashy green suit decorated with reindeer wearing Santa hats. Like the rest of the restaurant, he didn't appear to be done with the holiday season just yet. Sitting up straight, he ran a hand through his blond hair, rolling his eyes.

"Mr. Paranoid doesn't think so."

"I am not being paranoid, Julie is actually receiving gifts, and we don't know from who," Law retorted, his scowl deepening.

"I think that's kind of the point of a secret admirer." Q slid onto one of the barstools between them, amused. For some reason Law had a stick up his ass about Mistress Julie's secret admirer and that he couldn't quite figure it out.

The biggest problem seemed to be that a few of the gifts had arrived at times when Julie wasn't scheduled to be working, which Law felt was stalker-y. Considering how everyone knew everyone else's business at the clubs, Q thought it was possible that information was just getting around. Especially since the secret admirer seemed to know things like her favorite flower, her favorite kind of candy, her favorite brand for spanking implements...

"I don't like that they keep showing up here at the club."

"Because you're a control freak." Freddy shook his head. "I don't know how Iris puts up with you. Even Patrick isn't freaking out like you are, and I always thought he was the biggest control freak."

"That's because Patrick's main concern is Stronghold, not Marquis. He trusts Marquis to those of us who spend our time here."

"Olivia's not worried," Freddy pointed out. He turned to Q. "Anyway, what's going on with you and Sam?"

Law sat up straight, his expression clearing immediately as he focused in on Q.

"Something's wrong with you and Sam? How come Freddy knew, and I didn't?"

"Because Sam had Christmas with Morgan, and I hung out with Morgan yesterday, so I got to hear all about it."

Now it was Q's turn to straighten. That sounded like information he could use.

"Oh, you did, did you? What did she say?"

"Hmm... this is a conundrum," Freddy said, tilting his head and putting his finger on his chin. "Normally, I would never betray a fellow sub, but with you and Sam the lines are a little blurry. Are you approaching me as a fellow sub right now or are you asking as Master Q?"

"Sub. Definitely sub. I want to know how to fix this." He gave Freddy his most pleading look. "I don't know what I did to make her feel like she couldn't talk to me or trust me. I missed her this week, and I know we need to talk, but Sam, I mean Mistress Samantha, plays her cards pretty close to the vest. She always has."

"Well, that's something to think about. It sounds to me that what happened was she didn't tell you everything about her job search, you got angry when you found out, then you stopped talking to her because she didn't talk to you." Freddy raised his eyebrows at Q, as if asking if he wanted to challenge the summary of events.

Q opened his mouth and closed it.

Shit. When he put it like that...

"I needed some space to think," he replied defensively.

"Oh, you're not the asshole here. I don't think there are any assholes here, just a rough situation. Though I'd love to hear your side of it." Freddy beamed at him, and Law was now staring expectantly at Q, so he sighed and went over it again. At least one of the servers came by to get his drink order while he was doing so.

As he wrapped up, including the fact that they'd been texting since Christmas day, but he still didn't know what he wanted to say to her once they saw her in person, both Law and Freddy were looking thoughtful.

"I'm going to agree with Freddy—no assholes here. You were both upset and taking a step back isn't the worst thing in the world."

"Right, but what do I say to her now?" Q scrubbed his hand over his head, the bristles of his curls soft against his palm.

"Tell her that you were hurt she didn't talk to you, that you wish she had felt she could, and that you don't want her to go anywhere, but you'll support whatever decision she makes." Law shrugged his shoulders when both Freddy and Q stared at him. "What?"

"Iris has done good work with you," Freddy said, and then turned back to Q, jerking his thumb at Law. "What he said. You two are crazy about each other. I can tell. But you said it yourself, she's always kept her cards close to her chest. The real question is, can you accept her as she is?"

That was a hard question.

"I don't know if I can accept being kept out of the loop on something so important," he admitted.

"That's fair, but you should talk that through with her. Maybe she'll be willing to bend a bit, but you're also going to have to compromise." Freddy grinned.

"Have you ever thought about being a couple's counselor instead of a divorce lawyer?" Law asked, amused. "I think you'd be good at it."

"Of course, I would, but that's partly from years of watching people go through divorces. Half the time, the biggest problems stem from a failure to communicate, whether it's failure to listen or failure to truly try to see the other's point of view." He pointed a finger at Q. "You have to decide. What's a deal breaker? And what's an argument that you two can work through and come out stronger on the other side?"

It was not a deal breaker. Q didn't want things with Sam to end. He just didn't know where they went from here, which meant that Freddy was 100% correct.

They needed to talk.

He looked at Freddy and Law.

"It's not a deal breaker. I still want to be with her. I just want her to tell me when something important is going on in her life. I want her to let me in. Do either of you have any advice on how to make *that* happen?"

As it turned out, they did.

31

——————

YOU WERE SUPPOSED TO CALL!

Sam

Q had come home today but so far, he hadn't called *or* texted. Sam was about five minutes away from breaking out the emergency ice cream. She'd bought it months ago and saved it for when it was desperately needed, so it was probably frostbitten to all hell, but she was feeling the urge. It would be nice if she felt the urge to eat something cheaper, like saltines, but no, she wanted ice cream.

Grr.

She was sitting around her apartment, doing absolutely nothing, waiting for her phone to go off, like a pathetic caricature of a heartbroken girl. Ice cream was only going to add to that.

That didn't stop her from wanting it.

A knock on her door made her jump.

Oh, no.

He wouldn't have... would he?

Sam ran over to the door as quietly as she could and looked through the peephole. *Shit. Shit. Shit.* He would. Q was standing outside her door looking absolutely delicious in a forest-green button-down shirt she could see because he'd opened his coat. She looked down at her stained sweatshirt and yoga pants, her hand flying up to touch the messy bun in her hair.

It wasn't an artfully messy bun. It was a *messy* messy bun.

Shit!

She barely dared breathe as she tried to figure out what to do.

He knocked again, and she jumped.

Dammit, he was supposed to have texted! Or called! She was supposed to have had time to get herself together before he saw her!

"Sam, I know you're standing on the other side of the door. Let me in." Amusement threaded through his words.

She'd stopped breathing almost as soon as he'd started talking.

Dammit. How did he know she was there?

She glanced over her shoulder, wondering if she could run and change fast enough.

"Sam." He knocked again. "Let me in."

His voice was shifting, lowering, moving into Dom territory.

Crap.

"Now."

She groaned inwardly, even as she reached for the lock and flipped it open, her other hand turning the door's knob.

As she opened the door, her head ducked down. She didn't want to see his expression when he got his first look at her, especially considering how pathetic she felt. Dammit. She should have at least run to change her shirt before letting him in.

"There you are." The deep satisfaction in his voice gave no hint of disappointment or judgment. He sounded thrilled to see her, like it didn't matter about her hair or the stain on her shirt or anything else. Sam's head jerked up just as he stepped in to wrap his arms around her.

It felt so good to be in his arms again. Tears sprang into her eyes as he hugged her tight, inhaling like he was breathing her in.

Oh God. I hope I don't smell.

Whatever cologne he was wearing smelled fantastic. It wasn't fair that he looked and smelled so good. She clung to him. Partly because she didn't want to lose the sensation of being held so closely and partly because if he was holding her, he couldn't *see* her.

Eventually he pulled away. Sort of. Enough to get her turned around and moving into the apartment so they weren't standing in her doorway. Sam self-consciously rubbed at the spot on her shirt. Maybe if she covered it with her hand, he wouldn't notice.

"I missed you this week," he said, leading her over to the couch. Even though it was her home, it felt completely natural to let him take the lead.

Yeah. She was feeling super subby today. Subby and in need of a lot of reassurance. The hug had been a good start, but she needed more. She also needed to explain herself. Even though she understood some of her actions better, she wasn't looking forward to it.

She had a reason for why she'd interviewed for the job and hadn't immediately turned them down, but she didn't have a good reason for not telling Q about any of it.

"I missed you, too." Honesty was the best policy, right? Especially since, while she hadn't actually lied to him, she hadn't told him everything. Honestly and transparency. That's what Morgan, Kincaid, and Amy had all said. Kincaid had also suggested talking to Angel, which Sam had done, but Angel's advice had been, 'just talk to him, then if he's still cranky let him put it in your butt.'

Which... not that Sam objected to the idea, she just didn't see how it would solve anything.

To her surprise, Q didn't sit down on the couch. Instead, he came to a halt directly in front of it, then turned to her. What he thought of her messy hair and sweatshirt she had no idea, because he was looking straight in her eyes instead of anywhere else. He let go of her hand and grasped the bottom of her sweatshirt.

"Arms up."

She complied immediately, though confusion bubbled up inside her.

"Why?" She couldn't help but asking even though she followed his order. He tugged the sweatshirt off and over her head, revealing the utilitarian bra she was wearing underneath. At least it was clean, even if there was nothing inherently sexy about it.

Being stripped naked the moment he walked in the door had *not* been what she was expecting, and she felt wildly off kilter.

"It has been suggested to me that part of your problem is that you have trouble feeling vulnerable. We're going to make you vulnerable before we get to talking, so you're already in the right mindset." Q flashed a grin at her before crouching down and pulling down her stretchy pants.

"Who suggested that?"

"Law and Freddy."

Dammit. They would know. Not the same way Morgan or Noelle might, but they'd both worked with her and knew where she struggled. Which made it really hard to argue against Q stripping her down.

Did she even want to?

Heck. Maybe they had a point. Maybe it would be easier to talk when she was already feeling vulnerable.

A few minutes later, she was butt naked and draped over Q's lap, wondering if she'd made a horrible mistake, though his hand caressing her buttocks was nice. She wasn't sure the position made her feel more talkative, although not looking at his face seemed to help while she was explaining why she'd done the interview, even though she didn't plan on taking the job.

"I know it sounds a little weird to want to know if I have an option so I can reject it, but I needed to know if it was an option, so I could weigh it against my other options." She blew out a breath, wriggling a little as she felt his fingers tapping against her upturned ass cheek, as if he was thinking. "Especially since I wasn't exactly being offered any other job options."

There was a long silence, and she got the impression he was thinking about what she'd said. She tried to twist around to see his expression, but it wasn't exactly the easiest position. Feeling her movements, he rubbed his hand on her lower back, the other one sweeping over the curve of her ass and down to her thigh, making her body tingle with awareness.

This was the first time she'd ever been over his lap where he didn't have an erection. It didn't feel sexual, it felt intimate. Also, a little intimidating since she was pretty sure he wouldn't hesitate to spank her if he thought she'd earned it. That had the effect of making her very invested in explaining herself.

"I'll be honest, I can't say I understand it. It doesn't particularly make sense to me... but I get that it's how you feel and how you process things, so I can accept it." Q patted her bottom gently, as if in encouragement.

She bit back her lip against trying to explain it further, because she knew it wasn't how he did things, so he might never *get* it. That he accepted what she needed was what was important. She'd probably never understand how he could make a decision *without* considering every side of every single option.

"The real question is, why didn't you tell me about the interview and the offer? Why not let me know it happened?"

"I don't know." Even as she said the words, she knew they were a mistake, and she shrieked when his hand came down hard on her ass. "Ouch!"

"Try again."

Q

Rubbing his hand over the spot he'd just spanked on Sam's ass, Q had to admit he liked this way of talking. He felt a lot calmer. There was a lot to be said for having a serious discussion with a subbie while she was over your lap.

He didn't entirely understand why Sam felt the need to make her decision the way she had, but he understood it felt necessary to her.

That being said, he wasn't going to accept 'I don't know' as an answer for why she hadn't talked to him about it. Even if the answer was that she hadn't trusted him or she hadn't wanted him influencing her decision, he wanted to be able to talk about *that.*

Sam huffed out a breath of air.

"I wasn't sure what you'd say."

"So, you didn't want to know what I'd say."

There was a moment of silence.

"That's fair. I didn't want to know what you'd say," she confessed. "If you asked me to stay that would have factored hugely into my decision, but I also didn't want to make an important life-changing decision for a guy. I didn't want to be that girl."

Q gave her ass a little squeeze.

"Gorgeous, I don't think you could ever be that girl. Though I would also like to point out there is absolutely nothing wrong with including your significant other in life-changing decisions and taking their feelings into account. I know we haven't been 'together' that long, but I am completely serious about you. I want a future with you. Whether that future is here or somewhere else."

"You can't just up and move for me!"

"Why not?"

His fingers traced down her crease, brushing over her anus, down to her pussy, making her squirm in a way that had nothing to do with her protest. His cock was starting to harden, whereas before he'd been too focused on trying to understand her. Now he was getting turned on.

"I make my decisions based on what makes me happy. You make me happy."

"All your friends are here."

"So are yours. We can make new friends together. The ones we already have could come visit."

"We haven't been together long enough for you to be making these kinds of decisions just for me."

While he kind of agreed on the length of time thing, there was an odd note in her voice, and something bothered him about her words.

"I wouldn't be making the decision for you. I'd be making it for me. I would want to be with you because you are who I see my future with. I can do what I do from anywhere. I'm lucky that way."

"But you can't throw away everything else you have here for me."

"Sure, I can if I want to. You don't get to make that decision for me." He gave her ass a swat for emphasis.

"I'm not worth that!"

As soon as she half-shouted the words, she clapped her hands over her mouth, but it was far too late. They hung in the air, and Q finally understood why she'd kept him out of the loop. While part of her had known, deep down, he would want to go with her if she moved, she hadn't wanted to hear him say it. Hadn't wanted to admit it even to herself.

Because for some reason, she was insecure, felt unworthy, and she was anything but.

"Okay good. Now that we've identified the problem, we can work on fixing it. I think the first thing we're going to do is make sure that you understand that you don't get to decide what I think you're worth. So, what's going to happen now is you're going to say, 'Q thinks I'm worth moving for' and I'm going to spank you until I think it sounds like you mean it."

32

WORTHY

Sam

"Q thinks I'm worth moving for!" she shouted before his hand fell, but it didn't matter.

They both knew she didn't mean it. She couldn't even fake sounding like she meant it. She sounded slightly desperate, which was more about being punished than anything else.

Q's hand came down hard and fast and she squealed. He got a few swats in before she got her breath back.

"Q thinks I'm worth moving for!"

"That's a vast improvement, but I think you can do better, pretty girl," Q said as he continued to spank her, hard, crisp swats peppering her bottom and making her whine and whimper. "I want you to feel it, to mean it. What we have together is good. I want to be a part of your life, and I want you to be a part of mine. I don't want you keeping me out or making my decisions for me. I want to be part of making decisions together."

The heat flaring in her backside was becoming more and more painful, each swat coming down on spots that had already been smacked, adding to the growing fire. Sam wriggled and panted as she felt her skin changing color, knowing it was turning a brighter pink every time his hand impacted her flesh.

It was also cleansing. She knew she'd messed up. She'd known the right thing to do would have been to tell Q, but she'd pushed those thoughts away, burying them deep, thinking he'd never know. She hadn't wanted to face her feelings, but the guilt had still been there and got worse after he'd been so upset when he'd found the job listing.

Now, being punished for her wrongs felt right.

"Q thinks I'm worthy!" A bit different from what he'd said before, but it felt better. More like she was saying what she was really supposed to believe.

His hand came down again, smoothing over her sore buttocks.

"Good girl, that's a lot closer."

Her insides heated, but not nearly as much as her ass as Q's hand lifted and came down again.

Dammit!

The hard smack against her ass made her gasp. Her skin was becoming more and more sensitive, and the heat was burning through her, sparking off a new emotion—anger—not at Q, but at herself.

Why was she so down on herself? Why didn't she feel worthy? She'd always thought she had good self-esteem, but clearly, she'd missed something. There was no reason she should feel that way... except...

She'd always fought against the notion that money defined her worth, especially in high school. Pride had pushed her against telling anyone what was going on or what motivated her. She'd found her confidence in her grades, her AP classes, her intellect.

But in real life there were no grades. There was no one telling her she was top of the class. The only thing she could really measure her success by was her income.

Oh, yeah? What about measuring by the number of people who care about you? The number of people who would help you if you just let them?

What about measuring by the number of kids you've helped?

Her lack of money was causing issues in her life, but that didn't mean she was failing. Heck, she knew better than anyone that hard work didn't guarantee financial comfort. Otherwise, her dad would have been a millionaire.

She'd never blamed him or been ashamed of him.

So, why was she so focused on it for herself?

Because I wanted to make Dad's work and sacrifices worth it.

In her head, that had meant being financially successful enough to take care of him in the way he'd taken care of her. Sam sniffled, as much from the painful burning igniting in her butt as realizing that she'd been so hard on herself because she'd wanted to be able to give back to her dad—and do it on her own. So many people had talked about what promise she had and how successful she was going to be, she hadn't wanted anyone to know that she wasn't.

Granted, she was a bit of a loner, but feeling like she couldn't let anyone down, especially her dad, made it so much worse. He wouldn't want her to feel this way. He didn't care how much she made, only that she was happy.

And she was happier now than she'd ever been, though still worried about money. It was definitely time for a change, but she didn't have to sacrifice everything that was making her happy to get it.

"I'm worthy!" She said the words fiercely, not in reaction to the sting of Q's hand coming down on her ass—though that probably helped—but because she really truly believed it.

She was worthy. Even if she needed some help sometimes. Even if she hadn't met all the goals she'd set for herself when she'd graduated or when she'd gotten her job. What happened to her didn't define her worth, and she *was* worthy.

"Good girl."

Sam sniffled when she found herself being pulled up onto Q's lap, his arms wrapped securely around her.

"Ouch!" A freshly spanked ass rubbing against jeans was *not* comfortable. Q just chuckled, the big jerk, his hand coming down to rub against the side of her burning bottom.

Resting her head against his shoulder, Sam wiped away the tears adorning her cheeks, still sniffling and sighed happily. Despite the tears, despite her chastised bottom, she was happier and more at home here in Q's arms than she had been all week. This was right where she wanted to be.

"Now, then. I won't lie, I don't particularly want to move to Ohio, but if that's where you're going, I would absolutely consider it. Strongly." His arms tightened around her. "I want a future with you, Samantha Dupre. I'm hoping you want one with me, too."

"I do, I promise, I do." She pressed her hand against his chest. "I'm sorry if I ever made you doubt that. I just... I just realized that I had some ideas in my head that I don't particularly like. A lot of them about money and about accepting help. I might have a little too much pride sometimes."

"I don't think pride is necessarily a bad thing, but yeah, accepting help can be hard, but it can also make a huge difference. A friend got me my job. Sure, I've worked my way up through the company on my own merit, but I got the job because of a friend."

"Hmm." Sam blinked. She hadn't even though about reaching out to some of her past friends. She did have them even if they'd grown apart. As Morgan and Noelle had pointed out to her, if one of her old OT friends from either school or work reached out to her and asked for help, she would want to help them, right? Or if she'd found out they could have used her help and didn't ask, she would be upset.

She could absolutely reach out to her old college friends or some of the OTs who had left her practice for other jobs and ask them if they knew of any job openings.

Why hadn't she done that?

Because I didn't want to admit that I need help, that I had to do it all on my own.

People weren't successful all on their own. One way or another, they had help along the way, whether it was where they were born, what family they belonged to, the connections they made through their life, or even just being lucky enough to be in the right place at the right time. People didn't exist in a vacuum, and she needed to remember that.

She had friends. She had Q. She had her dad. She had help.

She'd get through this.

"Also, I would be happy to help you with any of your... needs." Q's voice turned husky and seductive. Lifting his hips, he rubbed the bulge of his erection against her thigh, making her giggle.

"Oh, yeah? I've missed you this week." She ran her finger up to the undone button on his shirt so she could stroke his chest. There were definitely more serious conversations in their near future and some things she needed to figure out, but right now, she really had missed him all week and her body was buzzing with arousal in the aftermath of her spanking.

Q

Sam's immediate response was a relief—he hadn't been sure he'd judged her mood correctly. Just because he was turned on didn't mean she was.

"I missed you, too." He really had, more than he would have thought possible a few months ago. He cleared his throat. There was one more thing they needed to talk about and he preferred to do it with her over his lap. "In the interest of full disclosure, I should also tell you that I've been paying your club fees that aren't covered by volunteering. Purely for selfish reasons because I want you there."

To his surprise and relief, she didn't seem upset. Jerking her head up, she looked over her shoulder, staring at him for a moment as if trying to assess whether or not he was being truthful, then her head dropped back down.

"I feel like I should be mad, but I'm not. I don't know if it's because of the spanking or because I missed you too much to be mad."

Thank God. Which meant he could get them back on track.

"I think you should show me how much you missed me." He gave her ass another little pat before shifting to tip her off his lap. Sam giggled but didn't protest when she ended up on her knees in front of him.

There was something incredibly hot about having her on her knees after a spanking, tear tracks still visible on her cheeks, her lips wrapped around his cock. He knew the tears weren't entirely from the spanking—she'd definitely had some kind of emotional reckoning— but the visual was still damn good.

And she was very eager to show him how much she'd missed him.

Q groaned, letting his head tip back, one hand atop her head, as her lips slid over the length of his cock, moving up and down. Her tongue curled and licked, pressing the sensitive underside, teasing the soft head. He groaned when she pushed it into the slit, lapping at his precum, before descending again.

His other hand reached for her breast, cupping the soft flesh and massaging it. Her nipple was already budded, and it hardened further under his touch. He tugged and twisted the little nub, enjoying the vibrations of her moans around his dick, the way the suction increased as he toyed with the sensitive bud.

It also reminded him of something he'd always wanted to do.

Taking hold of her hair with the hand he had atop her head, he lifted her head up, pulling her mouth away from him. His cock was wet and slick from the blow job, her lips swollen and pouty, eyes full of confusion, disappointment, and anticipation, wondering what he was going to do next.

"I want you on your back. Either on the floor or the bed, your choice."

Sam's eyes lit up, although he didn't think she had any clue what he was planning.

"Yes, Sir." He could almost see the calculation running through her mind before she made her decision, getting gracefully to her feet and moving to the bed.

Standing, Q followed her, a little more slowly because he was taking off his clothes as he moved. By the time he reached the bed, he was naked, and she was stretched out in the middle of the bed, arms above her head, elbows slightly bent in a position of repose. Her breasts had flattened slightly, nipples pointed to the ceiling, and she'd spread her legs wide.

Instead of getting on the bed and kneeling between them, Q got on the bed and straddled her ribcage. Sam's pretty hazel eyes widened in surprise as he palmed her breasts, cupping the soft flesh and pushing it together to cradle his dick in the plush valley.

He thrust his hips forward, and it felt good, her skin rubbing along his shaft, but that wasn't quite the sensation he wanted.

"Do you have any lube?"

"In the drawer," she replied, tilting her head at the nightstand. Her eyes were alight with interest and curiosity.

Leaning over, Q opened the drawer and pulled out the small tube of strawberry flavored lube. Perfect. He held it over her breasts, drizzling it down between them, making her pale skin glossy as the light reflected off it. Something about her expression, the completely focused way she was watching his every movement, made him wonder...

"Sam, has anyone ever fucked these beautiful breasts?"

Her gaze flicked up to him, then back down to his cock as she blushed hotly.

"No," she whispered.

Well, well, well. Virgin territory. He didn't know why but he really liked the idea of being able to do something with her she'd never done before, the same way he had when he'd let her peg him.

"Then I feel very lucky," he murmured as he cupped her breasts again, his thumbs teasing her nipples as he slid his cock into the now slick crease between the soft mounds. Sam shivered, still watching with fascination. The dark of head of cock peeked out between the creamy mountains. "To be the first to enjoy your breasts this way. Damn that feels good... give me your tongue baby girl. I want you to lick me while I fuck these pretty breasts."

The color in her cheeks turned even pinker, but she obeyed, her tongue flicking out and over the head of his cock. It was both a delight and a tease as Q thrust between her breasts. His hands held them tightly on either side, increasing the pressure on his cock as it ran through her cleavage. Every time the head made it through the valley, Sam's tongue was there to greet it.

The sight, as much as the feel, was what drove him, his thrusts coming harder and faster between her breasts. Having her pinned beneath him, offering up her body in a way that didn't give her a chance for climax, was so fucking hot. He moved his hips, sliding his cock back and forth, groaning as his pleasure bubbled up and over.

When hot liquid spurted, Sam instinctively jerked her chin up, leaving the white fluid to arc and land on her collarbone. The white cum flowed as Q groaned, shuddering as he created a pearl necklace around her pretty throat.

33

IT MEANS I LOVE YOU

Sam

Curled up in bed with Q, Sam was still horny, but she was starting to think that might be part of her punishment. It didn't feel like a mean punishment, and she was pretty sure she'd been forgiven—and she'd definitely forgiven him—but apparently, that didn't stop Q from being a bit sadistic. He was enjoying tormenting her, which was making Sam feel especially subby.

Even though they'd cleaned off afterward, she could still feel the liquid ring around her neck, like the phantom of the orgasm. That would make for a very odd musical.

Yeah, her brain was feeling a little floaty and distracted.

She never thought she'd enjoy titty fucking. She'd definitely never understood the appeal until now. It hadn't been something that would get her off, but it had been fun. Watching Q's face, watching his enjoyment had been incredibly arousing. And she'd always enjoyed having her breasts played with.

Was it going to be on her list of top favorite things to do? No. But she would totally do it again.

Q's fingers ran up and down her arm. Her head rested against his chest, arm wrapped over his body and one leg across his so he couldn't get up without moving her. Yeah. There was serious subliminal messaging going on.

Don't leave me.

She wasn't going to leave him, either. As soon as she got to her computer, she would do two things. First, she was going to turn down the Ohio job and let them know that while she was flattered, she didn't want to move and she hoped they'd consider her in the future for any Maryland openings. Second, she was going to contact some of her old college friends and colleagues to see if they had any suggestions.

Especially from colleagues who had moved on from her current practice.

"I can feel you thinking," Q murmured, making her giggle.

"You can *feel* me thinking?"

"Yup. I can feel all those little thoughts zinging around your head and pinging off the inside of your skull. Ping, ping, ping." He tapped her head with each 'ping,' and Sam laughed, swatting his hand away.

"I was just thinking about who to reach out to for help with my job search," she said, resting her hand back down on his chest, near her head. "I don't know why I felt like I had to do the whole thing alone. It never occurred to me to see if people I used to work with and have moved on might have some valuable information."

"You always were pretty independent, even in school. That's not going to change just because you're older if you're stuck in the habit."

Stuck in the habit was exactly where she'd been. Stuck in the habit of trying to do everything herself and not asking for help, much less accepting it, because she didn't want anyone to know she needed help. Which was silly because she loved to help people. Reciprocity was important.

If she could help others, she could let others help her.

"I do ask that next time, you talk to me about things, even if you don't want to." Q paused for a moment. "Maybe especially if you don't want to. If you don't want me to try to influence your decision or help you make it, I can respect that, but I want to at least be aware of what's going on and what you're thinking."

"That's fair. Trust me, I don't think I'll keep you out of the loop again—and not because of the spanking. I felt awful this whole week." She wrapped her arm back around him, hugging him tightly, and he shifted to face her, his arms wrapping around her as well. Next to her hip, she could feel his dick start to thicken, but he did nothing about it, just held her.

"I felt awful this whole week, too, but it was pointed out to me that couples fight. The important thing is we get through it, learn from it, and come out stronger the other side."

"That's nice," Sam said a little wistfully, rubbing her nose against chest hair. "The advice I got was 'if he's still grumpy, let him put it in your butt.'"

Q's entire body went still.

Sam went still.

"I mean... it's not the worst advice I've ever heard..." His hand, which had been resting against her upper back, slid down to cup her ass, making her squirm and wiggle—which, of course, made his slowly hardening erection go what felt like fully erect.

Sam had to laugh.

"So, what, you want my tits and my ass all on the same day?" A few lines of her favorite song from *A Chorus Line* ran through her head as she said the words. She was definitely going to have to play that for him later. Hopefully, Q liked musicals. It had been a while since she'd sat down and watched one, because she'd gotten so hooked on the home improvement shows, but suddenly she wanted to. With him.

She found herself rolled onto her back, Q grinning down at her.

"Nothing wrong with that," he said, the hand that wasn't still curved around her ass coming up to fondle her breast. "I know you have the lube."

Lowering his head, Q took her lips in a kiss as his hips thrust his cock against her. Yup. Fully hard. He wanted her ass bad. Sam grabbed his shoulders as he moved, lifting his lower body so he could kneel between her legs, hiking both of her knees up so he could grope her ass while their tongues danced. His cock rubbed against her inner thighs and pussy, which clenched emptily.

She wanted him. Wanted to give herself fully to him. Moaning against his lips, she tilted her hips up. Felt his fingers prying her cheeks apart, one tip brushing over her crinkled hole, and she made a small noise in the back of her throat as her nerve endings lit up with interest.

Pulling away from the kiss, Q grinned down at her.

"I want you on all fours, gorgeous girl. I want to see your pretty pink ass while I fuck it."

Heat bloomed in her cheeks, as well as her core, and Sam shivered a little at his dirty words.

"Yes, Sir."

Q was considerate enough to pile up some pillows beneath her hips, putting her ass in perfecting presenting position. She moaned as he massaged her cheeks, which were still sensitive from her earlier spanking, though she doubted they were still very pink. Maybe a slight blush.

A lubed finger probed her hole, then pushed in easily, making her moan and wriggle for him.

"That's a good girl, squeeze my finger like it's my cock. It's going to feel so good when I fuck your ass."

Panting, Sam obligingly squeezed her muscles, feeling the burn of friction increase as she clenched. Her head dropped to her forearms. There was something achingly intimate about anal play and sex—perhaps the trust it required since it could so easily be painful in a non-fun way.

A second finger slid in, Q murmuring words of encouragement and compliments for her sexy ass the whole time. Sam quivered and moaned. His other was stroking her pussy and toying with her clit, arousing her even more as his fingers moved back and forth in her ass, mimicking what his cock would be doing soon. Her body spasmed, and her pussy throbbed as the sensations built.

The fingers slid away, replaced by the thick head of his cock. Sam took a deep breath, doing her best to relax as he pushed in. He was thicker than his fingers, stretching her deliciously, and she moaned at the slight burn as he began to sink inside her. About halfway in, he rocked back, then thrust forward again, opening her up for his pleasure.

The feeling of fullness spread as he moved, going a little deeper with each thrust, leaving her panting and clenching until his groin came to a rest against her cheeks as his fingers gripped her hips. Sam whimpered when he flexed inside her, her pussy pulsing in response. She felt so full.

So good.

"Fuck, your ass feels so good, Sam." Q pulled out and thrust back in, hard enough to make her groan. It hurt and felt good at the same time as her body adjusted to the impalement.

Leaning forward, he slid his hands up her sides to her breasts, filling his palms with the hanging orbs. Sam moaned again as he rode her, slowly at first, using her breast to help leverage him forward. Every drag of his cock back and forth in her body was achingly sharp, and she throbbed around him. He pinched and twisted her nipples, and she clenched around him as pain and pleasure began to meld together, her pussy quivering in time with his thrusts.

As the sensations began to morph into ecstasy, Q moved harder, faster inside her, taking her just as roughly as he would her pussy, and she loved every moment of it. Each thrust slapped his body against her already sensitized cheeks, reigniting the sting of her spanking. She'd be feeling him inside and out tomorrow.

"Oh, fuck... Q... fuck!"

One hand still firmly massaged her breast, tugging on her nipple, while the other moved to delve between her thighs. Her pussy was soaked when his fingers dipped between her nether lips and rubbed over her swollen clit. Sheer pleasure zipped through her, tightening her muscles, and rousing her passion to a fever pitch.

Q

Sam cried out, her muscles clenching hard around his cock when she began to cum, her hips bucking as she rubbed her clit against his fingers. He could feel her climax, her body rippling beneath his, her tight sheath massaging his cock, sucking him in deeper.

Thrusting hard, he let go of his control, allowing the need take him over and pounding into her as she cried out in ecstasy until his own peak swelled. Hot bliss flowed through him as he buried himself inside her, pulsing and throbbing against her clenching muscles as they milked him, pulling every last wave of pleasure from him.

Panting for breath, he draped himself over her, still fully embedded inside her. His fingers moved in slow, lazy circles on her clit, making her twitch beneath him. With his ear pressed to her back, he could hear her panting, then her breathing slowly coming back to her now that their passion was spent.

Fuck.

That was just as good as he'd imagined it would be.

Hell, it was better.

"I love you."

Yeah, he hadn't meant to be that guy and actually say the words out loud.

Sam moved beneath him, so Q rolled onto his side, keeping his arms wrapped around her and pulling her with him, his cock still inside her. She tried to wriggle, trying to twist her neck so she could look at him, but he buried his face against her upper back.

Maybe she hadn't heard him.

Or maybe she thought she hadn't heard him correctly, and he could play it off.

He did mean to tell her... just not yet and definitely not like this.

"I guess butt stuff really does mean 'I love you,'" Sam mused.

Q started laughing.

Okay, so she'd heard him, but she didn't sound upset, so that was good. He still kept his forehead pressed against her back while he made his confession. Somehow it was easier than if he was looking at her.

"I know it's early in our relationship, and some people might say it's too early, but I do love you. And not just because of the butt stuff." He paused. "Though that doesn't hurt."

She burst out laughing and squirmed away, so she could turn around and face him. His cock fell free, and he sighed with the loss, but when she put her hands on either side of his face and tilted his head back so their gazes could meet, he found he didn't really mind at all.

"I love you, too," she said, before taking his lips in a kiss.

EPILOGUE – NEW YEAR'S EVE

Q

A black-tie kink party was a party like Q had never seen. The outfits ranged from fully covered to completely revealed and everything in between. Some people took the 'black tie' suggestion to mean wearing nothing but a black tie. Some, like Asad, had put on black underwear to go with their tie. Others, like Q and Law, were in full tuxedos.

Most of the women were dressed in long dresses or gowns, though some of those gowns were completely sheer, had lots of cutouts, or both. Sam had opted for a corset-style gown that showcased her breasts, but the skirt had slits on the sides up to her hips, and she wasn't wearing any underwear. Q liked to try to catch glimpses of her neatly shaved pussy whenever she moved.

Just for fun.

Marquis was decorated gorgeously, both upstairs and downstairs, with lots of sparkle, though no glitter. Patrick had expressly forbidden it. There were a lot of lights and shiny decorations that made up for it. The big man himself was moving through the space, Lexie tucked neatly under his arm. In deference to her brother in attendance, she was wearing a silvery gown rather than going naked.

Q was pretty sure that as soon as Jake and Sharon took their leave, so would Lexie's dress.

"It's almost midnight." Asad looked around the room. He was standing next to Q at the cocktail table where they'd parked themselves, so they had a place to rest their food and drink. "I need to find someone to kiss."

"Just kiss?" Sam asked, amused.

"I never said where I'd be kissing her." Asad winked before turning away. Grinning, he disappeared into the crowd, leaving the others to shake their heads.

"Are you going to find someone to kiss?" Q looked up at Connor, who had come on his own but hadn't seemed interested in mingling with anyone but his close friends.

"I'm still looking for someone to kiss, Master Connor!"

It was all Q could do not to flinch when Noelle's voice rang out behind him. On the other side of the table, Iris' expression went carefully blank. Law frowned before he quickly schooled his expression.

If he'd realized she was there, he wouldn't have said anything.

"Hey, I didn't know you were coming tonight," Sam said, appearing delighted as she shifted away from Q to give Noelle a welcoming hug. "I thought you had a hot date."

"Turned out to be not so hot." Noelle rolled her eyes, hugging Sam back, but her gaze was still on Connor, who looked a little bit like a deer in the headlights.

Thankfully, before he had to say anything, Morgan came up beside him, linking her arm through his.

"Hey, Master Connor, it's almost midnight!" The way she said the words made it seem like they had a prior arrangement, and Connor relaxed.

"Oh, is Master Connor your midnight kiss?" Noelle asked, looking disappointed.

"Yes, but... oh, hey I didn't know you were going to be here. Do you need a partner? We could share." Morgan blinked. She was so sincere, Q couldn't tell if she and Connor had actually made plans to be each other's midnight kiss.

"My date was a bust," Noelle said, stepping forward to give Morgan a hug.

Q glanced over at Law and Iris to see how they were taking this, but they'd both turned away. It looked like Olivia and Luke had come up behind them and were talking to them, taking their attention away from Noelle. Possibly a coincidence, but Q wouldn't be surprised if they'd seen Noelle and decided to stage a rescue.

Turning back to the others, he wrapped one arm around Sam to keep her by his side. They only had a few minutes left.

"I'll go find someone to kiss." Noelle tossed her hair. He wasn't sure, but it seemed like she was talking a little louder than she had been before. "I'm not going to take your man or ever do anything to jeopardize our friendship."

There was something in her tone that made Q think her words were a jab at Iris, but if they were, they missed the mark. Iris was laughing at something Olivia said and didn't appear to have heard Noelle.

It was hard to tell, though. Noelle didn't react to being ignored by Iris—if she'd been trying to get her attention in the first place. She just waved cheerily and walked off, disappearing into the crowd in search of someone to kiss.

He hoped Asad stayed clear of her.

Almost as soon as she was gone, Olivia looked up from her conversation with Iris and smiled at him and Sam.

"I see you two worked things out. I should have known Sam wouldn't need the Olivia hotline." She grinned at Sam. "Keep him in line."

"Hey," Q complained, sensing that he was being maligned.

"One more minute!" Someone yelled, cutting off any protest he might have made.

Suddenly there was a bustle of activity as everyone was passing champagne flutes. A server was skillfully weaving through the crowd with sparkling apple cider for those who weren't drinking, and Law quickly snagged a glass as they went by.

Sam turned to Q, her eyes sparkling, one hand held aloft with the champagne flute.

"Did you ever hear the superstition that whatever you're doing at midnight when the year turns over, that's what you'll be doing the next year?"

"You're so hot when you spout useless trivia," he said sincerely. "Let's make sure we're set up for next year."

Wrapping his free arm around her waist, he took her lips in a kiss as everyone else started counting down. He wanted to make sure that he was going to start his new year off right—and also set himself up for the future he wanted not just for the next year, but for the rest of his life.

Freddy

As the champagne was passed around, Freddy smiled, hiding his own feelings of discontent. No one wanted a party pooper for the new year. It was no one's fault that he was single, again, for the new year.

Out of the corner of his eye he saw Emery snuggled up with Mistress Red, the two of them practically glowing as they looked at each other.

"You sure you don't want to find someone other than me to kiss?" Steve asked, looking nervous.

"Hey, I thought we agreed we'd rather share a kiss with a friend than be kissing no one at all," Freddy teased, before becoming more serious. "But it's okay if you don't want to. We can wait."

Steve hadn't been 'out' as a gay man for long. Realizing that he was gay *and* kinky *and* submissive had been a lot for him, so Freddy had taken the other man under his wing. He usually watched out for the club submissives, anyway, but Steve was a special case because he was also the younger brother of Freddy's good friend Chris and because he was so new to every aspect of his sexuality.

Although Freddy was bi, he wasn't sexually attracted to Steve, but he didn't mind being there for a friend. Sure, he'd rather be kissing a hot Dominant at midnight, preferably a Domme, but this wasn't so bad. It was better than last year when he'd kissed his champagne flute at midnight.

The countdown started.

"Ten!"

Movement caught Freddy's eye, and he turned his head to see Master Eric headed for him and Steve with a determined look on his face.

"Nine!"

No, not toward him and Steve. Toward Steve. Oh, oh, oh! Freddy had told Steve that he thought Master Eric was interested!

"Eight!"

Steve had insisted that it was just a training relationship for the class. Didn't look like that from the expression on Eric's face.

"Seven."

Master Eric had his eyes trained on Steve and was moving like a man on a mission.

"Six!"

Stepping back, Freddy pivoted and pulled Steve with him so that he was facing the right way.

"Five!"

"Freddy, wha—?

"Four!"

Master Eric was in front of them, hands coming up to cup Steve's face.

"Three!"

"Say no if you don't want me to kiss you." Master Eric's voice was low, rough.

Freddy sighed out loud. It was like a moment straight out of a movie.

"Two!"

"Yes," Steve whispered.

"One! Happy New Year!"

Okay, well if he wasn't getting a kiss of his own, at least Freddy was getting a front-row seat to some of the juiciest gossip—and one of the hottest kisses of the night. Damn. Master Eric looked like he was going to devour Steve, and Steve seemed inclined to let him.

Apparently, last year's midnight did predict this year's. He'd be sharing a kiss with his champagne again. He brought it to his lips while he watched Steve rub himself all over Master Eric.

Envy pulsed through Freddy, which he hated, but he knew it was normal. Seeing so many of his friends pairing off made him more and more aware of what he ultimately wanted, what he wasn't getting, and what he didn't know how to get. He'd played with just about every Dominant at Stronghold and Marquis, yet he'd never sparked with anyone.

Not the way Eric and Steve were sparking with each other right in front of him.

Considering he wasn't picky about what gender he ended up with, he should have more chances than the heteros, yet here he was.

Someone tapped his shoulder, and he turned, holding back his sigh, expecting to see another of his friends there, someone who would want the gossip. But it was a woman he'd never seen before. Freddy blinked, his mind automatically running through his mental catalog of members, but no, he had definitely never seen her before.

He would have remembered.

She was about an inch shorter than him, but a quick glance confirmed she was wearing high heels, putting her another couple of inches shorter. Curvy as hell and currently packed into a light green corset dress that barely contained her breasts, which were threatening to spill over at any moment. Medium brown skin, dark brown eyes, and black curly hair that was styled naturally in a riot of springy coils that stood out around her head.

She looked like a goddess, and Freddy locked his knees against the instinct to drop and worship her.

"Hello, I'm so sorry, do I know you?" The urge to keep babbling about how he knew everyone at the club was strong, but he held it back.

Her lips curved in a stunning smile, and Freddy's knees trembled.

"I'm Mistress Camille, Mistress Julie's friend."

That's right. She'd been on the guest list, but Julie hadn't been sure she'd actually come. Freddy assumed she must have just arrived because he would have definitely noticed her walking around earlier.

"I'm Freddy, I help run the front desk here and well, all sorts of other things." *Do not babble. Do not babble. Do not babble.* He couldn't remember the last time a Dominant had had this kind of effect on him.

Mistress Camille's smile widened.

"So, I was told. I was hoping you could help me out with something."

"Yes, of course." *Anything.*

She leaned in, and he bent his head forward to make sure he'd be able to hear her, his heart thumping faster in his chest as she shifted closer to him so that they were almost touching.

"I don't have anyone to kiss for New Year's. Can you help me with that?"

Freddy and Mistress Camille will return in Legally Bound!

The End

ACKNOWLEDGMENTS

I have a lot of people to thank for helping me with this book.

My amazing beta readers, who are invaluable in helping me catch mistakes, doing the initial grammar and word checks, identifying continuity issues, and working through problems with me. Marie, Candida, Annie, Karen, Marta, and Katherine – you all make these books so much better!

Another extra special thank you to Katherine, who got me started down this career path and has been by my metaphorical side ever since.

Thank you to my husband for his continued loved and support. I could not do this without you.

And, as always, a big thank you to all of you for buying and reading my work... if you love it, please leave a review!

ABOUT THE AUTHOR

Golden Angel is a USA Today best-selling author and self-described bibliophile with a "kinky" bent who loves to write stories for the characters in her head. If she didn't get them out, she's pretty sure she'd go just a little crazy.

She is happily married, old enough to know better but still too young to care, and a big fan of happily-ever-afters, strong heroes and heroines, and sizzling chemistry.

When she's not writing, she can often be found on the couch reading, in front of her sewing machine making a new cosplay, hanging out with her friends, or wandering the Maryland Renaissance Fair.

www.goldenangelromance.com

Daddy Dom Deliciousness? CLICK HERE to for Foosball Daddies!

BB bookbub.com/authors/golden-angel

g goodreads.com/goldeniangel

f facebook.com/GoldenAngelAuthor

instagram.com/goldeniangel

OTHER BOOKS BY GOLDEN ANGEL

Stronghold: Closing Time Box Set

Masters of Marquis Series

Bondage Buddies

Master Chef

Law & Disorder

Switch Play

Legally Bound

Dungeons & Doms Series

Dungeon Master

Dungeon Daddy

Dungeon Showdown

Poker Loser Trilogy

Forced Bet

Back in the Game

Winning Hand

Poker Loser Trilogy Bundle (3 books in 1!)

Standalones - Daddy Doms

Chef Daddy

Foosball Daddies

Little Villain

Historical Spanking Romance

Domestic Discipline Quartet

Birching His Bride

Dealing With Discipline

Punishing His Ward

Claiming His Wife

The Domestic Discipline Quartet Box Set

Bridal Discipline Series

Philip's Rules

Gabrielle's Discipline

Lydia's Penance

Benedict's Commands

Arabella's Taming

Pride and Punishment Box Set

Commands and Consequences Box Set

Deception and Discipline

A Season for Treason

A Season for Scandal

A Season for Smugglers

A Season for Spies

Bridgewater Brides

Their Harlot Bride

Standalone

Marriage Training

The Duke's Pursuit

Rogue Booty

Sci-fi Romance

Tsenturion Masters Series with Lee Savino

Alien Captive

Alien Tribute

Alien Abduction

Standalone

Mated on Hades

Shifter Romance

Big Bad Bunnies Series

Chasing His Bunny

Chasing His Squirrel

Chasing His Puma

Chasing His Polar Bear

Chasing His Honey Badger

Chasing Her Lion

Night of the Wild Stags

Chasing Tail Box Set

Chasing Tail... Again Box Set